AN ERICK ANDERSSE

Death at a Distance

MARK A. NYSTUEN

RIVER GROVE
BOOKS

This book is a work of fiction. Names, characters, businesses, organizations, places, events, and incidents are either a product of the author's imagination or are used fictitiously. Any resemblance to actual persons, living or dead, events, or locales is entirely coincidental.

Published by River Grove Books
Austin, TX
www.rivergrovebooks.com

Copyright ©2014 Mark A. Nystuen

All rights reserved.

No part of this book may be reproduced, stored in a retrieval system, or transmitted by any means, electronic, mechanical, photocopying, recording, or otherwise, without written permission from the copyright holder.

Distributed by River Grove Books

For ordering information or special discounts for bulk purchases, please contact River Grove Books at PO Box 91869, Austin, TX 78709, 512.891.6100.

Design and composition by Greenleaf Book Group
Cover design by Greenleaf Book Group
Cover image © MaxyM, 2014. Used under license from Shutterstock.com.

Cataloging-in-Publication data
Nystuen, Mark A.
  Death at a distance / Mark A. Nystuen.—First edition.
    pages ; cm. —(An Erick Anderssen novel)
  Issued also as an ebook.
    1. Authors—Illinois—Chicago—Fiction. 2. Marathon running—Illinois—Chicago—Fiction. 3. Divorced people—Illinois—Chicago—Fiction. 4. Murder—Illinois—Chicago—Fiction. 5. Chicago (Ill.)—Social life and customs—Fiction. 6. Suspense fiction. I. Title.

PS3614.Y788 D43 2014
813/.6   2014933909

Print ISBN: 978-1-938416-82-8

First Edition

Other Edition(s)
eBook ISBN: 978-1-938416-83-5

For Susan, Kevin, Connor, and Scott.

Eventually, I think Chicago will be the most beautiful great city left in the world.

—Frank Lloyd Wright

Acknowledgments

My thanks to . . .

Susan, for her unending love, unstoppable sense of humor, and unswerving belief that someday I would finish the book. And I did. I did.

Kevin, Connor and Scott, for their love, support, input, and ideas.

Jocelyn, for her enthusiasm, excitement, and creativity.

Sue B, for taking on the herculean job of the first edit.

My friends and family for encouraging me and promising to buy the book when it's done. I've kept a list.

River Grove Books and the outstanding talent that helped tell Erick's first story.

The LaSalle Bank Chicago Marathon team (you know who you are!) whose excitement, energy, and plain old-fashioned hard work made the event into an enormous success on so many fronts.

Norm, for believing that the LaSalle Bank Chicago Marathon could be more than just a race . . . it could be a force for good in the city.

Finally, my late parents, Otto and Lila, for always encouraging me to read (except on the tractor) and learn and grow.

1

I've always been lucky. About me, the French would say *rôtir le balai*, or "to live the good life." They tell me it literally means "to roast the broom," but that's the French for you.

Even when things didn't go the way I thought they should, they always seemed to turn out for the better. Take my divorce—it was painful at the time, but look how happy I am to be rid of that cunning, ambitious she-devil. Lucky me.

My surprisingly successful writing career is proof of my good fortune. I'm Erick Anderssen: yes, that Erick Anderssen, author of the best-selling series of how-to books for people who want to defy age and fate. I hit the right idea at the right time. Just as seventy-five million baby boomers ran smack into middle age (at thirty-nine, I almost counted among their numbers), I showed them how to stave off old age—at least temporarily—by testing themselves through exotic new adventures.

With my latest book, you might say that my luck has continued. After all, with everything that's happened around the topic, it's become a publicist's dream. And yet it's a nightmare for me. Who would have thought that such a healthy topic could prove so deadly? Would I have chosen something else to write about? Would lives have been saved if I had? Perhaps. Probably. But I chose what I chose. And I'll live with the consequences for the rest of my life.

As with many of my books, this idea started with yet another nagging email from my agent, Barbara Bronfman. Granted, Barbara didn't work unless I worked, but I really had hoped she'd find a hobby or a new husband so she'd have less time to think up new adventures for me and my readers to conquer. I have to admit that up to now, she'd been right on target. For eight years I had invited readers to share my experiences as I faced new challenges.

My first effort, *Conquer the Colorado*, was relatively tame: a week of white-water rafting down the Colorado River at high water. The success of that book (twelve weeks on the *New York Times* best-seller list) was followed in quick succession by *Intense Ice* (climbing glaciers in Alaska), *Mission to Morocco* (traveling the ancient caravan routes of the Maghreb and Marrakech via camel), and *Africa Alive* (living and hunting with Maasai warriors). My latest book, *Himalayan High*, about backpacking among the monasteries of Tibet, was a big hit for those seeking inner knowledge and strong thighs.

While I'm no John Grisham or Tom Clancy, I had achieved enough success to give up my day job as a mid-level editor at the *Chicago Tribune* and still keep bread on the table. Not that I ever ate at my table. It had been some time since I had seen the knotty pine finish. All that shiny blond woodiness has been long buried by past, present, and future book research, notes, and memorabilia. The thought of clearing a spot or two on which to serve a meal always sends me out of my Lincoln Park townhouse and into one of Chicago's welcoming taverns.

So here was the latest e-brainstorm from my agent in New York. Barbara (one of my publisher's least favorite agents, but someone who has fought for me like a mother bear protecting her cub) told me, in her usual knowing way, that running, and marathon running in particular, has been growing in popularity in the US—and worldwide—for decades.

She told me that my readers were becoming runners in record numbers. Not that Barbara ever laces up a sneaker. She might if Jimmy Choo made a shocking pink, size five little number. But she's never going to take up the sport, if you can call it that.

I've always classified sports in two ways: real sports (football, basketball, baseball) and faux sports (golf, ice dancing, synchronized swimming). The difference is crystal clear to me, but I'm sure there are those out there who would disagree. As for running . . . come on. Put on a pair of $39 Keds, an old, well-worn Pearl Jam t-shirt, and a pair of shorts, and then put one foot in front of another just a bit faster than plain old-fashioned walking.

But as usual, she was insistent. "Help your readers achieve something more . . . show them the incredible experience of running a marathon after forty."

"Barbara," I said in a quick email response, "that would be one of the shortest books on record. Here's the outline: Get dressed, go to the starting line, run for 26 miles, and you're done. The end. Who would pay $29.95—$9.95 on Kindle—for that? It's dull. And I don't do dull."

She fired back, "Erick, you can't believe how challenging a marathon is for anyone, but especially an older runner. It takes an incredible amount of time and dedication to train. Besides, the publisher is all over this (unlike the other ideas you've sent me). You could get a six-figure advance. You have GOT to do this book!"

Was she forgetting that in order to do this book I'd actually have to run a marathon? Sure, I knew that marathons had become big business, a big charity draw, and even a made-for-TV event. I probably knew more about marathons than many participants did (but more about that later). I was surprised to read in Barbara's email about elite runners who make seven-figure incomes for two days of work a year. Two days? My first thought: Is it too late for me to make yet another career change? Probably.

Don't get me wrong. It's not that I don't believe in exercise; my love of food and drink (not necessarily in that order) requires me to participate in some form of exercise. I must have inherited the spare tire gene from my Norwegian-American father (along with his love of scotch, his blond hair, his fair and frequently sunburned complexion, and, I'll admit, his stubborn streak a mile wide). At just over six-feet tall, I can't hide excess weight the way some of my taller brethren can, but a solid frame built up from years of high school football and swimming helps a bit.

For me now, exercise is a leisurely trot along Chicago's stunning jewel of a lakefront with my buddy Max. Lucky for me, Max is a serious chick magnet. A five-year-old Pyrenean Mountain Dog who knows just when to turn on the charm and blink those big almond shaped eyes. Gets 'em every time. Okay, not every time, but often enough.

Back to Momma Bear Barbara and the book. So far she'd only convinced me that, like most things, marathoning was more complicated than I imagined. "What you haven't given me," I wrote, "is a good reason to spend the next four months of my life training for a risky, painful experience while researching a quasi-sport that's the obsession of a few crazies who love to spend several hours a day in a solitary pursuit with only an iPod to keep them company."

"You do have a contract that calls for two books every eighteen months," she wrote back. "Spring is now upon us with no concept on the horizon and a book due to your publisher, Regency Press, by year's end. And this is a good concept!"

I was suitably outraged, reminding her of the six or seven fantastic story ideas I had in my head for my next blockbuster. In her amazingly accurate way of bringing me down to earth, Barbara reminded me that at least half of my fantastic ideas had already been done by someone else (she implied "and better") and that the rest required either courage I did not possess (heli-skiing) or an upfront investment that no publisher in the world would even consider (being the next civilian in space).

The exchange went on and on. I could just see Barbara sitting in her office overlooking New York City's bustling Columbus Avenue. She'd be impatiently shoving her pink reading glasses up into her carbon black hair (still so unexpectedly black as she nears seventy) and glaring at the screen, willing me to do her bidding. In one last pleading, begging, and threatening email of the day, Barbara asked, "Would you at least have lunch with the race director of the Chicago Marathon? As one of the biggest and most successful running events in the world, focusing on that marathon will have two huge advantages for you. First, being in your hometown would greatly reduce the demands on the advance money. And second, the race director is offering unprecedented access to the event. What do you have to lose by talking to her?"

It made sense that the race director was doing this. She's a publicity hungry, self-absorbed, egomaniacal bitch who would do anything to get her name in print. And I should know. That's exactly how she was when we were married.

2

I knew it was a mistake to meet with Kate even to discuss the subject, but Barbara wouldn't drop it. Hating Kate with all my soul just didn't cut it as an excuse with Barbara. So I gave in at least a bit and agreed to meet for lunch, under the condition that Kate would pay. She could easily afford it, with a multimillion-dollar budget that no one looked at too closely. The race sponsors were willing to shell out essentially any sum without even asking where their money was going. They were just happy to see their logo on a big event, thus satisfying whomever in their marketing department was responsible for spending the company's millions.

I should have known that I was in trouble when Kate suggested we meet at noon at Flannigan's. Chicago is a wonderful city for fine dining at the highest level, but the heart of Chicago is its bars and pubs. I had two favorites: one for work-related meetings, and one where I went to escape from everything and just be around friends and a great bartender.

For work, I loved Flannigan's. It was one of the last great Irish pubs in Chicago that hadn't been ruined by the tourists—or, even worse, the drunken convention-goers from every small town in America. It was a true Chicago watering hole and perhaps the greatest living reminder of our city's long and distinguished history of great bars. In the 1940s, an enormous, highly polished oak back bar with a slightly foggy mirror had been shipped over from Ireland. With brass sconces along the sides, it was the pride and joy of the Flannigan family who had owned the place since just after Grandpa Flannigan snuck into the country in the early 1900s. Grandpa's portrait hangs proudly above the original beer taps with their small, highly polished brass plates announcing what's available on tap that day. All of this came with a hammered tin ceiling, classic bar food (greasy and delicious), and bartenders who know when to stop talking and to never, ever sing along with the jukebox.

But Kate detested Flannigan's. The only reason she would ever go back to the scene of our only public knock-down, drag-out fight was to get something from me. Something big. And there she was, walking into Flannigan's wearing one of her St. John power suits, the bright pink one. She used to correct me and tell me the color was "daiquiri." Like anyone cared. It was the one she always wore to impress people when they had money she wanted to move from their pocket into her last-year's Moschino clutch. Although it looked like she was carrying this year's edition for a change. Pricey.

What I didn't expect was the person who walked in a few steps behind her. After all, how many husbands does any woman want at one lunch?

. . .

Despite my lifelong disdain for running as a sport, I married a runner. Kate and I met as freshmen at the University of Missouri. I was in their world-class journalism program; she was a second-tier runner getting a tuition break in their middling track and field program. You could say that both of us learned a lot at Mizzou. I learned how to be a journalist and began to develop a suitably skeptical and sarcastic view of the world. She learned that she would never be a world-class athlete, but she quickly figured out that her best path for fame and fortune was to learn how to promote herself in an arcane but growing sport.

We both graduated with value for our parents' investment in the Missouri higher educational system. The money they spent on our wedding turned out to be a less successful investment, however, and we were divorced less than four years later. Kate was unhappy in a series of random jobs, traveling way too much while I slogged through entry-level journalism at the *Tribune*. What little we had in common in college soon disappeared after we moved to Chicago. She was the first to figure out that there was no future between us. After that, the divorce was inevitable.

Soon thereafter, Kate found her niche. She turned a volunteer job with the Illinois Runners' Alliance into a paid job as the office manager, slept with enough influential people, and then became president of the alliance. A few short years later, she snagged one of the best jobs in running: executive race director of the Chicago Marathon. Oops, I'm sorry: the GrandHotel Chicago Marathon. For all the money they're shelling out for the event, GrandHotel had always felt pretty strongly that they should get their name mentioned. Often. I knew from my days at the *Trib* that the Marathon's public relations people would call and whine every time one of our writers missed that point. Unfortunately, that was about all I really knew about the current state of the Chicago Marathon. I tried hard to ignore the entire thing.

Kathleen Marie O'Callahan Anderssen would say that she was born to succeed. I'll grant that she's a bright woman with a load of personality, but judging from the speed of her rise, she apparently had management skills I'd never known about when we were married. It also helps to have a personal trainer at the Peninsula Hotel's swank spa and club (of course she slept with him), personal shoppers at Saks, Nordstrom, and Jil Sander, and a weekly refresh of her honey blond rinse at Hugo's too chi-chi Oak Street salon (she hasn't slept with Hugo, but I hear Hugo is doing Kate's trainer). Lord only knows how she pays for all of that personal treatment.

In short, Kate knows how to surround herself with the right people, and her smarmy squad of slick PR shills also aided in her rise to prominence. She paid them well to guarantee that they would lose no opportunity to promote her name or face (preferably both) in every possible media outlet.

You may find my discussion of Kate and her background to be a bit of ancient history (colored perhaps by my disdain for her and her manipulative ways), but trust me; it will matter before this is all over.

In the case of Jackson Clark—Kate's husband number two—the less said the better. A California golden boy surfer dude runner, he swept Kate off her feet just as we were melting down. Coming after a couch potato who spent most of his time either at Tribune Tower, Flannigan's, or some combination of the Wrigley/Soldier/Comiskey ballparks (sorry, I don't care what they paid for naming rights, I'm still calling it Comiskey), a tall, tanned, and toned stud with an Olympic gold medal must have looked pretty good. In my nightmares, I see him wearing the medal when they have sex. After all, he wore it at every other possible opportunity; why not then?

Jackson had faded a bit since that time. He was the running world's equivalent of Dexys Midnight Runners: one hit then gone. But he was smart enough to keep a Nike endorsement deal that somehow got renewed every few years, and I had heard he was doing quite a bit of private coaching for CEO types and B-list celebrities that wanted to run a marathon. He even wrote a book on training, although one reviewer called it more of a photo album than a book, since it contained more pictures of Jack than actual words. One of my favorite book reviews ever. I framed it for my study and it makes me smile every time I read it.

. . .

Besides the unwelcome presence of Jackson, there was one other troubling part about watching Kate walk in a couple of minutes before noon: Kate hadn't been on time for anything since 1997. Why the hell was she early? Of course, she was on both her BlackBerry and her other cell phone, apparently texting while she was doing yet another interview, using the same empty platitudes about running that she'd been using for years. It didn't appear that she was even listening to herself. It sounded as if she was talking to one of those countless running magazines. There seemed to be one for every state: *Illinois Runner*, *Wyoming Runner* (are there enough people in Wyoming to have any kind of a magazine?), and the other forty-eight. Plus, there was *Women's Running Universe, Gay and Lesbian Runners, Bored by the Whole Thing Runners* . . . okay, I made that last one up.

Anyway, Kate smiled at me with that plastic little smile of hers while she chatted and texted away. That left me with the challenge of making conversation with Jack. Always painful. Once you got past the weather and the Cubs (hey, maybe this year is the year!), there really wasn't much that interested Jack besides Jack, or maybe name-dropping the rich and famous wanna-be marathoners that he was training.

I was too tired and too pissed off at Barbara for talking me into this meeting to put any effort into it, so I took the easy way out.

"So how's the Nike deal going?" I asked him. "Are they still happy?" This was something I wondered about. When he signed with them years ago, it was the most lucrative contract in running, with an annual $250,000 payout plus incentives for appearances and product placements. There were even more incentives for winning marathons, but that was far past Jack by now, and I'd heard he had some problems when he showed up at appearances.

"Nike should be very happy," Jack said. "They have exclusive access to one of America's only two gold medal marathon men. Why shouldn't they be happy?"

To avoid starting a fight so early in the meal (we hadn't even ordered drinks), I kept quiet rather than pointing out Jack's well-publicized reputation, his late-night bar fights, and his habit of flirting with every blonde under thirty. It was a miracle that Nike kept him on. Instead, I asked him how the training business was going.

What happened next came as a complete surprise to me. Jack gave me an articulate, coherent description of his philosophy toward training non-athletes for competitive running. He had a business plan in place, several training plans, and a team of nutritionists and physiologists on retainer to support his clients. None of my previous encounters with Jack had given me any indication that he'd had such a head for business. I reluctantly decided that perhaps I had underestimated him.

As Jack was describing one of his training programs to me, I noticed for the first time that he had the new TAG Heuer Champion watch on. I knew he'd paid at least $10,000 for the watch, and recently: the Champion series was new for this year. Coaching must be paying well.

You may wonder how I know whether someone's carrying this year's Moschino clutch vs. last year's, or when new pricey watch styles are released. It's my mother's fault. A buyer for Saks Fifth Avenue in

New York, she lived for the latest fashion and talked about designers and beauty nonstop. To make sure we were paying attention, she'd quiz us at dinner to see whether we could tell this year's Chanel from vintage. My father would always smile and retreat behind his *Wall Street Journal*. Eventually, my sister followed her into the business, and I kept a casual eye on these things in her memory. I may be a little obsessive on the topic, but there are worse obsessions. I guess.

Just as Jack finished telling me about the latest celebrity right out of rehab that wanted to run a 10K for charity (and for a commensurate boost in his troubled public image), Kate chose that well-timed moment to finish her call. That took me off the hook conversation-wise and prevented me from having to ask whether this was going to be the Cubs' year. It never will be, of course, but it does make great conversation filler when you're stuck with the terminally dull of any persuasion.

"Erick, so good to see you and Jack getting along," Kate gushed. Kate always gushed. "I'm sure that you would be great friends if you'd just get to know each other better!"

With that bit of fiction floating in the air between us, we ordered drinks. Helen, the server who had been working at Flannigan's since before any of us were born, knew from years of experience that noon for me meant a Bloody Mary (celery, no horseradish, and for God's sake, no olives). Jack ordered some pricey vodka on the rocks (the man had no clue how to pick up a bar tab, so ordering pricey wasn't a concern for him), and Kate ordered Evian water with a lemon twist—never a slice. I'm convinced she asks for a twist just to be difficult.

We slogged our way through small talk (my last book, her recent glam photo shoot in Jean Paul Gaultier for *Chicago* magazine) and our first round of drinks (Jack's first and second round, actually). At last, Helen strolled over to take our lunch order. She took pride in never writing down orders, instead keeping all the orders straight in her head. She normally got about half right, but no one had the courage to correct her.

I had the double cheeseburger and fries, both crisped to a shade just past mahogany in Flannigan's well-aged kitchen grease. Kate somehow convinced Helen that they had a salad on the menu (a challenge for a kitchen that only had wilted lettuce and condiments from which to build said salad), while Jack tried to be healthy and gambled on the turkey club, hedging his bets by adding a bottle of Heineken. Kate quickly turned the subject to my agent's suggestion. Kate and Barbara were clearly colluding on this one. And I knew who stood a good chance of coming out on the losing end.

"Erick, it'll be a huge best seller! Running is incredibly popular with your darling boomers. Help them achieve something they never thought possible—running a marathon! You'll get access to our staff, see all the behind-the-scenes action, interview the elite athletes, and get the tips and techniques that your readers need to finish all 26.2 miles of the marathon."

I made a note to myself: it's 26.2 miles, not 26. I'm sure that matters somehow. To someone. Somewhere.

"Kate, I frankly don't think that people care about the behind-the-scenes stuff," I replied. "They just want to finish what they start and not to break a leg or die."

If I'd known then that death would be a big part of this story, I would have found another adventure to write about. At least that's what I tell myself. And my lawyer.

Kate shook off my protests with a wave of her well-tended hand. Was she wearing a new diamond tennis bracelet? I'm sure I would have noticed it before.

"You are so wrong, Erick," she said. "People will definitely want to read a book about your marathon experience. I mean, who would have thought that people wanted to read about all the disgusting habits of camels? Or how the Maasai prepare their ritual cattle blood brew?"

"You've read my books?" I was surprised that she would read any book that didn't make *People* magazine, much less something by me.

"Of course I have," she replied. "Cover to cover!"

Jack stopped peeling the label off his beer bottle long enough to say, "Only the front and back of the dust jacket. And she goes on Amazon to read the reviews whenever one of your books comes out. She wants to make sure it isn't about her or your marriage."

Kate didn't even blush when caught in her lie. I think she lost that ability a long time ago.

"Okay, so I haven't exactly read them," she said, "but my point is still valid. And second, everyone loves behind-the-scene stories. Especially ones that involve glamour, fame, and fortune!"

"Come on," I replied. "I don't know much about what you people do, but I do know that the only fame involved in a marathon is for the winner, and that's pretty fleeting. Fortune seems to be pretty limited, too. And there is no way that anyone would associate glamour with 40,000 sweaty people all trying to find a port a-potty at the same time."

"Ah, but that's why I wanted to have lunch with you," said Kate. "This year's GrandHotel Chicago Marathon is going to be all that and more. GrandHotel is about to announce that they've done a huge deal with Ashley!"

Jack set his beer down with a crack. "Ashley? Seriously?" he exclaimed.

I must have looked as blank as I felt. Jack stared at me with amazement—one of the few facial emotions that Botox had left him with. "Dude, have you been living under a rock? You don't know who Ashley is?"

My gut reaction was to respond that I had spent a good part of the last year not under a rock, but in Tibet with the lamas. But it would take too long to explain to Jack that Tibet was not West Lafayette and that the lamas were religious men in robes rather than hoofed animals with great hair. So I went another route.

"Dude, I'm just not totally connected like you are. Ashley who?"

Not surprisingly, he didn't get the sarcasm. "She's just the biggest new thing in music and fashion! A top ten song with the hottest video, plus her own clothing line that's being rolled out by Lagerfeld in the fall. And a national concert tour this summer."

That Ashley. "Of course I've seen her name," I said, "but I have trouble keeping all of those blond pop stars straight. Is she the one that slept with what's her name's husband?" Okay, I'll admit it. I check out people.com once in a while.

"No, that's Patti-Ann," Jack said. "Seriously, Erick?"

Kate continued her pitch to me. "GrandHotel is rolling out a whole new campaign related to the Ashley endorsement. And they're going to open a new nightclub and restaurant in all their major hotels and casinos called Ashley's. She's going to design the whole place, from the logo to the menu to something sexy and sultry for the servers. Best of all, she's going to run in the GrandHotel Chicago Marathon to raise money for her charity!"

Jack was impressed, naturally. "Ashley's running the marathon? You'll get international media coverage for weeks before and after!"

"I know!" Kate replied. You could see the gleam in her eyes. I used to think that gleam was love. Then I realized it wasn't love: it was lust. Lust for anything that would advance her cause. That was me, for a while.

3

I had to admit that by this time I was confused. Kate had an enormous public relations opportunity in front of her that would get coverage for her and her race in every news outlet from *TMZ* and *People* to the Food Network and Fox News. So why did she need me? My book might sell 200,000 copies if I was lucky. She'd be in millions of homes worldwide every day for weeks. I knew her well enough to know that she had a plan, but I was damned if I could figure it out.

"Erick, here's where you come in."

At least I didn't have to wait long. That was some comfort.

"Ashley has read all your books. She truly has."

I was always skeptical when Kate used the words *truly*, *honestly*, or *frankly*. What usually followed was the opposite.

"She honestly does love your work, and she wants you included in the project. She has an amazing idea. She's going to use Chicago as her base of operations for the next three months. She'll be working on her first concert tour, her new album, and the GrandHotel project. And—are you ready for this? She wants to train with you every day!"

I didn't know quite how to respond. Luckily for me, Helen chose that moment to deliver our food.

Helen and her memory were having a good day. My burger and fries were perfect. And somehow the kitchen made a salad appear. I doubted that it would make the permanent menu, but it didn't look half bad.

Unfortunately, Helen was only batting .667. Jack's turkey club had morphed into Flannigan's famous beer cheese soup in a bread bowl. Jack stared at it as if trying to figure out where it resided in the food pyramid and how it came to be sitting in front of him. After a minute or so of contemplating that question, his attention deficit disorder kicked in, and he moved on to me.

"You, training with Ashley? Totally outstanding. You'll be getting sweaty on a daily basis with a woman who's on the cover of every magazine in town!"

Not, I suspected, my beloved *National Geographic*, but any argument with Jack would only frustrate both of us.

"Erick, aren't you thrilled?" Kate asked. "An exciting new adventure for your readers. Running a marathon with the entertainment world's newest sensation! It absolutely guarantees your book's success."

I briefly closed my eyes and took a deep breath before responding. I was trying to figure out how to send a clear and final message without sounding like the insensitive and uncaring jerk Kate often accused me of being.

"Kate, let me be clear on this," I said. "I am not interested in the topic. My readers are not interested. My goal is to find challenges that stir the soul, to bring readers to someplace they've never been, and to do things they never dreamed they could do. I show them that they can challenge themselves in a whole new way, even if they aren't twenty-three anymore."

"That is the whole point of the marathon," Kate snapped.

"That may well be," I snapped back, "but there must be dozens of books on how to run. The world doesn't need one more. I also don't give a damn about some girl singer who is going to run your race as part of some corporate deal. I want nothing to do with her or you or your stupid race. Do I make myself clear, or should I use smaller words?" So much for good intentions. I may have been a wee bit sarcastic there for just a minute.

During all of this, Jack gave the impression of someone watching a tennis volley, his coiffed and toned head turning back and forth between us. Kate's sudden silence after my little tirade gave both Jack and me pause. Our collective years of being her husband had trained us to expect the tantrum that was sure to come.

The silence at the table continued. I would have said something, but I was too pissed off to speak. Jack was clearly too afraid to say a thing. Finally Kate broke the silence.

"Erick, I fully understand," she said. "This isn't like taking your readers to Morocco or Africa. It won't submit them to the life-or-death thrills of being on the face of a glacier or hunting some beast in Africa. But it will change their lives. And there is one more thing you need to know."

I bit back my automatic sarcastic response. Instead, I just asked, "And what is that?"

"Ashley has done her research on you. And to show you how much she wants you in on this project, she and GrandHotel are offering to donate $250,000 to the Alex Project if you'll do the book."

Suddenly all my sarcasm was gone.

4

Alex was nine years my senior, out of the house before I got to know him very well. As my parents tell the story, he was fine until toward the end of high school, when he became increasingly reclusive. He gave up on sports, friendships, and, worst of all in my parents' eyes, school. He graduated (barely) and was admitted to one of the smaller state colleges. Alex didn't last long there, dropping out and taking a series of part-time jobs at which he failed with regularity. Mom and Dad tried to get him help, but he refused and finally just left. Left our home, left our family. We would hear from him now and again, sometimes at Christmas, sometimes on my mother's birthday. A different city each time, or so he told us. And he sounded worse and worse with each phone call.

When my parents finally got the call they were dreading, two years had passed since they had last heard from him. As we later pieced together, he had been in Chicago for the last couple of years, in and out of shelters, no longer able to work as whatever disease was fighting for control of his mind began to win the battle. What finally defeated him, though, wasn't a disease of the mind but of the body: leukemia. One of the doctors at County Hospital had diagnosed him, but they didn't have the budget to care for the terminally ill poor. St. Helena's shelter took in the indigent, but they didn't have the staff to handle the diseases of his mind, and Alex was impossible to control in the later days of his life. And so Alex died alone and abandoned on the streets of Chicago a few weeks before his fortieth birthday.

When I sold my first book, I vowed that I'd do what I could to help people avoid what Alex suffered in those last few months. With the help of some friends and former *Tribune* colleagues, we started the Alex Project hospice in a two-flat in West Rogers Park. Three years later, we have a waiting list too long to imagine and a sweetheart lease in the West Loop, but still too few resources to count on. We'd been scraping by for the past few years with volunteer time and money from my book sales. It kept us going, but every month we faced the worry of paying the bills. The amount of money Ashley and Grand-Hotel were offering would keep the hospice open for a long time to come and enhance the last few days of many, many people who would otherwise die alone and abandoned. Just like my brother Alex had. It was a gift that couldn't be rejected.

So why was I thinking about doing just that?

. . .

Kate's voice cut in. "You've got that look again. You're going to be Norwegian stubborn and say no because your precious little moral compass is telling you to. You aren't even thinking about what this could mean for the hospice."

"There you have it wrong," I replied hotly. "I am thinking about how much the hospice needs that money. I'm also thinking about what a truly rotten idea this book is and how a quarter-million-dollar bribe doesn't make it any better. How convenient that this Ashley found my soft spot. Why is she so hell-bent on having *me* write this book? And why me instead of one of the young studs who write about the X Games or something equally mindless?"

Kate sat quietly for a minute. She was clearly working through something in her mind. We waited while Helen cleared away lunch. Kate had barely touched her salad, while Jack's soup in a bread bowl was nothing more than a soggy mess. I, on the other hand, remained a member of the clean plate club.

"That's a good question," Kate said. "I see that old journalistic radar of yours is fully lit. You think there is something odd about all of this and you want to know what it is. That's the only possible explanation for why you haven't walked away from this like you used to do."

She had learned a thing or two about me during our brief marriage. Despite my less-than-stellar career path at the *Tribune*, I always was drawn to understanding the "why" of a story. Why would an increasingly famous person bribe me so extravagantly to write a book that would only minimally be about her?

"Erick, you think on that one, and get back to Barbara with your answer. This is important. More important than you know. But talk to Barbara. I know she's already been in contact with Ashley's people."

Kate then did the very best thing she could have for her cause. She stood up, dropped money on the table for Helen, and grabbed Jack by the arm. They headed for the door. She glanced back at me once with a strangely serious look, and then she and Jack were gone.

. . .

Wondering why Barbara and Kate were so eager to get me to do this book, I left a little something extra on the table for Helen (Kate had always been a lousy tipper) and headed out into the warm April day. As I strolled the few blocks back to the townhouse, I wondered about Ashley's motives, Kate and Barbara's collusion, and Jack's presence at lunch.

I climbed the front steps and heard Max's deep bass of a bark, challenging anyone who had the effrontery to come to his front door. That fierce, protective beast turned into a sloppy welcoming committee of one as I turned my key and opened the heavy oaken door. I braced myself for the onslaught as Max came at me full tilt. I was able to stay on my feet, but I could feel the pent up energy of a big dog that needed to stretch it out.

A little bit about my home. When the royalty checks from my first book began to come in, the out-of-work me insisted that I put them into something safe and secure. Like a bank account. When the next two books sold even better than the first, I remembered something my father had said: They aren't making any more land. So I used the proceeds from those two books to buy a stone-clad townhouse on North Hudson Avenue in Chicago's trendy Lincoln Park neighborhood. Lucky for me, the owners needed to sell quickly—an ugly divorce, I heard—so I got a great deal.

When I moved in, most of the three stories were empty, since Kate had taken much of our furniture (except for the knotty pine table I fought so hard for). Over the years, I've filled it with an eclectic mix of antiques and newer pieces and am pretty damn proud of how it looks.

As I went upstairs to change into my running clothes (good pair of Sauconys, shorts, and Led Zeppelin t-shirt), Max waited patiently by the front door. He sat with his leash in his mouth, having dragged it from its normal spot by the back door and thus putting even more scratches in the old wooden floor.

I hooked him up, and we headed down the street, cutting over to the lakefront on one of those small, shaded side streets that add so much charm to this city. Once we crossed Clark Street, we circled around South Pond and hit the lakefront paths, headed north for a mile or so, made a big turnaround, and came panting back toward home. The lake glistened in the sun with a fair number of sailboats dotting the water. I was surprised to see so many people at the beach. Not because it was April—Chicagoans get a little stir crazy after our long gray winters and seek the beach the moment a warm day shows up. My surprise was rather how so many people had jobs that enabled them to be out here in the middle of a weekday. They probably wondered the same thing about me.

As we walked, I considered the marathon book. While I normally accepted Barbara's advice in nearly every situation, this one just didn't feel right. It didn't have the drama or the high adventure of my previous books. It felt a little pedestrian. Pun intended, of course. Still, I kept thinking about it as I headed home. I saw an older man wearing a tattered Chicago Marathon t-shirt from many years ago. I began to look more closely at the runners going by—how many of them had run a marathon? Which ones were training for this year's race?

A few more minutes and we were back on our block, slowing down to cool off and to allow Max to check out all the new scents that had been deposited on the cast iron lamp poles and well-tended shrubbery that lined the sidewalk. I looked up as we got closer to the house and was pleasantly surprised to see a friend waiting for me on the front steps. The beat-up galvanized metal pail on the steps made me all the happier, as I could see frosty beer bottles peeking out from some serious chucks of ice. After all, what's better after a run than your best friend waiting with an icy bucket of beer?

I didn't notice that Ted wasn't nearly as happy to see me as I was to see him.

5

Ted McCormick and I had been friends since my *Tribune* days. Back then, he was a novice writer and photojournalist who did travel stories for the newspaper. He would move back and forth between full-time staffing and freelancing, all based on how well his real job (as he described it) was doing. Being an actor in Chicago—even a reasonably talented and quite handsome one like Ted—is a tough, erratic way to make a living. For most of his career, he needed to supplement his acting income through writing and photography projects, including two of my most recent books. While my books are certainly much heavier in words than pictures (unlike Jack's homage to himself), some of Ted's spectacular images added to the excitement for my readers and helped me tell my stories.

Through all our work together, both here in Chicago and around the world, Ted was always the unflappable one. He faced every missed flight, every bad hotel, and every minor official looking for a bribe with equanimity and endless good humor. His notoriously bad memory was his biggest challenge, but he prided himself on taking good notes. Not a bad habit for anyone.

But for someone capable of dealing with the third canceled flight of the day with a laugh and a joke, what was behind the somber, serious look on Ted's face as Max and I climbed the stairs? As Ted leaned over to scratch Max behind his big floppy ears, even the dog could sense that something was wrong and sat uncharacteristically still.

After a suitably chaste bro-hug, Ted and I sat on the steps and opened the first Heineken. Max gulped noisily and gratefully at the huge bowl of water that Ted had set out for the dog.

We tried making small talk, gossiping about former colleagues from the paper and Ted's latest fling (a strikingly attractive young man from Los Angeles that Ted had met during the Chicago filming of one of the *Transformers* movies). None of the conversations went very far, soon dissolving into what for us was uncomfortable silence.

"Ted, are you going to tell me what's wrong? Because something is clearly bothering you."

"You aren't going to like this," my friend replied. "I mean you seriously aren't going to like this."

I suddenly knew that one of the next words out of his mouth was going to be "Kate" or "Barbara." And I was right.

"Erick, buddy, it was Barbara. She called me this morning with news from Lord Greene."

Lord Greene? The British billionaire who bought out my publisher last year? He had news for Ted? Barbara had introduced me to Greene early on, but I'd only spoken to his lordship twice, both times at the annual parties the publisher threw for all their authors. They're always held at the same staid New York City club, with the same tiny appetizers passed on gleaming silvery trays. Slipping through the guests with those trays are the usual would-be actors moonlighting—at least in their minds—in their black cater-waiter tuxedos.

Fortunately, those events featured plentiful bars and mercifully short speeches. I knew they did a nicer event for their best-selling authors, but I was relegated to the "large" party along with the biographers, faded politicians-as-autobiographers, and the second tier of cookbook and self-help writers.

"Ted, why would Lord Greene have news for you? He doesn't even know you exist!" That may have been unkind on my part, but it was true.

"Barbara has convinced him to sign me for a book deal. It's only a one-book deal, but it's my big chance. But . . ."

"But what?"

"Barbara told me that I should talk you into doing this marathon book. She said it would be in everyone's best interests to do so," Ted explained.

"What the hell does that mean?" My anger was apparent even to Max, who quickly lay down and watched me warily.

"Barbara said that I should do everything I can to get you to write this book. She told me that Greene might cancel your contract and drop you entirely if you didn't cooperate. She said Greene can drop a few well-placed words in high places to make sure that you're never published again"

I was stunned. Why would Greene give a shit about some ego book about a road race and some pop sensation? Besides, I had a contract. Even his lordship can't just arbitrarily walk away from a legal agreement.

I looked over at Ted but saw he couldn't even look me in the eye. Something else was up.

"Ted, we've been friends too long and been through too much together for you to hold out on me. Tell me the whole story."

"She told me not to tell you the last part. Greene said that if he found out that I told you he'd walk away."

"Walk away from what?"

"My deal—my reward."

I was totally lost. "Your reward? For what?" I asked.

"If I can convince you to write the marathon book, Greene will give me this deal. My photography, my writing, my stories. No more being the understudy to someone else's story. No more being an afterthought on a dust jacket. No more having my name in small type, barely noticeable. My own book. My own dream." He stopped, too emotional to say any more, tears welling in his eyes.

"Ted, man," I began. "Why didn't I know how badly you wanted this? Why didn't we ever talk about this?"

"Erick, you're my best friend in the world, and we've had some great times together. But man, you don't spend a lot of time looking around you. You've created Erick's world, and the rest of us are players in that world. I've watched you bring in the big bucks for every book while I get paid a pittance. I need money, Erick. I'm tired of being poor. And this is my chance to score big. You can make it happen for me."

I didn't know how to respond. Was I really that self-absorbed? Did I blithely go through life ignoring the dreams and needs of those around me? I didn't want to believe that about myself, but would anyone?

Max interrupted my self-recrimination by shoving his big, wet friendly nose into my hand.

"Ted, why didn't you ever force my stupid egocentric self to see this from your perspective? Why didn't you smash it into my thick Norwegian head a long time ago?"

"I tried. I really, really tried. I tried in God knows how many airport bars, beat-up taxis, and cheap hotel rooms. Somehow, you were always able to turn the conversation around to your next project, your next adventure. You really have a gift for keeping the focus always on you and your work. Maybe that's why you've succeeded, and I'm the poor sidekick." He sighed. "I haven't made any money or achieved anything on my own. My only real success has been as an underpaid bit player on your stage."

"Ted, let me explain," I started, but Ted stood up abruptly.

"I just can't right now. I just can't. I never wanted you to know about this deal, but when I heard it said out loud—my own book—it just became real for the first time. I never should have told you. I may have ruined my chance with Barbara and Greene and destroyed our friendship. I don't know which will hurt me more, but now I've got to go."

He touched my shoulder gently as he hurried down the stairs and away from the townhouse. His head was down, body language conveying sorrow with every step.

If he had looked back, he would have seen that same sorrow on my face, mixed with shame at being such a poor friend.

6

I sat there for many minutes, my mind a blank. Max again broke my reverie with a sharp, deep bark. A squirrel strayed a bit too close to Max's turf.

"Come on, buddy, let's go in. At least I haven't let you down today."

Max dutifully picked up the end of his leash and waited by the door as I gathered up the galvanized pail and two empty bottles. Those green bottles were now a sad reminder of what I had hoped would be yet another evening shooting the breeze with my best friend.

My best friend. Well, he'd certainly been more of a friend to me than I had to him.

As I filled Max's bowl with his favorite chow, I poured myself a small glass of Glenmorangie ten-year scotch. As Max chomped away, bits of food escaping his big jaws and falling onto the plastic mat that valiantly tried to protect at least part of the hardwood floors, I began to think about Lord Greene's involvement in this whole affair. Why did he care at all, much less so much? Why would he get personally involved in offers that came perilously close to blackmail and bribery?

Bribery. How did someone whose days were spent in the isolated mahogany splendor of corporate power even know that Ted existed, much less know that he had a dream that even I, his supposed best friend, didn't know about?

Clearly, there could be only once source for that information: Barbara. My agent was fond of Ted and had even tried to get him more money for my last book. Had they talked about Ted's dream? Did she figure out what I had missed? More importantly, why had she convinced Lord Greene to give Ted a book deal?

Leaving Max behind, still deeply involved in his dinner, I went to my study. I dropped myself into the old leather armchair in front of one of the smaller piles of material and called Barbara's cell phone. I knew she'd be out to dinner, entertaining another round of editors, authors, or publishers. I had once very carefully suggested that perhaps a night or two dining at home would help to reduce her formidable figure and ease the strain on her well-taxed heart. Being the genteel New Yorker that she was, Barbara promptly told me that I should mind my own "effing business and focus on improving my first drafts, not her waistline." I wanted to ask, "What waistline?" But even I had some sense when it came to imposing women who wield considerable control over my life.

After a few rings, she answered in a quiet, subdued voice. The background was devoid of the sounds I expected from an evening in Manhattan: silverware clanking, glassware tinkling, and egos clashing.

"Erick. I expected you to call me tonight. Neither one of us is going to enjoy this conversation, are we?" Her preternatural calm was unsettling, and although she and I had been through a lot of turbulent times already, I didn't know if we'd survive this maelstrom.

"Barbara, you've been busy behind my back, haven't you? First Kate, now Ted. I don't know what you've got over them or why you've abandoned our friendship after all of these years. What I do know is that I want to get to the bottom of this right here and right now."

"Why? Why are you asking me questions? Do you think I really wanted to get involved in all of this?"

"All of what?"

"All the pain I've caused people—and the pain yet to happen," she said. I was confused—were we still talking about my book? "I never intended for any of this to hurt anyone. It all seemed so simple, so easy, and so foolproof—but now I'm the real fool. Do you remember the party I threw for you when you came to New York on your first book tour?"

"Of course I do. It was everything I ever thought a dazzling New York City bash would be."

"Do you remember what you called me?"

"Distinctly. I said you could be the next Martha Stewart."

"Little did you know how right you'd be."

"I have no idea what you're talking about. Martha Stewart gone wrong? Frankly, this is really starting to piss me off. What have you done to us?"

"What do you mean, us? In the long run—if you write the book, that is—I'll have done very little to you. You, Kate, Ted, and the Alex Project—all of you will make it through just fine. As long as you write the goddamn book." Her voice held a strange mix of sorrow and supplication. It was almost as if she was begging me to stop her from doing something she had to do.

"Barbara, just tell me what's going on. I'm sure we can work it all out, and everyone will be okay."

"That's just not possible anymore. It's just a matter of time, don't you see?" She paused. "Of course you don't see. You're there in your little world, oblivious to those around you. Even now I bet you think Kate is in all of this for her own glory, don't you?"

"First, Kate's in all of *what*? You still haven't told me a goddamn thing. And second, of course she is. Every waking breath she takes is about her glory." It always was and always will be about Kate.

"Erick," she sighed, her voice getting softer still. "She's not the same Kate you married, but you've never taken the time or effort to notice that she's changed. I've seen it. But you won't let reality get in the way of your anger toward her."

"Look," I said, "even if she has changed, what the hell difference does it make, anyway? What does me writing this book have to do with any of this? And how do you know so much about Kate? Maybe I should be asking Kate these questions."

"You can't do that. Don't start asking questions. It's too dangerous for you and Kate." Barbara's voice had risen in fear.

"Dangerous? How can this be dangerous to anyone, much less the one person most likely to benefit from my writing a flattering account of the Chicago Marathon? She made the event what it is today. She can't possibly be hurt by a glowing portrayal endorsed by a pop icon."

My initial anger toward Barbara was beginning to fade and becoming replaced by a growing sense of anxiety. Had I been more astute or more caring, my anxiety would have turned into full-blown fear.

Barbara was increasingly nervous, gasping slightly between phrases.

"Erick, you truly have no idea. Don't get in the middle of this fight, for your sake and for the sake of your friends and family. Don't ask questions. Just write the book and everyone will be happy."

"Even you?" I asked.

"Me? When my favorite author is happy and successful, I'm happy and successful." She said the right words, but I didn't like the tone in her voice.

"Barbara, what the hell is bothering you? Whatever it is, we can take care of it."

"If it only were that simple, Erick darling." She paused again. "I really didn't think it would go this far. I had hoped you'd just do the book, and it would end there. At least end as far as you and your friends are concerned."

"Now you're scaring me. I'm coming to New York tomorrow, and we're going to sit down and straighten this out. We'll figure it out over lunch at the Four Seasons. They still do an okay lunch, right?" If nothing else worked, I hoped that bribery with Barbara's favorite ultra-luxe lunch spot would tip the scales.

She gasped, barely able to speak. "No! Don't do that—it's not safe here, and you can't be seen with me. Let me think about all of this and call you tomorrow. But for God's sake, don't come to New York." She hung up.

. . .

Barbara's last few words had raised my anxiety level substantially. My first reaction was to call Kate, but Barbara's warning made me hesitate.

As I was hesitating, my cell phone rang. I automatically checked the caller ID before answering—a holdover from those angry years of the Kate breakup—and saw that it was Ken Hamlar, the volunteer executive director of the Alex Project. Ken was a true find, a retired corporate executive from the local utility company who lived off his pension and investments and who shared my passion for the project and the people it served. When he retired, he was the most senior African-American corporate officer in the company's history. Instead of running corporate affairs or another such pigeonhole for diversity obligations, he had been chief financial officer and wielded considerable power both at the company and in the utility industry nationwide.

Under his leadership, we renovated a small, decaying commercial printing facility into a free clinic with a six-bed hospice for the homeless and terminally ill. We had just turned the old massive shipping bay into a kitchen and dining room that served nearly one hundred meals a day. Ken found volunteers, scraped together government grants, and guilted funders all across the city. The Alex project was as much his passion as it was mine. He ran the day-to-day work of the project on his own and rarely called unless it was important. I took the call.

"Ken, let me guess. The governor changed his mind and put an extra $500,000 in the state of Illinois budget for Alex."

"Erick, I wish. We have a problem. A serious problem. We may have to shut down Alex."

I suddenly flashed back to Barbara's warnings about how this could hurt my friends and family. With no family left, the Alex Project was as close as it came.

"What's wrong?" I asked.

"I just got a call from Steve, the building manager. Our building was sold last week, and he says we're going to have to move out. And soon."

"What? What about our lease?"

"I checked the lease right away. One of the reasons why it's such a sweet deal is that the landlord has the right to move us out at any time. We never thought it would be a problem." No, we didn't. When we moved in, we were the only occupied building on the block. It wasn't, as they say, a bustling industrial center. The gentrification of Chicago's West Loop was slowly moving toward us, but we were sure we had years to go before our lovable dump saw a Starbucks or Jimmy John's nearby.

"So what happened? How long do we have?" I asked, panic edging into my voice.

"Apparently this all moved very quickly," Ken said. "The building wasn't even for sale, but the owner got an offer too sweet to resist.

Unfortunately, part of the deal was that it had to close quickly. We've got thirty days to move out."

"Thirty days? How in the hell are we going to find anything even close to what we have, much less raise the money to afford it and move everyone over? We can't leave people out on the street!"

"We've got thirty days to figure that out," Ken said. "The landlord was told that he had to get us out and out fast. He negotiated the thirty days for us with the new owners, who weren't very happy about it. Turns out they gave Steve the same thirty days."

"They fired Steve? He's been with the building for years. Doesn't he have a bunch of small kids, too?"

"They're not so small anymore—one is in college and one in high school. He's really upset. This is a tough time to find jobs in real estate."

"So who are the bastards doing this to Steve and the project?"

"I'm not sure. Some New York company called Regency Realty. A lawyer from there is the contact person."

Regency Realty. My publisher is Regency Press. Lord Greene.

You know what Tom Stoppard said: all mystical experience is coincidence, and vice versa, of course. Yeah, I didn't get the quote either, but I also didn't get why Lord Greene was suddenly so interested in my life.

"Ken, let me make some calls. Send me an email with the lawyer's contact info, and I'll see if we can get this stopped."

"All right, Erick, but don't get your hopes up. Steve said the lawyer was as cold as the Cubs in September."

"Ken, just send me the info on the lawyer. I'll sic Ross Peters on them." Ross was an Alex Project board member and a newly minted partner at one of the Loop's big law firms. They require pro bono work by all the partners (more, I suspect, from those whose billing rates hadn't yet gotten stratospheric—why give up the big dollar guys to little nonprofits like us?), and we were lucky enough to get Ross. A lawyer with a heart, Ross gave us far more of his time than the firm required, even coming in as a volunteer on his rare days off.

"Okay, Erick, I'm sending it now. But I'm still going to start with all my old real estate contacts, in case we have to find a new home in a hurry. We'll never find such perfect space at this kind of price, but I'll do my best."

"I know you will, Ken, I know you will." And I did. Although I was the public face of the Alex Project (and the source of much of its financing), I knew that Ken was the engine that kept the project moving forward. This was a crisis—and I was furious at whoever this new owner was—but we'd come through plenty of similar crises and survived.

. . .

As I hung up from the call with Ken, I realized it was getting late, and Max was the only one of us who had eaten dinner. I didn't feel like going out again, so I called in my usual order to the Thai place around the corner. Max has become a huge fan of Thai food, and yes, I know I shouldn't give table food to a dog, but did I tell you about his big brown eyes and how they look at you?

After enjoying my Pad Gai Mamuang Himmapan (chicken gently sautéed with cashews, water chestnuts, crispy vegetables, and just a little too much spice), I went to the study to check my email and do some investigative Googling. My goal was to find out as much as I could about the Chicago Marathon, which was not a huge challenge with Kate's PR army and the even larger army of marathon nerds who filled every chat room, conversation board, and Facebook page with endless stories of the personal trials and tribulations of running.

I read on and on, getting deeper into the serious runner sites, the professional runners' blogs, and the national reporters who covered Olympic sports like the marathon. Nothing I found helped solve the mystery of why Lord Greene was so desperate to have me work with Ashley on her Chicago Marathon run. Running continued to be one of the largest sports in the country and clearly the largest participatory sport, with more than half a million people running marathons each year. Like most well-organized running events—and trust me, there are thousands of them—the Chicago Marathon continued to be successful, selling out each year.

The race draws runners, their families, and their credit cards from around the world, so the city supports the event with thousands of cops, city workers, and 26 miles—excuse me, 26.2 miles—of closed streets and pissed off drivers. Sponsors love the high-end demographics of the runners, so funding dollars flow freely. The only downside I saw through my Googling efforts was that the media couldn't quite figure out how to cover the marathon. Was it a sports event with highly paid athletes? An I-overcame-great-obstacles-to-run-this-race story? Or a great opportunity to find oddballs and costumed freaks looking for their fifteen minutes of fame? (With all due respect to the late, great, and overrated Mr. Warhol, YouTube can give anyone at least three and half minutes of fame with no effort whatsoever.)

How *would* someone cover the marathon, say, in a book? How do you make something so inherently boring . . . interesting? Well, that was one challenge I didn't have to face.

7

Restless, I moved from my laptop to the overcrowded dining room, seeking inspiration from the stack of books, clippings (yes, I actually keep paper clippings from the pile of newspapers I read each day. Call me a Luddite, but I still crave the tactile pleasure of holding newsprint in my hands), and scraps of random paper that dominated the blond expanse of my table.

I was aimlessly sorting through an old folder of travel brochures when my cell phone rang. Devo's *Whip It*. I really need to change my ringtone one of these days.

It was Barbara. Instead of the unnerving silence of the background of her last call, the sounds of a busy airport intruded as she began to speak.

"Erick, I'm at LaGuardia, and I'm ticketed on the last flight out to Chicago. I should be at your place before midnight. Promise me you'll wait there and not go out. Not go anywhere."

"Of course I'll be here."

"You'll understand why I'm so concerned when I tell you what's really going on. And I have proof of all of it. Written proof. A file packed with proof. I just hope you can forgive me when you know the truth about what I've done." She sounded subdued and even a little resigned, as if she knew, even then, what was about to happen.

I tried to sound confident and cheerful, hoping to lighten her concern. "Go catch your flight, and I'll see you in a few hours."

"Good, Erick. I booked first class, so hopefully I'll sleep a bit."

That was odd. Barbara loved the service and style of the forward cabin, but she wanted it at a back-of-the-bus price. She always fought for upgrades but had never, to my knowledge, shelled out cash for a full-fare ticket before.

With a final good-bye, she clicked off. In my mind's eye, I could see her slipping her rhinestone encrusted iPhone into her couple-of-seasons-ago Prada tote, the one that teetered on the edge between carry-on and checked luggage. She loved that bag and carried it everywhere. If you asked, she'd tell you that she bought it at a thrift shop whose owner had no idea what it was really worth—that woman loved a bargain.

I had a couple of hours to kill before Barbara arrived. I knew that despite my promises to her, I couldn't stay cooped up in the house. I'd use Max as my excuse to get out. The poor pooch had to go out, right? Even Barbara couldn't blame me for that. So I quickly changed into my running gear (Genesis t-shirt and semi-ratty shorts), hooked Max up to his leash, and headed out into the evening. I couldn't have known it then, but in a few short hours I'd hear a knock on my door that would change my life forever.

. . .

It was a beautiful April night in Chicago, with no signs of the thunderstorms that had been in the forecast. Max and I knocked off a couple of lazy miles through the park where, despite my doubts, I kept us on the crowded parts of the running path and well away from the quiet sections of the park where some unknown threat might be lurking. I guess Barbara's call had me a little jumpy.

We arrived back home both feeling better for the exercise and the sheer accomplishment of getting something done. I refilled Max's water bowl (in recognition of his size, it was frankly more like a tub than a bowl) and took a quick shower, changing into khakis and an often-laundered J. Crew button-down. I felt at least somewhat obligated to dress up for my guest.

Having known Barbara for years, I was confident that she would walk in the door, drop that enormous bag at my feet, and ask what a girl had to do to get a glass of wine in this joint. I pulled a bottle of Barbara's favorite chardonnay from my built-in wine fridge (an indulgence purchased from the first royalty check of my second book. *Intense Ice*. Appropriate, right?) and pulled the cork. Of course I had to have a taste to make sure it hadn't gone bad, as if a bottle of wine would last long enough in my house to go bad. I felt it was important to respect the ritual.

As I sampled the wine, an enormous flash of lightning accompanied a crack of thunder that sounded awfully close by. The forecasted thunderstorms—straight into Chicago from the prairie where they were born—had arrived. Max, brave heart that he is, immediately hid under the dining room table where he would wait out the storm. I always worried for my table when that big lug of a dog ran under there like a frightened little kitten.

At a loss for what to do next, I popped my iPod into its dock and pulled up one of my favorite playlists. This one featured great Chicago jazz legends like Koko Taylor and Otis Rush. After getting it started, I realized that my glass was empty and got a quick refill. I chose one of the big Hepplewhite armchairs bracketing the fireplace and settled in to wait.

8

I awoke sometime later to the sound of frantic barking from Max. Moving my empty wine glass to the kitchen counter, I glanced at the clock on the microwave and was surprised to see it was already close to 1:00 a.m. I had been asleep much longer than I had thought and certainly longer than I intended. The doorbell sounded, sending Max into a fresh frenzy of barking.

Much to my surprise, my late night guest wasn't Barbara.

"Ted! What the hell are you doing here at this hour of the night?"

"Is Barbara here?"

"Barbara? No, but she should have been here long before now ... wait, why are you looking for her here?"

"Erick, I think we have a problem. Barbara's missing."

"Missing? No, she's not. She's on her way from O'Hare—"

"Barbara called me yesterday and asked me to pick her up at O'Hare tonight. She sent me an email with all the details, but I waited and waited and she never showed. Have you heard from her?"

"Wait, she called you yesterday? She told me this afternoon that she had just decided to come."

"We were talking about my book deal and at the end, she asked if I would pick her up."

"So, what happened? Where is she?"

"Her flight was due in at 10:30, and the website said it was on time. I was waiting at the arrivals area where she told me to pick her up but she never showed. I left four or five messages on her cell, but there was no response. I figured she missed me, grabbed a cab, and came straight here."

Normally, I would have attributed Barbara being a no-show at O'Hare to her decidedly fickle personality. But not this time. Not after the unsettling pressure surrounding Lord Greene. Not after those disconcerting phone calls and the mysterious proof she'd said she had for me. I didn't know why Barbara wasn't where she was supposed to be, but I was sure it wasn't good.

We immediately called Barbara's cell, her office (no answer, of course; it was the middle of the night), the airline she always flew (who refused to tell us anything, citing some asinine TSA rule), and the Chicago Police Department contingent at O'Hare (who was coolly efficient but really no help at all). We called her cell phone again and again, leaving increasingly frantic messages.

Her disappearance made no sense to either of us—unless, of course, her earlier warnings of danger had been real. I shared some of her concerns with Ted, whose slightly paranoid personality led him to read significance into all Barbara had to say. I was a little surprised, but then again, I hadn't just been coerced into working behind the back of a long-time business partner (me) by a billionaire lord of the realm who wielded power with the delicacy of a blowtorch.

Increasingly anxious, we decided our best option was to divide and conquer. I sent Ted back to O'Hare to talk to the airline and the airport police. I said I would keep trying Barbara's phone and email, as well as her assistant, Martha, and I'd wait at home in case she showed up. We made promises to call if and when we heard from Barbara.

After Ted had left and I had made another series of calls, I let Max out one more time in my pocket-sized backyard and then checked the locks and armed the home security system. I felt a little foolish checking the lock more than twice, but I did it anyway. Then I waited by the phone.

. . .

When I woke up it was barely 6:00 a.m. My dreams had been filled with thoughts of Barbara. I immediately checked my home and cell phones for messages from Barbara or Ted, checked my email, and even checked the old-fashioned mail slot in the front door. No word from Barbara. A call to Ted verified that he hadn't learned anything new at O'Hare.

A morning bowl of kibble for Max and a pot of very strong Jamaican Blue Mountain coffee for me led to a quick read through my stack of daily newsprint and a check of email. Every ping from the laptop made me quickly look to see whether it was from Barbara. But nothing; no word.

I didn't know what to do. Should I go to New York and look for Barbara? I even thought of calling Lord Greene's office at Regency to see if he knew where she might be, but Barbara's anxiety convinced me to avoid my publisher, at least for now. So now what to do?

Soon it was late morning. With my iPhone and cordless phone in hand, I ran upstairs, took a quick shower, and returned downstairs. A sharp knock on my front door echoed through the house like last night's thunder.

9

I opened the door to find a uniformed Chicago police officer and a man in a suit standing on my top step. My heart dropped. Barbara.

"Mr. Anderssen?" the cop asked.

"Yes." My mouth was suddenly dry.

"I'm Officer O'Brien of the Chicago Police Department and this is Detective Hanson. May we come in?"

"What's this about?" Hell, I already knew. "It's about Barbara, isn't it?"

I stepped aside and silently invited them into the living room. The formality of the space seemed right for what I knew was going to be a very somber discussion.

They were guests, and I needed to offer them refreshments, said the voice of my prim and serious Norwegian Lutheran mother. But despite my mumbled offer of coffee, tea, anything, they seemed to want to get to the issue at hand. We all sat down, with my beautiful Hepplewhite chairs flanking the fireplace suddenly looking less comfortable, filled as they were by serious people on a serious mission.

While O'Brien's name should have signaled the stereotypical florid and overweight Irish cop, this O'Brien was quite different. She was as blond as any of my Norwegian ancestors, with startling blue eyes and the build of a long distance runner. Hanson was equally fit, but dark where O'Brien was light, wearing what looked to be a designer suit and handsome tie, both far more expensive than I would have thought possible on a detective's salary. I think I was staring again. His gold detective badge caught the light from the room's leaded windows. Now I knew I was staring.

"How do you know Barbara Bronfman?" the detective began.

"She's my agent," I replied. "Is she okay? Have you found her?"

"When did you last speak to Ms. Bronfman?" asked Hanson, pen poised over his notepad as if to not miss a word from me.

"Yesterday. We spoke on the phone early in the day and again in the late afternoon. She was coming to Chicago last night and wanted to see me when she arrived."

"Do you know the reason behind her trip?"

"Not really. I assume it was business related—everything was with Barbara. I'm a bit late with my new book, and she had been after me to develop the next great idea."

The detective looked puzzled. "Why would she come all the way here in person to talk about that? Couldn't she accomplish the same thing on the phone or by email with a lot less hassle?"

"She tried, but I still hadn't sent her anything. Maybe she thought this would be a big dramatic gesture that would get me motivated."

He continued. "Did you see her last night or speak to her?"

"No, she never showed up at the airport. So what's going on here? Why won't you tell me why you're here?"

"Where were you between nine o'clock and midnight last night?"

Now they were seriously scaring me.

"I was here all night."

"Did you have any guests? See anyone who can verify that you were here?"

"Ted McCormick was here. He's a friend, and we've worked on books together."

"We've already talked to him, and he said pretty much the same thing."

During all of this, O'Brien just sat and stared at me with those icy blue eyes. Clearly some type of bad cop/staring cop routine. Trying to break me down. No, I wasn't feeling the least bit guilty. Even though I had nothing to feel guilty about. I didn't. Really.

As I turned my attention back to Hanson, I saw him look up from his notebook, briefly close his eyes, and sigh. I went cold all over.

"Mr. Anderssen, I'm sorry to be the one to tell you, but Ms. Bronfman is dead."

Despite every scenario that had gone through my mind since last night, and despite every sign, signal, and sense telling me that this was why they came, I was stunned.

10

"What happened?" I found my voice but barely, and tears were beginning to flow.

"That's what we're trying to figure out," Hanson said. "We got a call from CPD O'Hare last night saying they had found a body in one of the parking garages. Her wallet was next to the body. We identified her from her driver's license."

"So how did you find me?"

"A handwritten note in the pocket of her jacket—kind of a quick itinerary that she had written for herself. Your name, Mr. McCormick's, and both of your cell phone numbers."

"Did you find her big Prada bag and phone? She'd never travel without both of those."

"We've got people retracing her steps from the gate to where the body was found, but so far, nothing. We also have a team looking at the airport security camera video to see if there's anything there. There's been a rash of purse snatchings at the airport lately. We think this may have been a robbery gone bad, although she had a pretty impressive emerald ring that wasn't taken."

An emerald ring? I had never seen Barbara wearing anything that expensive. Then, thinking out loud, I said, "So no file either."

I immediately realized what I had done. I had needlessly opened myself up for a whole new set of questions.

. . .

Thirty minutes later, I had finally extricated myself from the hole I'd dug for myself with my stupid mutterings about a file. I explained to Hanson that if Barbara was coming to see me, it must be about my rapidly approaching book deadline, and she would have brought her file of ideas so we could go over them. I would be naturally anxious to get my hands on that file so that it wouldn't fall into the hands of other writers. I hoped they believed me.

As they were leaving, Hanson asked me if I had talked to anyone in Barbara's office since last night. I explained that Barbara was a freelance agent who worked out of an office in her Upper West Side townhouse with only a part-time assistant, a quiet young lady named Martha Johnson. Martha handled her research, travel, and occasional special events. Giving the detective Martha's name and contact information, I promised I wouldn't contact her until I knew the detective had talked to her. I also promised I wouldn't leave town without contacting Hanson.

It wasn't a difficult promise to make. I couldn't begin to understand how, but I sensed all the pieces would soon fit together: Barbara's death, Lord Greene's involvement, and the Chicago Marathon. I wasn't going anywhere until I made sure that whoever killed my friend paid the price.

. . .

I left a message for Ted asking him to call me back right away. I wanted to know more about the conversations he and Barbara had regarding her visit to Chicago.

While I waited to hear back from Ted, I spent the rest of the morning and afternoon answering emails, taking a long conference call with a producer who was working on turning my books into *National Geographic* specials, and paying the bills, tears coming to my eyes whenever I thought of Barbara. I rummaged through the leftovers in the fridge, piecing together a simple meal of bread, cheese, and an only slightly overripe apple. As tempting as it was, I avoided the obvious glass of wine that would have made the meal complete. I wanted to concentrate on the problem of who had murdered Barbara.

I knew I had to approach the problem logically, no matter how much I might be grieving for her. With no callback from Ted, despite more messages left on his cell and at his apartment, I sat down with a notebook and started listing everything I knew so far:

- Barbara was pressuring me to write this marathon book.
- She wanted me to have lunch with my ex to talk about it.
- Barbara and Kate were bribing me with access to one of today's disposable pop stars and unfettered access to the marathon.
- I was being further bribed with money for the Alex Project.
- Barbara was working with Lord Greene to bribe—and threaten—Ted in order to get me to write the damned marathon book.
- And it looked like Greene (via Regency Realty?) was threatening the Alex Project with eviction.

Yet despite Barbara's active role in all of this, something was going on that disturbed her enough to make her get on a plane to Chicago to see me. Had the answer been in the file that she was carrying?

Lord Greene seemed to be the common denominator in several

of these items, but that just didn't make sense. Why would a British lord with business interests all over the world care about one book on running a marathon? And how did this Ashley fit into the picture? As I thought about these questions, I realized that there was one other common denominator in this list: me. There was something I had that Lord Greene wanted. I just needed to figure out what it was.

My first thought was to look closer into Regency Realty, so I started a little digging on my own via Google. There wasn't much there, or at least not much that could help me out. I called Regency's office to get a copy of their most recent annual report, but they referred me to the skimpy online version. I knew I had to learn more about this shadowy Regency Realty and how it might connect with my publisher, but I needed a way in—or someone with well-placed sources. And no one fit the bill like Bruce Mays, a freelance investor and researcher I had used as a reference for financial questions regarding previous books. Bruce had worked for one of the big brokerage firms for years, building networks that bridged the industry. He knew half the open outcry traders at the Chicago Board of Trade, a bunch of runners at the New York Stock Exchange (the runners always had the best scoops), any number of investment bankers, and some semi-unsavory individuals associated with some of the big international trading firms. If anyone could get the real scoop on GrandHotel, it would be Bruce. Of course, I'd pay dearly for the information. I might as well make the reservation now at Chicago Cut, Bruce's favorite steak place, and start saving for what was going to be a costly evening. Would the wine bill exceed the cost of the food? If so, it was always the sign of a good time.

I sent a quick email to Bruce asking him to do some digging for me.

While I was on a roll, I thought I'd check out this Ashley person. Googling celebrities was usually an exercise in sensory overload, and Ashley's story wasn't an exception.

I found that she had started her ignominious climb to stardom as a backup dancer for Britney Spears. Oh yeah, that's impressive. Sort of the poor man's Julliard.

I read how she was "discovered" by some star maker and crammed through stardom school like the 1980s boy bands. After a couple of well-placed appearances on *American Idol* and a tribute show or two, the industry started to take notice. Before you knew it, she had a few hit songs, a Grammy for best new artist, an upcoming national tour, and the rest is Internet history. I checked out the Google images and saw a pretty, generic blonde with too much makeup and not nearly enough fabric in her clothes. She seemed to range from Juicy Couture to Jean Paul Gaultier, but she couldn't carry off either of them. Maybe she was coming out with her own clothing line so that she'd have something respectable to wear. I had to admit that she seemed to be making the most of her fifteen minutes of fame.

11

It was another beautiful spring day in Chicago, but it didn't seem so beautiful to me. I still couldn't believe that Barbara was dead. Murdered. My mind was full of questions and no answers.

Picking up my phone from the bedside table, I sat down in front of the big bay windows overlooking the street. I saw I had several voice mails and even more missed calls. Caller ID showed only one call from Ted but several from Detective Hanson, as well as one voice mail from Ted and one from Hanson. The detective was going to have to wait; I needed to talk to Ted.

His voice mail was brief. "I just can't believe it. Barbara, gone. That is so messed up. Call me." He sounded odd, not like himself. I guess that was to be expected. I called him back but got his voice mail again. After leaving a message, I waited a few minutes in case he called right back. He didn't.

I didn't want to talk to Hanson until I had a chance to sift through my thoughts, so instead I changed into my running gear, grabbed Max, and headed back toward the park.

We stopped at the South Pond so that Max could bark at the ducks. Tuning him out, I thought again about my last conversation with Barbara, about her troubled tone and deep concern over something dangerous that could affect all of us. I tried to think of a clue that she might have given me, but nothing resonated, nothing helped make sense of all that was happening. Having no brilliant insights, Max and I headed north before looping back to the house.

I checked my phone, but there were no calls from Ted. Another call from Detective Hanson, but no new message. Sure that it could wait, I showered and dressed. After mindlessly working through a couple of days' mail that had accumulated on the front hall table, I resigned myself to calling Hanson back. Just my luck. He answered.

"Detective, this is Erick Anderssen. You called?"

"Yes, I did. Several times. I have a few more questions for you. I'd like to stop by around 5:00 this afternoon."

"I'm sorry, I won't be here. I have a previous commitment." And I did. I wasn't making it up. Really.

"Can you change it? This is important."

"No, I really can't. Can we do this tomorrow?"

"All right. I'll be at your front door at 9:00 a.m. And if you talk to your friend Ted, have him be there too. He's not returning my calls either."

I agreed to give the message to Ted. Hanson hung up.

I was suddenly exhausted. I'd had next to no sleep in the last day, and I was emotionally drained from the news about Barbara. I made it as far as the living room, where I collapsed on the big sofa and quickly fell asleep.

12

My phone's calendar reminder woke me just in time to change and head out for my evening's commitment, one that I had been looking forward to for a very long time. And something that would take my mind off of Barbara, even if it was just for an evening.

After waiting to have my application approved, I was finally being welcomed as a new member of the Adventurers Club of Chicago. Founded nearly one hundred years ago, the club exists (to quote its motto) *"To provide a hearth and home for those who have left the beaten path and made for adventure."*

The club boasted a pretty impressive list of former members: Admiral Byrd, Theodore Roosevelt, Thor Heyerdahl, and Sir Edmund Hillary. The clubhouse was this incredible loft space in the South Loop filled with mementos of the members' adventures all around the world. I'd been there for lunch as I was being vetted for membership, and I was fascinated by the stories the members told of this item or that, including what they claimed was the largest privately held collection of shrunken heads in the world. Who doesn't want to belong to a club like that?

The organization is a serious one, of course, and features lectures and study programs, while its nonprofit foundation gives grants to students for scientific and conservation studies. I'd been asked to join after one of the members read my book *Africa Alive*. She had just returned from a project working with the Maasai on improved healthcare for their people and thought I would be an interesting addition to the club. I jumped at the chance, and now I was headed downtown for my welcoming event and what I was sure would be a fascinating evening.

. . .

I was absolutely right about that. When I finally stumbled home up the front steps of my townhouse it was well past midnight, and I was well past my limit of full-bodied red wines. I hoped that I would remember all the wonderful stories the next morning and forget the number of empty wine bottles on the club's famous "Long Table."

I turned my phone back on after receiving Max's always-exuberant welcome home. No messages, no missed calls. How odd that I hadn't heard from Ted. But it was too late to call him, so I let Max out in the backyard for a brief moment and then headed up to bed. I knew that Detective Hanson would be at my door, as promised, in a few short hours, and I needed to be at least reasonably sharp so as to not get myself in any deeper with him. So, setting my alarm for 8:30, I fell into a restless sleep.

13

The doorbell rang at precisely 9:00. I opened the front door, blocking Max as best I could given his size and eagerness to greet our visitor. Hanson was alone this time, dressed as impeccably as before, this time in a dove gray suit with a crisply starched white shirt and beautiful sky blue tie. I was less well suited out, dressed for a run instead of a LaSalle Street board meeting. I gestured for Hanson to go to the living room, where we took our seats as before: me on the sofa and him by the fireplace across from me.

"Mr. Anderssen," he began, "as I told you on the phone, I have a number of questions for you. I appreciate your willingness to meet with me."

"No problem, Detective. I'll do whatever I can to find out who killed Barbara."

"Good to hear, sir. First, tell me again where you were the night Ms. Bronfman died."

"As I told you before, I was here. Alone. And I have no alibi, unless you can interrogate the dog."

"As much as I'd like to, I can't. So no one can place you here—you didn't order food, talk to a neighbor—"

"No, but I was online. Can't my internet service provider verify that?"

"With your permission, yes. But all they can tell us is that someone was online—no proof that it was you, sir. You'll have to authorize them to release what information they do have."

"Happy to do so."

"What about your friend Ted?"

"What about him?"

"He—like you—was home with no alibi."

"I've known Ted for many, many years. If he said he was home, he was home."

The detective paused before asking the next question. "I gather he was in communication with Ms. Bronfman without your knowledge."

This time I paused. I was trying to figure out how best to answer that one. I thought the truth was likely to be the best course to follow. It was certainly the easiest.

"Yes, I guess that's so. I can't tell you exactly what led to that. You'll have to ask Ted."

"I certainly would like to, but he isn't returning my phone calls or answering his door at home. We really need to talk to him. Have you spoken with him lately?"

"No. We've traded phone messages, but I haven't talked to him since he was here the night Barbara died."

"When you do talk to him, tell him that he isn't doing himself any favors by not responding to my calls. It just puts him under suspicion."

"I will," I replied, not convinced that the detective was doing much more than offering idle threats so that he could check one more interview off of his to-do list. There is no way Ted could really be a suspect. But why was he avoiding the cops? And why wasn't he at home? Where was he?

"Mr. Anderssen, are you and Mr. McCormick involved?"

"Involved?"

"Romantically."

"I can't imagine how that is any of your goddamn business, but no. We are not."

"I understand. You can appreciate why I'm asking."

"I don't understand, and I don't appreciate it. Whether Ted and I are sleeping together has nothing to do with Barbara's murder, and I resent the implication."

"Fine, sir. One last question," said the detective. Only one more? That surprised me, given how important this interview had seemed when the detective called yesterday. "I talked to Ms. Bronfman's assistant Martha Johnson yesterday. We actually talked for quite a while. She tells me that over the last few days, Ms. Bronfman had been quite upset. And most of what she was concerned about seemed to involve you. Ms. Johnson didn't know the details, but she thought you might. What had Ms. Bronfman so concerned?"

"To be honest with you, I have no idea. She mentioned something about a problem when we spoke on the phone, but she gave me no details."

"When we last spoke, you asked about a file folder that Ms. Bronfman might have been carrying. Was that file related to Ms. Bronfman's concerns?"

"I don't know what was in the damn folder or even if there really was a folder. She said she was coming to talk to me about my next book. Like I told you, I'm a little behind in developing the idea and beginning research. She always has notes on book ideas, copies of my contract. I assume that's what was concerning her in the file." I knew that I was making it up as I went and hoped, again, that Hanson didn't see through my song and dance.

There was another awkward pause as Hanson quietly stared at me, hoping, I thought, that I'd say something stupid and incriminate myself. Again, I knew that my best option was to say nothing, especially since I was so angry. After a minute, he made yet another note in his book, closed it, and stood up.

"I'm sure I'll have more questions for you, sir. Please don't leave town without checking with me first."

"I'll be attending Barbara's funeral." My voice broke at that. "In New York."

"The body is still waiting for autopsy, so it will be a few days. Make sure you check with me before you leave town for any reason."

"Does that mean I'm a suspect?" Perhaps a stupid question, but I wanted to know.

"No, but it does mean that I need to know where you are and to make sure you don't disappear like your friend Ted has."

"So who are your suspects? What's going on with the investigation? Why the hell haven't you found out who did this?"

"Sir, I can't tell you anything about our investigation. Just know that we're actively pursuing a number of leads. Now, if you'll excuse me."

"Gladly."

I ushered him out the front door, restraining myself from slamming it shut behind him.

14

I tried Ted again via phone, email, and text, but still there was no response. I called a number of mutual friends, but no one had seen Ted for days. They all assured me they would let me know if they had a sighting.

Restless and deeply concerned about all that was happening, I settled into my Saturday routine, hoping that the customary grocery, laundry, and dry cleaning stops would bring some semblance of normalcy after the horrible events of the past few days. A late afternoon run with Max and a grilled chicken Caesar salad completed a day that was, in many ways, very ordinary despite the extraordinary circumstances in which I found myself.

Sunday began normally enough. I had made plans to meet old friends at Ann Sather's for brunch and wanted to keep the commitment. Spending a couple of hours catching up on gossip regarding absent friends over Sather's famous Swedish pancakes with lingonberries sounded like a good distraction.

. . .

And for the most part it was. I happened to mention that people were trying to convince me to write my next book on running the marathon and was inundated with stories from nearly everyone at the table.

They'd run themselves, someone in the family ran, friends ran to raise money for charity. My friend Chris, who had battled breast cancer for years, ran side-by-side for 26.2 miles with one of the nurses who helped her win her fight. They raised more than $20,000 for breast cancer research that day.

I had forgotten—if I had ever known—how broadly the marathon touched everyday Chicagoans.

Listening to their stories (and the pancakes) helped me forget—if only for a few minutes—about Barbara's horrific death and how much I was going to miss her. I could forget about all the problems being caused by Lord Greene's strange machinations. But all my worries came crashing back when I got home and there was still no word from Ted. No calls, no emails, no text messages. I was now truly scared for Ted and knew I had to track him down.

Ted lived in Wrigleyville, the now trendy neighborhood surrounding the Cub's century-old monument to frustration. Ringing the bell at his three-flat apartment building, I wondered what I was going to do if he didn't answer. I didn't have a Plan B, so I considered myself fortunate when the buzzer sounded and the front door clicked. I headed up to Ted's third-floor apartment and found his door slightly ajar. I slowly pushed it open while calling his name.

"I'm in here, Erick," was the soft reply from the living room. Despite it being another beautiful spring day, Ted's shades were pulled tight, leaving his artfully decorated home in deep shadows. I could barely make out his expression as he looked up at me from the sofa.

"Ted, buddy, are you okay? I've been trying to get a hold of you for days!"

"Yeah, I don't know who has left more messages—you or some cop who wants to talk to me about Barbara."

"So why haven't you called me back?"

"Erick, I just couldn't. This whole mess—Barbara's murder, Lord Greene's threats—I just couldn't talk to anyone. And I'm not sure I can now. It might be best if you just left."

"There is no way in hell I'm going anywhere until you talk to me about all of this. You've already pointed out my shortcomings as a friend. Well, it's time I stepped up and became the kind of friend you deserve. And, frankly, it sounds like you could use that kind of friend right now. I know I could."

With a sigh, Ted looked down at his folded hands. He didn't reply for what felt like a very long time.

Finally, he started talking in a low voice, almost a monotone.

Once he started, he kept talking for almost fifteen uninterrupted minutes, telling me again the story of the book offer from Lord Greene (via Barbara) and his conflict over his sense of betrayal toward me while being excited about his first real opportunity to shine on his own. He told me about the many conversations he'd had with Barbara about that conflict. She was understanding and compassionate while at the same time being the pragmatist she always was. This book would be very important to Ted's career. He couldn't live in my shadow forever. I would understand, Barbara told him. She was also adamant that Ted do everything he could to talk me into the marathon book.

"Bro, she talked about that marathon book like it was life or death." Upon saying that, Ted paused, fully realizing what he had just said.

A beat or two later I broke the silence.

"Ted, it seems like Barbara suddenly came into some money. She flew first class, and she wore that emerald ring. Did she just get a big advance for someone?"

"Yeah, something like that," Ted said guardedly.

"What does that mean?"

"I can't tell you. I really can't."

"Why the hell not? What secrets are you keeping from me?"

"Nothing good will come out of you knowing. Especially not you. It's not safe. None of us are safe—except maybe you, if you'll agree to cooperate."

"Safe from whom? Ted, what the hell?"

"Greene is a very powerful man. Don't get in his way."

"I just don't understand why Greene is putting so much pressure on everyone around me to get me to write this stupid book. Maybe I should go see Greene and ask him directly."

"You'll have a chance on Tuesday," Ted said.

"Tuesday?"

"Yes, I got a call from Martha Johnson just before you got here. They've completed the autopsy—God, what a horrific word—and are releasing Barbara's body today. She'll be flown back to New York tomorrow, and the funeral is on Tuesday. I assume Greene will make an appearance."

"Why did Martha call you and not me?"

"I don't know the whole story, but she's pretty pissed off at you. Barbara was upset these last few weeks, and for some reason, Martha blames you for whatever trouble Barbara was in."

"I have no fucking clue what any of this is about! What the hell is going on with everybody?"

"That's all I know," Ted said. "I wish I could tell you more."

My anger died as quickly as it had flared. I asked dully, "Are you going out for the funeral?"

"Yeah, I guess."

"We could fly out Monday night. Maybe it won't be so bad if we go together."

"Good idea. The Waldorf?"

Ted's mention of the storied Park Avenue hotel brought a smile to both of us. Barbara was a lifelong New Yorker who had firm ideas regarding just about everything New York. She tended toward the classics. The Four Seasons for business lunches, Sardi's after the theater, Bergdorf, Dean & Deluca, Zabar's, and—lately, it appears—Tiffany's. And in her mind, the Waldorf Astoria was the true New York City hotel. After forty years of putting her clients and friends up at the Waldorf, she knew half the staff and everyone important at the hotel.

As we talked more about Barbara and our plans for New York, day slipped into early evening. Ted suggested we grab dinner nearby. I was glad to see that he wanted to get out of the apartment, so I readily agreed.

We continued our conversation over beer (well, beers) and wings at John Barleycorn, just steps from the friendly but frustrating confines. I told Ted about calls I'd received from other authors that Barbara worked with, although I hadn't heard anything from the publishing company.

Setting that oddity aside, I passed along Detective Hanson's message that he wanted to talk to Ted again. Unfortunately, that seemed to darken Ted's mood and effectively ended the evening. He picked at another wing or two, but he was clearly thinking of things other than our conversation. We soon parted with my promise to make our travel arrangements and send them on to Ted via email that same night.

I stood there for a moment, watching Ted's forlorn figure walk north on Clark Street toward home.

15

The morning dawned with heavy clouds overhanging Chicago with the promise of rain and more thunderstorms later in the day. Packing for New York, I carefully wrapped my best dark suit in a dry cleaning bag to hold down the wrinkles and pulled the rest of my clothes into my carry-on. Flying thousands of miles a year taught me to pack well and never, ever to check luggage.

The doorbell rang, and it was Julie from PetSet, Chicago's best doggie daycare, who was there to pick up Max with a promise to take good care of him while I was gone.

Minutes later, the cab pulled into the airport. I'd agreed to meet Ted at the American Airlines Admiral's Club. We had a travel ritual. Ted was terrified of flying, so we started every trip with a glass or two of champagne. So far, our routine had worked. Thousands of miles of flying, and we hadn't crashed yet. Why push your luck?

16

The predicted thunderstorms moved through Chicago just in time to give us an hour delay, but the flight itself was uneventful, and we made up a little time in the air. Once on the ground, we made a speedy exit from LaGuardia and headed in a cab for the Waldorf. Why New York City thinks it's necessary to hear recorded cautions from a famous New Yorker in every cab is beyond me. Today it was former mayor Ed Koch. Really? Ed Koch?

With no more delays, we were soon in our rooms with plans to head out for dinner. One of my favorite New York City restaurants was only minutes away from the Waldorf. Daniel was the flagship restaurant of famed chef Daniel Boulud and was a temple to food, design, and service. With New York's weather more accommodating than Chicago's had been, we had a pleasant fifteen-minute walk up Park Avenue.

We hit our 8:30 reservation spot on and soon were enjoying the best of Daniel's creations. The roasted black sea bass was exquisite. Ted had the lamb. We chatted throughout the dinner, but I realized that from O'Hare to the Waldorf to Daniel, neither of us had mentioned Barbara, his lordship, or any of the troubles surrounding us. We finished dinner and headed to Daniel's Bar and Lounge where Xavier was presiding over the bar as usual. We both had a scotch. Then, suddenly, a silence fell over us, and we both knew it was time. We spent the next half hour talking about

Barbara and toasting her with a second (and perhaps a third) scotch. I shared some of my favorite Barbara stories, telling Ted about how I had relentlessly begged her to represent me for my first book.

"I was rejected by so many people. I was getting incredibly discouraged when I read about Barbara in an online article about new authors. There must have been something in my email to her that caught her eye because she asked for more details about my idea. When I look back on what I sent her, I realize how needy I sounded, but I was convinced that baby boomer adventures had an audience. I'm sure I made her crazy with my repeated pleas to represent me, but later, well after she agreed, she said she admired my stubborn streak but pointed out that not everyone would appreciate it. After I told her about my stubborn father, she shared with me stories about her family. Barbara was very proud of her Jewish roots.

"She used to tell me stories that her grandparents told her about the pogroms that reached even their small town in Austria. Fortunately for them, they were able to escape to England thanks to some business connections her grandfather had made as a craftsman. The rest of their family was lost to the Holocaust."

Talking about her family's tragedy led us to speculate again on what might have caused her to be murdered and how it all fit together. Nothing new presented itself, no new answers.

Knowing that tomorrow was going to be a long and troubling day, we strolled back to the hotel and—for me at least—a fitful night's sleep.

. . .

Tuesday arrived, bringing low, gray clouds and a cold drizzle. Appropriate for the day and location. I headed for the lobby to meet Ted, who was waiting for me outside Peacock Alley, looking as sad as I felt.

I had reserved a Town Car for Ted and me after learning from Ted that we had a number of miles to go before the day ended back at LaGuardia. We threw our bags into the back and headed for the funeral.

. . .

As we pulled up to Riverside Memorial Chapel on West 76th Street, I told Ted that Barbara had planned out her service. At first glance, it appeared that her arrangements were being followed to the letter. With little of Barbara's family in the US, I wasn't surprised to see Martha Johnson in charge. When I went up to speak with her, she suddenly became very busy and turned away.

We were ushered into Riverside's smaller chapel, which was already crowded with people I didn't know. With one exception. I saw Lord Greene near the front, looking like the elegant and wealthy patrician he was. His perfect posture, beautiful bespoke suits, and full head of silver hair were every bit the British lord. I vowed to keep an eye on him so that I could catch him as he left.

The service was brief but moving. A reading of Psalm 23 and excerpts from other Psalms opened the service, followed by the Memorial Prayer, the Kel Maleh Rachamim, or so the program told me. The rabbi, who told delightful stories of having known Barbara for decades, spoke briefly. There were two eulogies: one by her nephew, who was clearly grief stricken and who had a hard time getting through his remarks, and one by Martha, who eulogized her mentor in what I thought was an incredibly moving tribute.

"Barbara was the most wonderful mentor a young person could ever have," Martha began. "As busy as she was, she never failed to stop and explain why she did something, where her ideas came from, who inspired her. She told me stories of authors she had found, famous people she had met. She shared her knowledge and years of experience with me from the very first day we met. I was incredibly fortunate to have met Barbara and even more fortunate to have worked so closely with her. We were very, very close, especially over the last year. It's as if she knew she wouldn't be around much longer and couldn't wait to impart to me what she knew."

As Martha spoke, I watched Lord Greene from across the chapel. He seemed uninterested until Martha spoke of Barbara's last year. His silvered head shot up and he looked intently at Martha, who seemed to find his stare. She finished her eulogy looking only at him. I wondered if there was yet another piece to the puzzle that I was trying to solve.

Following the service, we were directed to follow the hearse to Mount Carmel Cemetery, one of the largest Jewish cemeteries in the New York area. As we stood and watched, a group of somber men in black carried Barbara's casket from the hearse to the grave, pausing several times along the way. This pause, I was told, would happen seven times to indicate an unwillingness to end the service. Led by the rabbi, the pallbearers reached the open grave and labored to lower the casket.

Since I had missed Lord Greene at the end of the service, I looked for him at the cemetery but didn't see him in the crowd. I wondered why he had chosen not to follow the casket to Mount Carmel.

The rabbi led a short service which included psalms, a prayer, and, as the grave was filled in, the Burial Kaddish. As the Kaddish finished, we slowly drifted to our cars and headed back to Mid-Town for the reception at the Yale Club. I knew Barbara had chosen the site and planned the menu to include all her favorites. I knew she would have loved this party. Ted and I exchanged only a few words during the drive.

17

As tuxedoed waiters passed champagne and hors d'oeuvres, I chatted with people I knew from Barbara's life, mostly other authors that she represented. I'd met many of them on joint book tours or at one of Barbara's famous launch parties. Unfortunately, the two people I really wanted to talk to—Lord Greene, who was here despite having missed the graveside service, and Martha—seemed to be moving in perfect cocktail party ballet, constantly putting as much space (and as many people) as possible between them and me. I saw them pirouette in the same direction twice. The first time they exchanged a few brief words. The second time Martha began to speak, but Greene shook his head and quickly turned to greet someone else. That didn't sit too well with Martha, but she moved on with more grace than I would have given her credit for. I wondered how the owner of the entire company would know Martha, a part-time assistant to an agent.

As I introduced Ted to a couple of fellow authors, I looked over Ted's shoulder just as a strongly built young man in a black suit and earpiece leaned over to whisper something to Lord Greene. Greene immediately smiled at the woman he was talking to, kissed her on both cheeks in the French style, and strode out of the room through the big double oaken doors that led to the lobby. Hurrying, I caught up to him just outside the club under the navy blue awning with its interlocking Y and C.

His bodyguard stepped between us, but Greene touched the young man's arm.

"Wolfgang, it's all right. I know this gentleman."

"Lord Greene." My mouth was dry and my heart pounding in my chest.

"Mr. Anderssen. Nice to see you, despite the circumstances."

"Thank you. I wish I could say the same."

"What's this?"

"You know goddamned well what this is. You think your wealth and title let you push people around and manipulate them. Well, it doesn't work that way, and it's about fucking time you figured that out."

"Ah, so hurt, so angry."

"I am hurt. And angry. My friend is dead. People—you—are manipulating everyone around me. What you're trying to do with the Alex Project is especially underhanded. Those people haven't done anything to you, and you're threatening their home. I want to know what's going on."

"I too am sad about Barbara's death. But I have no knowledge of any manipulation. Perhaps your writer's imagination is taking over, Mr. Anderssen."

"I write fact, not fiction, Greene. I know what you're up to; I just don't know why. But I'm going to find out."

"Be very careful, young man. Stay out of my affairs. I have nothing to do with this imaginary conspiracy of yours."

"I don't believe you, Greene. I'm going to get to the bottom of this."

"People who ask too many questions soon learn to regret their actions. I hope you won't be one of them."

With that, he turned and got into the backseat of the big black Daimler that had been idling at the curb. The young bodyguard hurried around to the front passenger side door, barely shutting it before the car pulled away from the curb.

Knowing that the threats meant I was getting somewhere with Greene, I hurried back into the reception to try to find Martha in order to ask her about Greene. A bit of my famous luck showed up. Martha stepped right in front of me just as I entered the room.

"Martha," I said, watching her startle as she saw me. She looked left and right as if to find a way out, but there was to be no easy exit for her. Apparently resigned to the confrontation, she gave me a chilly smile.

"Erick."

"Martha," I repeated. "Let's cut to the chase. Why have you been avoiding me all day—in fact, ever since Barbara's death?"

"You mean Barbara's murder."

"Yes, I guess that's what I mean."

"What would I possibly have to say to you? You're the cause of her gruesome death. I've lost my job and my shot at being an agent. All because of you."

"Why is any of this my fault? I had no involvement in what happened to Barbara."

"You most certainly did. It was you she went to Chicago to see. It was you that dominated her last few weeks. It was you that caused her so much pain—all the phone calls that ended with her being so upset. And the file—she carried that big purple file with your name on it everywhere. You might not have been the one who slit her throat, but you were the cause of her death."

"I knew Barbara was concerned about me and had something important to tell me, but I have no idea what it was. I knew she was pressuring me to write my next book about the Chicago Marathon, but I don't know why it was so important to her and Lord Greene. That's all I know, I swear to you."

"You know, Erick, I don't know if you are telling the truth or not. And, in fact, I don't care whether you are or not. It doesn't change the fact that Barbara is dead."

It sounded like my sheer existence was causing people to be hurt—even killed—and I didn't know why.

"Martha, where is the file that Barbara was talking about? The police told me that she didn't have it with her when they found her body."

"Well, she had it with her when she went to the airport. I saw it sticking out of her bag when she left the office."

"The Prada?"

"No, it was a Marc Jacobs—a new one. What difference does the bag make?"

Those bags cost $500 or more. What was Barbara doing splurging on something like that? It didn't make any sense.

Ted had been watching our exchange from a few feet away with concern in his eyes. He came closer, ready to intervene. Always the protector. He gently touched Martha's arm. She turned toward him and gave him a gentle hug, and then she walked off without a single glance in my direction.

Ted and I made small talk with the other mourners, and then headed down to the Town Car and our return flight to Chicago.

18

I was grateful that the week went quietly and uneventfully. A nice, routine week with no drama. I had an Alex Project board of directors meeting coming up, which meant working with Ken on a report for the board on the project's finances and main projects. Other than our space crisis—for which Ken had already identified a few potential solutions—everything else was on track. I lunched with friends, made sure Max had a good run every day (well, almost), and stayed in touch with Ted.

I also continued my research on possible subjects for my next book. Barbara's death didn't change the fact that I had contracted obligations to Regency Press that I had to fulfill. I had scraps and pieces of ideas scattered all over the dining room table, so I spent some time organizing all those little bits and parts into ideas, concepts, and notions. Unfortunately, while I was now better organized, none of the ideas seemed to catch fire with me.

Frustrated and increasingly concerned about the approaching deadline to deliver a completed book by year-end (and without my mother bear of an agent to defend me against the publishers' minions), I thought I'd clean out my email box in case there was an idea floating around the ether. No amazing new inspirations were to be found.

But as I sorted through my electronic correspondence, I came across the original email from Barbara that seemed to have started all of this—her suggestion that I focus on the trend of older runners tackling a marathon. At the time, I had been furious with the idea of it and the pressure she was bringing to bear on it; now, with her gone, it made me think of her and how she was always looking out for me. Always steering me in the right direction whether I liked it or not. I wondered if I had been too quick to dismiss the idea. Was I still so bitter about the divorce that I wanted nothing to do with Kate or anything that involved her? I printed out Barbara's email, cleared off a section of my dining room table-cum-research center, and laid it in the middle.

Over the next couple of days, I pondered the idea using my now-standard book development process. I chatted about the idea with friends, ran the idea past Ted, and did a pro-and-con list while raising a pint or two at O'Shaughnessy's. I even did some old-fashioned research, reading two of the definitive books on marathoning and on our famous local race: Hal Higdon's *Marathon: The Ultimate Training Guide* and Professor Andrew Suozzo's *The Chicago Marathon*.

I found myself talking about the marathon more and more with the circle of friends that had become my unofficial sounding board over the years. And while there wasn't a runner in the group, everyone knew at least one person who had run the Chicago Marathon, and nearly all of them had amazingly inspirational stories to tell. Recovery from a serious illness. Weight loss that added years to a life. Raising money in memory of a lost loved one. By the end of the week, I had to admit that I was intrigued.

Maybe this *was* my next book. And not just because Greene or anyone else was pressuring me to do it. Because now it felt right.

19

I knew I couldn't go any further without talking to Kate, a conversation I was dreading. Or should I say yet another conversation I was dreading. Seemed to be a trend these days.

I would need her help to get the inside track that would make my book more than just another runner's story. With no time like the present, I dashed off a quick email, suggesting that we have lunch as soon as it was convenient. No topic given, no agenda broached.

Hearing Max by the door, I hooked him up to his leash for a leisurely walk. The spring weather was having its impact on my beautiful neighborhood. Tulips, daffodils, and hyacinth were all beginning to bloom. Many of my neighbors had finished their spring planting, with colorful bursts of pink, purple, and yellow in pots flanking their front doors. I resolved to do the same thing this coming weekend, a resolution I confirmed as Max and I returned home and I saw the empty pots outside my own door.

After unleashing Max, I checked my iPhone and saw that among my new emails was one from Kate. Her response to my brief email was agreeable but terse. *One o'clock Saturday at Nellie's.* Yeah, Kate was pissed.

Don't get me wrong. I like going to Nellie's. Outstanding food, great service. But Nellie has rules. And if you don't follow the rules you don't get fed. Literally. People have been known to sit for an hour without service for breaking one of Nellie's unwritten rules. Wearing white after Labor Day. Talking on a cell phone at the table will get you a glare from Nellie's eponymous owner. And I knew that as much of a rule follower as I was, Nellie took it one step further and made a meal a tense affair for many.

The time was also a giveaway regarding Kate's mood: I hated eating lunch late. In Kate's passive-aggressive way (versus her plain old bitchy way), she was doubly punishing me while seeming to be cooperating. So very her.

. . .

Saturday started out like a typical Midwestern spring day. Clouds, mist, more clouds, rain, and the occasional glimpse of sun. I knew I couldn't just show up at Nellie's in a golf shirt and cargo pants, so I looked through my wardrobe to see what would impress. After much deliberation, I picked out a black Alexander McQueen silk and cotton blazer that Kate had given me years ago, plus a grey Paul Smith shirt and Jack Victor slacks. I thought the dark colors were particularly slimming.

I arrived at Nellie's just before one o'clock. I certainly didn't want to be late and risk the wrath of Nellie.

Kate was already seated at a small table in one of Nellie's big bay windows overlooking the charming neighborhood of Chicago's Gold Coast. Nellie turned what was the huge formal dining room of one of the great mansions of Astor Street into a blizzard of Pierre Deux: florals, stripes, and toiles in shades of pink and green, crisp white linens with a quiet monogrammed N on the table, and huge bunches of flowers everywhere. Sparkling crystal and silver serving pieces finished off the room, reflecting the beautifully restored cypress walls.

I walked up to the table with some degree of trepidation, both about Nellie and about the conversation to come.

A small smile for me but no air kiss. Bad sign.

"Hello, Erick."

"Hello, Kate. You look lovely." And she did. The woman knew how to dress. Her pink and green Lily Pulitzer sundress and little sweater may have rushed the season a bit, but she fit into Nellie's décor so perfectly that I was confident that our hostess wouldn't complain.

As I settled in at the table with some small talk, we ordered. Kate had the sole meunière while I had Nellie's famous toasted ravioli, which she claims to be an homage to her hometown of St. Louis. Like I said, if you got the rules right, there was nothing better than lunch at Nellie's. We each ordered a glass of chardonnay to accompany our meal. I thought a little more alcohol could smooth things over a bit.

"So, Erick, why did you need to see me so urgently?"

"I think I might have been a little hasty regarding the marathon book. I wanted to talk with you about what I could expect from you if I were to go ahead and do the book."

It was as if the sun had just come out after a dark, heavy thunderstorm. She lit up, with the old charming Kate smile, the one that always did me in.

"Erick, I can't believe my ears. Do you mean it?" Her enthusiasm was so strong it caught the attention of nearby diners.

"I do—well, I mean I'm thinking about it. No commitment yet, but I wanted to talk to you first."

"Erick, this is just thrilling. Everyone will be so excited!"

"I said I'm thinking about it. I need some answers from you, first."

"I'll give you anything you want if you do this book. Just ask away."

"First and foremost, I want unfettered access to everything. Your staff, the elite runners, the sponsors—everything."

"Done." I could see the excitement building in Kate and again asked myself why she cared so much. But not knowing the answer to that question, I moved on.

"I don't want to be burdened by this Ashley person. If she can't keep up with me, she's on her own."

"Done as well. I don't see that as a problem." I wish I had known to ask a follow-up question to that answer, but I didn't. Her answer was correct, just not how I understood it to be.

"Nobody has editorial control over my book except me and the publisher. Not you, not your PR people, not Ashley. No matter what I write, neither you nor anyone associated with you can change it."

"Done, done, and done. You'll get no interference. None." She was almost bouncing up and down in her chair and beginning to draw some attention from Nellie.

"Okay, settle down. You don't want to get us kicked out of here."

"I'm sorry, Erick, but I'm just so excited that you are going to do the book. It's going to be awesome and will be a huge success for all of us."

I frankly didn't care if it was a success for anyone but me but thought better of sharing that with her right now. Instead I told Kate just what she wanted to hear. "Assuming I can finalize the details with my publisher, I'm in."

I swear she almost burst into tears. But she pulled herself together, leaned over and gave me a quick kiss on the cheek, grabbed both my hands, and stared intently at me. "Erick, you'll never regret this decision. Never."

Something in me already did.

After a celebratory glass of champagne, Kate insisted on picking up the check, so I let her. I can't stand watching people fight over the check. Miss Manners would certainly not approve.

We parted at the front door, Kate off to some glamorous destination (I assumed) and me back home.

. . .

Realizing that I had just committed to a very public exhibition of my running prowess, I figured I'd better step up my running regime as of that afternoon. I pulled on my running gear and headed out the front door, leaving behind a very disappointed Max.

About a mile from home, the combination of chardonnay, champagne, and toasted ravioli came back to haunt me. I found myself throwing up in a Lincoln Park hedge, not too far from the children's zoo. Honey, stay away from that dreadful homeless person throwing up in the bushes.

Afterward, I carefully strolled home, mindful that any misstep would result in the last of my lunch ending up in someone's front yard. As I walked into the house, Max took a sniff and almost smiled, as if to say that it served me right for leaving him at home.

The phone rang. It was Ted.

"Buddy, I am so excited that you are going to do the marathon book. Martha Johnson called a few minutes ago to tell me!"

"What the hell? How—and why—does she know?"

"So it is true! That is just outstanding!"

"Outstanding or not, how the hell does she know about the book? I just decided to do it this afternoon."

"Apparently Kate called her at Regency Press."

This wasn't sounding good.

"Why is Martha at Regency Press?"

"I guess I forgot to tell you. She lost her job when Barbara died. Lord Greene felt sorry for her and gave her a job. Her first project is to shepherd your marathon book through Greene's publishing company."

I was rarely caught speechless, but I certainly was at that news. Since when did a part-time assistant get a job at a major publisher working with an established author? Plus, I couldn't imagine working closely on a major project with Martha.

We spoke a bit about our collaboration, the kinds of photos he thought would be best to take and how they would work with my text, and then I finished with Ted, agreeing that the new book was going to be great. I was glad that despite his new deal, he was still interested in working with me on this book. Somehow I'd known that our longstanding partnership would survive his attempt at solo success.

As the evening wore on, I received more and more calls, emails, and texts from friends in the publishing world who heard that my next book was marathoning for boomers. Kate—and others?—clearly were getting the word out before I could change my mind.

20

After giving Max his breakfast and a little quality one-on-one time, I settled in at my desk and started looking into GrandHotel, the marathon's title sponsor. I knew I couldn't spend too much time, as I would start the marathon office visits and staff interviews in only a few days. Quickly I found that the GrandGroup was privately held, with its legal headquarters in Switzerland and its main offices in New York. They had an impressive portfolio of luxury GrandHotels around the world with a management team that seemed to be relatively new, almost all of them having started in the last two years. While most of the team were experienced hoteliers, two or three, including the CEO and the chief financial officer, were consultants who seemed to have no hotel experience at all.

Since the group was private, there were no financials available other than some analysts' guesses regarding revenue, room nights, and other hospitality industry key indicators of success. It seemed, at least to the analysts, that GrandHotel had weathered the worldwide recession and subsequent malaise fairly well. That meant that like most hotel groups, GrandHotel had to be low on cash reserves and desperately waiting for business to pick up. It seemed like an odd time to be investing in celebrity-driven luxury makeovers like health clubs and investing in sports sponsorships. A day or two earlier, I had emailed a list of

GrandGroup questions to Bruce Mays, and sure enough, minutes later, there was an email waiting for me from Bruce. The message was brief and to the point.

Running into some roadblocks with your inquiry. Seem to have stirred up a hornet's nest as well. Lunch at Manny's? My treat.

The only part of the note that made sense was the invitation and offer. While Chicago Cut may be Bruce's favorite restaurant, it is so only when someone else is buying. When he's buying (which he does rarely), it's Manny's.

A word or two about Manny's. An institution since the early 1940s, Manny's is an enormous deli on the near South Side (Roosevelt Road to be precise—which should be pronounced Rowww-se-velt, not, as many South Siders say, Roooo-se-velt). Fiberglass trays, a big long cafeteria line, and pretty funny servers who give you anything from a hot meal to their signature corned beef. You could always count on a great mix of locals, politicians (every Democrat who wanted votes out of Chicago had to make an obligatory appearance at Manny's), cops, and wise guys. Each group had its own space, but it was sometimes hard to tell the pols from the mob guys. I highly recommend trying a crispy potato pancake. Or three.

I sent Bruce a quick response. Thirty minutes later I was on my way to Manny's.

Bruce was waiting for me outside. He's easy to pick out of a crowd, especially a Manny's kind of crowd. Tall, just enough silver in his hair to look distinguished and wise, but as trim as he had been when he played football for Virginia. How he had kept his Southern drawl after thirty years in Chicago never ceases to amaze me. But don't let the persona fool you. Bruce was as financially savvy as anyone I knew. He just had a couple of weaknesses. Don't we all?

As I got closer, I saw Bruce eyeing what appeared to be two somewhat disheveled elderly gentlemen arguing their way toward the front door from the somewhat seedy back parking lot. He looked skeptical as they approached the front door at the same time we did. I stepped in front of him and held the door open for the two men.

"Alderman, nice to see you," I said to the less disheveled of the two.

"Erick, always a pleasure. You know Judge Reilly, don't you?"

"Of course, Judge, nice to see you again. Enjoy your lunch."

As I followed the politicians into Manny's cramped entrance, Bruce pulled me back a bit.

"Alderman? Judge? Seriously?"

"Absolutely. Brendan has been the alderman representing our ward for much longer than I've owned the house, and Reilly is his brother-in-law and lives about a block from me in the biggest house for six blocks in any direction. We pay our judges well in Illinois, don't we?"

"And when did you suddenly get involved in politics?"

"When some big money developer wanted to turn three of the brownstones across the street into a high-rise. We formed a neighborhood group to oppose it, and by making the right donations to the right politicians, we got it stopped. I've helped the alderman with a couple of issues along the way."

"I'm impressed. I'll have to remember that next time I get a speeding ticket."

"Sorry, they won't let the aldermen fix those anymore. Remember the City Council reforms under the last mayor?"

We both chuckled at that one and headed toward the steam tables and our lunch.

. . .

If I was to run a marathon soon, I knew I had to lighten up on the diet. Turkey breast (no bread) and a small salad constituted my lunch, while Bruce loaded up on chicken soup with a matzo ball as big as a child's head, six inches of salami on rye, and a big slice of cheesecake. To say I was jealous understates my emotional state. Dieting sucks. Running sucks.

"I don't have much time, Erick; I need to be back at the office before the European Central Bank issues their latest economic outlook. I have a client with a boatload of money riding on the Euro dropping like a stone this afternoon, and if things go wrong, I need to be there to put the pieces back together for her." By his smile, I knew my Southern gentleman was giving his client more than just financial advice. No surprise: that's what got him fired from his last two firms. And they wondered why he had a disproportionate number of female clients.

"Fine with me. What have you found out about GrandGroup and GrandHotel?"

"I haven't found out much. Every path I go down, even some of the obscure ones, I only find shell corporations, dummy transfers, and companies who seem to exist just to obfuscate the truth. I think I'm on to a document that shows the last change of control of the company was about two years ago, when one of these shadowy entities I'm trying to track down bought control and moved the headquarters to Switzerland. If I can get my hands on the change of control filings, we'll know a lot more about who runs GrandHotel now."

"That's great, Bruce. Any luck with their current financials? I just can't understand how they can afford to invest millions in hotel upgrades and fancy spas when the economy is in the gutter."

"No luck at all. As a private company, they have no obligation to file any financial reports anywhere. I have a source in Europe who is trying some, shall we say, extraordinary means to get into the files, but it's a long shot."

"What about the management team? It seems to be a mix of seasoned hotel people and a group of consultants."

"All true, all true. The hoteliers are very well respected and have been in the industry for decades. They are well known for managing luxury properties and seem to be aboveboard. The consultants—including that CFO and CEO you wanted me to check out—are a different story."

"How so?"

"They all come out of a niche consultancy in Knightsbridge called Regency Advisors."

"Wait, Regency Advisors? Are you sure?"

"Yeah, Regency. Why?"

"Regency Press is my publisher. Gotta be the same people, right?"

"Again, there's very little public information on Regency Advisors. Just a simple website with their consulting capabilities and contact information. They seem to specialize in corporate turnarounds, especially in media. Interestingly, I found an archived website for Regency with bios for the consultants, but they've been removed from the current site."

"Why?"

"I don't know. But the top three people—out of five—are now running GrandGroup."

"That's odd. Why would turnaround specialists in a completely different industry essentially shut down their practice to run a hotel chain?"

"My guess is the oldest reason in the book: money. I'm trying to track down the two managing directors who didn't go to GrandHotel, but I'm having no luck. One of them died last year, and the other seems to have dropped off the grid."

"How did he die?"

"She. She was mugged outside of St. Pancras station in London. Died of her injuries. There was a ticket for the Eurostar to Paris and a large number of Euros and English pounds in her bag. She looked like she was running away from something."

"You said mugged."

Bruce set down his drink. "Actually, her throat was slashed. Scotland Yard tried to pass it off as a mugging so as to not panic the public. That's a very popular station and is generally pretty safe."

The similarities to Barbara's death were disturbing.

"Bruce, you've got to find out more about Regency. I'm certain there's a connection between all of this."

"All of what?"

"Regency, GrandHotel, the marathon book I'm doing—"

I didn't know what to make of all of this. Publishing. Barbara and Kate. Lord Greene. Ted. People with a publishing background were now running a mysterious hotel chain that found connections to my book and my friends. What could that mean?

As I pondered that mystery, Bruce finished off his cheesecake and started to get up.

"Last question, Bruce. See what you can find out about Regency. A Regency branded firm bought the Alex Project building, and I'm sure they're connected."

"Will do. And, as promised, Erick, I'll pay on my way out. I'll get back to you as soon as I hear anything from my sources. But don't hope for too much. Things seem to be buried pretty deep when it comes to GrandHotel. I'll keep digging into Regency. They have a very complicated corporate structure with lots of little Regencys all over the place. And it's pretty closely held with very little float in the stock, so there isn't much out in public hands to be traded on a daily basis. A bunch of institutional investors and trusts own a big chunk of the company."

"Thanks, Bruce. Thanks for lunch and for the info."

"You're welcome. I'll send you my bill when I'm done, and I'll be looking for a nice, expensive Chicago Cut dinner as my bonus if I come through with the nasty details."

"Can't wait."

With a smile, Bruce left.

21

My head was spinning with facts that seemingly were connected but that still didn't make sense. Since I didn't know where to go next with this conundrum, I decided I would approach it a little like I did when I got the occasional writers' block. I'd walk away from the puzzle and head over to the comfort of my friendly neighborhood tavern. Nothing brought on solutions like a pint or two and the advice of a good bartender.

Grabbing my notebook, I gave Max a scratch behind the ears and the promise of a run in the morning. I headed out the door, double-checking the locks as I left.

My next-door neighbor, Amar Singh, was headed up to his front door, loaded with packages. I ran over, offering to help him navigate his armful into his townhouse. With a grateful smile, he handed me one set of bags as he reached into his coat for his house keys. Amar had been a neighbor for several years, buying the stone clad townhouse next to mine just after he had become the youngest physician ever to be named head of Northwestern University's neurosurgery program. Amar and his beautiful wife, Minu, an assistant state's attorney with the Cook County state's attorney's office, were neighborhood favorites, always out working on their home, entertaining their large family with huge traditional feasts, and then having all of us over the next day for a backyard cookout with every classic American picnic basket item. We all wondered when they would have a family. Both had hugely successful careers, but they spoke longingly of having lots of children to fill their townhouse with noise and activity.

There was no shortage of noise and activity with my other close neighbors. The owners of a successful Midwest chain of gift shops catering to the GLBT community, Pam and Leslie were consummate entertainers, always hosting an eclectic crowd in their beautifully restored Victorian next door. The two women had been together for more than thirty years and divided their time between Chicago and the location of their first store in Saugatuck, Michigan. In addition to being a regular at their parties, I was their designated house-watcher and plant-waterer when they were gone, and they did the same for me.

Thinking I was lucky to have such good neighbors, I headed back up the street toward my destination.

. . .

If you had asked me to create my own neighborhood hangout, I couldn't have done a better job than O'Shaughnessy's. Cozy small but not too small, popular but not jammed, good bar food from a classic menu, O'Shaughnessy's bartenders in starched white shirts and black ties knew when to chat and when to just shut up and pour.

As I walked in, seeing Dennis behind the bar lightened my mood just a bit. One of my favorite bartenders ever, Dennis was presiding over the huge oak and copper bar. An equally welcome sight was my favorite seat near the corner of the bar being vacated just as I walked in. I slid onto the well-padded seat, put my feet up on the wooden rail, and dropped the notebook on the bar top. "Dennis," I sighed, "It's definitely a Miller moment."

Dennis stared at me for just a moment before he smiled. He knew full well that I was kidding and that I wouldn't deviate from my usual routine of a cold, frothy Smithwick's in a classic pint glass. No mugs with handles, no little juice glasses, just a classic Irish ale in a classic Irish pint glass. He turned away and quickly returned with my beer, setting an O'Shaughnessy's coaster underneath to protect the beautifully polished finish of the bar. He gave me a quick "How ya doing?" before moving on to refill a couple of pint glasses that had recently been drained by their renters.

I sat for a moment, listening to Sinatra on the jukebox. It was a classic jukebox with a quarter a song, five songs for a dollar, and blessedly free of what passes as today's pop and rock music, instead focusing on jazz and ballads of the last fifty years or so. Michael Bublé was a radical new addition to the O'Shaughnessy's play list.

Opening my notebook, I continued to stare at my list of recent events. Sometimes staring made something new leap out from the page. Most of the time, like today, it just gave me a headache.

I leaned back against the backrest of the stool, closing my eyes for a second. But then I heard the familiar voice greeting Dennis from the other side of the bar. I was looking for answers, for solutions, and for cosmic enlightenment. I certainly wasn't looking for America's favorite marathon runner-cum-beach bum. Why was Jackson Clark invading my sanctuary?

Like a teenage girl trying to avoid a boy with a crush on her, my first reaction was to look away and hope he hadn't seen me. Maybe I could hide behind the brass beer taps. Unfortunately, O'Shaughnessy's cozy space and u-shaped bar didn't permit a lot of avoiding. Jack had already seen me.

"Erick!" he shouted in a voice already slurred by what must have been several of the oddly colored concoction in the nearly empty glass he was barely carrying. "What a fucking surprise to run into you here!"

Now I really wanted to disappear. Jack was drunk, of course. While you do find your occasional happy, cheerful drunks, Jack was a loud, profane, and oftentimes angry drunk who more often than not found himself being asked to leave for one reason or another. He also got touchy as he drank. Not touchy in the sensitive sense, but touchy in the hugging, backslapping, and arm-over-your shoulder sense. I hated that. And you didn't swear at Dennis' bar. You just didn't.

"Jack, I sure didn't expect to run into you here. What brings you to O'Shaughnessy's?"

"Is that what this place is called? I came here with a buddy after dinner, but let me tell you, I'm not likely to return. Took the bartender too fucking long to make a simple fucking caipirinha! Can you believe that? And every refill seems to take longer and longer!"

I see Dennis is up to his old stall tactic. Make the near-drunks wait long enough between drinks and you'll either frustrate them so they leave or force them to get reasonably sober so they aren't a menace to society. Dennis takes his bartending responsibilities to the public very seriously.

"Gosh, Jack, I usually just get the beer."

"Yeah, that makes sense, doesn't it?" I think that was a slam, but it was hard to be sure.

"So where's your friend?" I was desperate to find someone to take Jack off my hands before he could get either maudlin or belligerent. It was sort of a coin toss.

"He ditched me for some woman he knew. Just left me here on my own. That's why I'm so glad to see you, buddy!"

Thinking that Jack's friend clearly got the best end of the deal, I reluctantly asked Jack to join me on my side of the bar. At least I could try to keep him somewhat restrained and less of an embarrassment. After all, I live at this bar.

I think Dennis was surprised to see me talking to Jack, who clearly wouldn't have fit into my regular circle of O'Shaughnessy's friends. Dennis' skepticism was confirmed when Jack asked Dennis why there weren't any TVs in the bar.

Yes, in total repudiation of the "there must be at least half as many big flat screen TVs blaring some sports programming as there are seats in the bar" tradition, O'Shaughnessy's had no TVs. None. Never. Ever. Dennis, who was a part owner of the bar, explained to me once that he thought bars were for enlightened conversation and not meant to be a room full of people with their mouths open staring up at some football game or soccer match or professional bowling championship (just because you are paid to do something doesn't make it a profession). Before Dennis could start his anti-TV diatribe, one of the servers reached around me to drop a tray of empties on the bar. She took a quick glance over, said hello, and then seemed to take a second look at my new companion and me. (And I mean companion in the traditional way. Not that there's anything wrong with the new form of companions.)

"Hey, Erick, is that your brother?" she asked.

Suppressing my initial horror, I glanced over at Jack and realized that there was a passing resemblance between us. Same height, same coloring. I had a few pounds on Jack, who almost certainly ran many miles more a week than I did. I was a little bigger across the shoulders, but I was fighting a losing battle against my hairline. Jack, one way or another, still had a full head of his thick blond hair.

"No, Kathy, not brothers. Just acquaintances."

"Hey," Jack interrupted, suddenly serious. "We almost have to be friends. After all, we married the same woman, didn't we?"

Yet another chill of horror hit me. Kate had married a younger, fitter version of me. I decided I could delve into this latest bit of psychology once I had solved the current mysteries of my life.

Knowing I wouldn't solve those mysteries tonight, I decided to give up that struggle for now and keep an eye on Jack. It helped that one of my occasional running partners came in and joined us. Within a half hour, there were three or four others in our group, and Jack was telling one of his great London marathon stories. With a stunning course that rambled through hundreds of years of British history, it was one of the great sporting events of the year. Jack had enjoyed the pubs a little too much the night before and ended up making an unexpected stop to relieve himself not too far from the Tower Bridge. Unfortunately, London's finest didn't take well to someone pissing in the Thames in the early afternoon, London marathon elite athlete or not. Race organizers had to bail him out of gaol that afternoon. I have to say, the man tells a great story, and none better than when he's the butt of the joke.

After Jack rambled through yet another story (I'd heard this one as well: tall blond Jack lost in downtown Tokyo less than an hour before the Tokyo men's marathon, only to be found by a reporter who noticed Jack towering over the local citizens at a subway station) his phone rang, and he headed for the door to take the call on the somewhat quieter sidewalk in front of O'Shaughnessy's. I decided to take advantage of his temporary absence to call it a night. I dropped some bills on the bar for Dennis, gave him a quick good night, and headed out the front door.

Or rather, I almost used the front door. There seemed to be an incident of some kind just outside, so I turned and left through a side door that opened onto one of Chicago's better-kept alleys. Knowing every way out of a bar was something I had learned about in college when I earned spending money as a bouncer at one of Mizzou's more popular student bars. Having that knowledge may have saved my life.

22

Blissfully unaware of how lucky I was, I headed home, let Max out for one more time, and got him settled for the night. After double-checking the window and door locks and activating the home security system, I got ready for bed and was quickly asleep. I wasn't sure how long I'd slept when my bedside phone startled me awake.

"Hello," I croaked.

Kate's terror-stricken voice hit me.

"Erick, oh my God, you have to come right away! Jack's been hurt."

That snapped me wide awake.

"What happened? Where are you?"

"Northwestern Hospital. Jack was beat up outside some bar on the North Side. They don't know if he's going to make it."

"Jack? Outside a bar? What bar?"

"How the hell should I know? Erick, you've got to get here!"

I promised Kate I would be there as soon as I possibly could. I jumped out of bed, threw on the first clothes I could find, and ran out the front door. I ran over to Clark Street where I knew I could find a cab. All the time I was wondering what had happened to Jack and whether it was connected to all the other incidents that seemed to be piling up around me.

The cab made good time—it was almost 1:00 a.m., which explained the lack of traffic—and I stormed through the doors of the ER. Though it was surprisingly crowded for that time of the night (or morning, depending on your perspective), I immediately saw Kate across the room. Not too hard to pick out of the crowd, given that she was in a floor-length, shockingly blue Peter Soronen gown. I knew Kate couldn't afford to shop where Michelle Obama got her state dinner outfits.

Walking closer, any thoughts of the family finances disappeared. I had never seen her look so frightened.

"Oh Erick, it's just awful!"

"What happened?"

"I don't know for sure. I was at the Hospital Gala at the Hilton when I got a call from the police. They said a patient had been brought in at Northwestern's ER with my name as his contact in case of emergencies. I rushed over here just as Jack was being taken into surgery. He has internal injuries of some kind, but they won't tell me anything. Erick, what am I going to do?"

"Kate, just calm down. This is a great hospital, and they've got some of the best ER docs in the country."

"But who would want to hurt Jack? I don't even know what he was doing in that bar. He was supposed to be out for dinner with a friend."

"What bar? When did it happen?"

"I have no idea where or when or why. I just know that he's hurt, and no one is telling me how bad it is. I want to see him!"

"Kate, I'm sure someone will come and find you as soon as they know something." As I was trying to calm Kate down, I saw a policeman in the background, filling out paperwork of some kind. Thinking he might be the one who had called Kate, I settled her into a seat with the promise of finding someone with answers and headed over toward him. Glancing back over my shoulder to make sure that Kate was staying put, I realized I could have chosen a better seat for her. One of Chicago's unfortunate homeless seemed to be trying to make Kate's acquaintance. Knowing that I would be back to her soon, I continued to work my way through the crowd and the noise. Despite attempts at soothing lighting, rental plants, and pastel furniture, the ER reminded me of every other facility of its kind. Cold and institutional. And scary.

. . .

I knew the policeman was watching me approach even as he filled out his paperwork. I guess cops develop peripheral vision soon after joining the force.

"Officer, I was wondering if you could help me."

"Will if I can, sir."

"A friend of mine was brought in a while ago. Someone from the police department called his wife to let her know that he was here, and I wondered if you might be working on his case."

"What's your friend's name, sir?"

"Clark. Jack Clark. He was beat up outside some bar earlier this evening."

"Sir, may I see some ID? How are you related to this Mr. Clark?"

"Here's my driver's license." It was an awful picture—made me look like I'd gained twenty pounds and almost that many years. "And I'm not related. Well, sort of related by marriage."

"Sir?"

"He's married to my ex-wife," I clarified.

"And where is she?"

"Over there, in the blue dress." As I turned to point, I saw Kate with not just one but two would-be suitors. Neither one of which looked like they would win any hygiene contests.

"Let's go talk to her, and I'll tell her what I know." The officer folded up his paperwork, shoved it in his back pocket, and started working his way through the crowd toward Kate. I hurried to follow, moving in his wake.

As he reached Kate, her two new friends peeled away and moved to different sides of the ER. The cop saw but didn't appear to give them much of his attention. He stepped in front of where Kate was sitting.

"Ma'am? I'm Officer Wilson. Are you Mrs. Clark?"

"I'm Jack Clark's wife, but I don't go by Clark. I'm Kate O'Callahan."

"O'Callahan? Aren't you that marathon lady?" The officer started to smile as he recognized Kate.

"I guess I am, Officer. But how's—"

"I'm training to run the marathon in October. I'm part of the CPD team!"

I could see Kate trying to be polite no matter how desperate she was for news of Jack.

"That's terrific, Officer Wilson. You're running for the Gold Star fund, right?" Gold Star raised money for the families of officers killed in the line of duty.

"Yeah, we are. We've got a great bunch of guys—and gals—training, so I'm sure we'll beat those bastards from Fire this year." Each year, a friendly (or not-so) rivalry existed between the Chicago Police Department marathon team and the one made up of runners from the Chicago Fire Department. "Pardon my language, ma'am."

"Not to worry, Officer, but please tell me what happened to Jack."

"Sorry, ma'am, just got excited when I realized who you are. Let me fill you in on what we know."

As I listened, Wilson described how he and his partner were on their regular patrol of the Lincoln Park neighborhood, focusing on the bars that were full of late night patrons. They got a call reporting an incident just a few blocks from where they were, so they responded within minutes.

"As we pulled up, we found your husband on the ground on the sidewalk in front of a bar and in pretty bad shape. There were a couple of people standing near him; one of them had called 911 just a few minutes earlier. We called for an ambulance and I checked on the victim—sorry, your husband—while my partner started to question some of the bystanders. I saw that he was in pretty bad shape, so I did what I could while we waited for the ambulance."

"Oh, dear God. Poor Jack!" Kate was in tears, holding my hand in a death grip.

The officer continued. "My partner wasn't getting very far in questioning the crowd. They'd mostly just come out of the bar and had clearly been there for some time."

I had an eerie feeling that I knew the answer to the question I was about to ask, but had to ask it.

"Officer, what was the name of the bar?"

"Funny you should ask. It wasn't one of those places that seem to generate trouble on a regular basis. This was more of a neighborhood spot: O'Shaughnessy's."

I doubt that I turned as pale as I felt, but Kate did give me an odd look as she watched me respond to Wilson's announcement. She knew that O'Shaughnessy's was one of my favorites.

While I wondered whether Jack's injuries were related to the disturbance that sent me out the side door, Wilson continued.

"Luckily, an ambulance was there within minutes, so the paramedics took over. I know he was beat up pretty bad, and he had a cut on his neck." Cut and neck are two words that really should never be used together. Then I realized that I'd heard them used together very recently in my living room when I heard how Barbara was killed. As I was trying to figure out the odds of two incidents like that happening to people in my life in two short days, I realized that a fourth person had joined our conversation.

23

"Are you Jackson Clark's wife?" asked the blond woman in well-worn blue scrubs.

"Yes, yes I am," Kate answered.

"I'm Dr. Fraley. Your husband is going to be fine." She clearly knew how to deliver good news. Short and to the point. I wondered if she followed the same approach toward bad news.

"Thank God!" Kate exclaimed.

"He's had a rough go of it, and the surgery was more extensive than we first thought. He had internal bleeding, which we were able to stop during surgery. He sustained a cut on this throat, but it missed the jugular vein, so it wasn't life threatening. His right leg is fractured. He won't be awake for some time yet, so if you want to go home and rest, we'll call you when he wakes up."

"Absolutely not. I'm staying here by his side. Take me to him." I had seen that look in Kate's eyes before, and Dr. Fraley might as well just give up and take Kate to see Jack now, because it was going to happen one way or another.

"Mr. Clark is in recovery," said Dr. Fraley, "and he will be there for another couple of hours. You can't go in."

"Then I'll wait right here until he's out. I am not going anywhere."

Knowing that Kate would fight this to the death (another bad thing to think about in an overcrowded ER), I suggested what I thought was a reasonable compromise.

"Kate, why don't I run you home so you can change out of your gown and grab a few of Jack's things. I'll wait with the cab, and we'll head straight back here."

Kate looked at me skeptically and was ready to start her protest again when the officer intervened.

"Mrs. Clark—or, I'm sorry, Ms. O'Callahan—that seems like a reasonable idea to me. I know how these things go. It always takes longer than you'd think for people to come out of recovery. You really don't want to be hanging around here in that beautiful dress." Just as he said that, Wilson flushed like a schoolboy asking out his first girl. Kate noticed, and I think his attention settled her down a bit.

"You're right, Officer. I will go home, but I'll be back in thirty minutes. I expect a full update, doctor, and I want to know how your investigation is going, Officer. Are you both clear on that?"

The doctor had already begun making her way back toward the closed off section of the ER, but she halfway turned and gave Kate a wave of acknowledgment. Wilson, on the other hand, didn't leave Kate's side.

"Good choice, ma'am. We'll need to ask Mr. Clark some questions when he wakes up, but we'll come back for that in a few hours when he's ready to talk to us. I'll see you then."

"Okay, then, we have a plan," I said, hoping to get the newly cooperative Kate moving in the right direction.

With one more look back toward the foreboding doors of surgery, she turned and walked to the elevators. I followed, and we were soon down at street level.

She climbed into the back of a waiting black Town Car.

"Tim, take us home, please."

I looked at Kate with what must have been a confused yet inquisitive look.

"Jack's been using Tim and his car service for some time. He says he can be so much more productive when he can work during trips back and forth from the airport and to meetings."

"But the cost . . ."

"Jack says not to worry, but I do wonder sometimes. But I guess that's Jack's concern, not mine. Erick, thank you so much for being there for me." For a moment, I saw the old Kate that I had fallen in love with. That, of course, didn't last for long, and the smile was replaced by an angry glare.

"So tell me what the hell is going on."

"What do you mean, what's going on?" Even I knew I wasn't going to get away without telling the story.

"Why did you ask the name of the bar? Why did you look like you knew he was going to say it was O'Shaughnessy's?"

I knew Kate too well. I had no chance of winning this one. I briefly protested, but then I gave up the battle and told her about running into Jack at the bar and the disturbance that led me to leave through the side.

"Kate, you know that I had nothing to do with this, nor did I know that Jack was in trouble. For all our disagreements, you've never seen a violent side of me."

"No, I know better than that. Despite all your faults, you're not that big of a son of a bitch."

Again choosing discretion over valor, I didn't inquire as to my faults. I'd heard the litany before, during, and after our divorce proceedings. Instead, I took the higher road.

"Kate, can you think of anyone who might want to hurt Jack?"

"No, I really can't," Kate replied with a troubled look on her face. "God knows he's pissed a lot of people off over the years, but it was never that serious. Unless—"

"Unless what?"

"Never mind, just some business problems Jack's been having. But he assured me that everything is under control, so that can't be it."

I didn't know much about Jack's business acumen, but I could see him getting into financial difficulties, especially the way he and Kate liked to spend money. After all, how much can the person in charge of a footrace make in a year? Were they living off of Jack's endorsement and coaching?

As I was trying to conceive of Jack having any business sense, the car pulled up in front of Kate's building. The drive from the hospital to her South Loop high-rise had only taken minutes.

"Kate, do you want me to go in with you?"

"You're sweet, but no. I'll just be a minute."

Before I had much of a chance to ponder how—or if—all of this made sense, Kate was back out. After the many fights we'd had over how long it took her to get ready to go out, I was shocked at how quickly she had changed from her Gala gown to bedside jeans and a sweater. The jeans were Dolce & Gabbana and the sweater had that sloppy, elegant look that only comes with a hefty price tag. She had a biggish Louis Vuitton bag over her shoulder. I started to wonder again where the money came from for Kate and Jack's lavish lifestyle, but my ruminations were interrupted with a terse "Let's get back to the hospital."

I couldn't get much conversation going on the return trip, and minutes later we were there. She rushed out of the car, leaving me to trail behind her back into the ER.

Unfortunately for Dr. Fraley, the surgeon was just about to head back toward surgery when Kate caught her by the arm. "How's Jack?" she demanded.

With an infinite patience that seemed more like something learned by those wonderful nurses (rather than the seeming lack of patience ingrained in high-powered surgeons), Dr. Fraley turned toward Kate and smiled.

"We're actually very pleased with Jack's recovery and will have him in a room within the next hour. Why don't you wait here, and I'll make sure that someone comes to get you when he's settled in his room?"

Kate was taken aback by the quick response and offer. She clearly couldn't think of what to complain about, so she basically sat down with the bag in her lap. I joined her and we waited. She still wasn't interested in conversation, seemingly lost in her thoughts. So was I. Threats, death, and serious injury were suddenly swirling around me. Was I at the center of all of this? And if so, why?

24

What seemed like only minutes later, a nurse walked into the waiting room and called Kate's name. My ex immediately sprang to her feet and hurried after the nurse, her bag falling to the floor. As she hurried off, I picked up the pricey luggage. One of the side zippers was open, so I reached down to close it. As I did, I caught the glint of steel reflecting the all-too-bright ER fluorescents. Making sure that Kate didn't see me snooping, I pulled open the zipper just slightly. Only enough to see what that bit of shiny metal was. A gun. Kate was packing heat.

I froze for just a second, unable to take my eyes off of the revolver in the side pocket of the bag. I snapped back to the present as I heard Kate calling my name. I quickly zipped up the bag, hoping she thought I was just fumbling for the handles. She didn't appear to have noticed anything, just annoyed that I wasn't by her side as she strode through a side door, following the nurse. I quickly caught up just as the two of them entered an elevator. Catching the doors as they started to close, I earned a glare from Kate for my tardiness.

"He seems to be doing well, but he's still groggy from surgery and is on some serious pain medication. I'm not sure you'll be able to talk to him for some time yet."

Kate said, "I just want to see him. I don't care how long I have to wait to talk to him."

The nurse nodded. "I understand. I'm not sure the police are going to be as patient. They've been waiting outside surgery. They seem to be quite anxious to talk to him."

Kate instinctively looked toward her bag, then to me. I returned her gaze as innocently as I could. She was about to say something to me when the doors opened and the nurse strode out, quickly turning left at the nurses' station. We followed to a room halfway down the long, bright hallway. I noticed a policeman, a big, broad football player type, standing with one of the nurses. He quickly looked up as we went by.

Then there we were—in the room with Jack. Kate gasped as she saw him. I almost did too.

It was hard to recognize Jack. His face was bruised and swollen, with small skeins of stitches scattered here and there. A huge bandage wrapped his throat. A cast covered one leg. His arms and hands were scratched, and I could see what appeared to be bandages under his thin hospital gown. He was pale as death and his eyes were closed. Aside from his chest moving slowly up and down, I couldn't see any signs of the vibrant, excitable Jack that had barged into the bar just a few hours ago.

Kate sobbed and rushed over to his side. She had to restrain herself from hugging him, but even my overly emotional ex-wife knew that she would only be causing him more pain. Instead, she leaned over and gave Jack a gentle kiss on the forehead, carefully working around the areas where his skin had been scraped raw. The nurse checked his monitors and all seemed well enough for Kate and I to be left alone after an admonition to let Jack rest.

I waited for Kate to say something while suppressing all the questions I had for her. Just as she was about to speak, there was a not-so-gentle rap at the closed hospital room door. It was the officer I had seen by the nurses' station.

"Ms. O'Callahan?" the officer asked, stepping into the room.

"Yes, can I help you?"

"I'm Officer Wachowski. You met my partner, Officer Wilson, earlier?"

Kate was distracted by a quick start of breath from Jack, so I answered for her.

"Yes, we met him in the waiting room. You can't tell me that you're here to get Jack's statement. He's just out of surgery and not even conscious."

"Not quite yet, no," the officer replied. "I just wanted to drop in and let you know that we're here and that we need to talk to him as soon as he's awake. We'll be right outside."

With that ominous closing, Wachowski closed the door.

Kate turned her attention back to Jack. She stroked his blond hair back from the raw wound on his forehead, making gentle cooing sounds that I had never before in my life heard from her. I was momentarily taken aback, and suddenly I felt like I was watching something that I had no business seeing. I certainly wasn't close to Jack, and my relationship with Kate can best be described as chilly. So why did she call me, and why was I here?

There were two chairs in the room. One, which looked more like a recliner than a standard issue hospital chair, was on Kate's side of the bed and was likely there for family members who would sleep by the side of their stricken loved ones. The other, which I slipped into, was a hard-backed chair best suited for short visits. Which mine was going to be if I had anything to say about it.

I sat quietly for a minute or two as Kate continued to stroke Jack's hair and stare into his closed eyes, as if her willpower could make him come awake. But even Kate's indomitable personality couldn't pierce the veil of narcotics that were lessening Jack's pain.

She finally sat down with a sigh, her eyes still not leaving Jack. After a moment or two passed, I offered to get Kate something from the hospital cafeteria, coffee, perhaps. With a slight smile, she nodded and said that a coffee would be nice.

"But would you mind going to Starbucks? I can't face hospital coffee."

If for no other reason than to get out of that room, I agreed.

The woman at the nurses' station directed me to the chain's nearest location: the main lobby of Northwestern's gigantic complex. With more than one thousand beds, the facility is spread over several very expensive city blocks, and it felt like it as I wound my way through corridors and mini-lobbies.

Turning what I hoped would be one last corner, I saw Starbucks ahead of me. Skylights brought the early morning sun into the lobby, eerily illuminating the once-topless mermaid that symbolized overpriced and overcaffeinated drinks.

Remembering Kate's preferences from years ago, I asked the cashier for a large skim latte. Smiling in that sort of creepy-Stepford Wife way that seems to be part of the Starbucks training program, she turned to the man behind the coffee machine and shouted, "Grande non-fat latte." I knew it was grande and not large, and that for some reason they insisted it was non-fat, not skim (there's a difference?) but the contrarian in me couldn't speak those words.

After paying and putting in the requisite two packets of the blue stuff ("Never the pink stuff," Kate would always tell me), I began my trek back to Jack's room. After finding a shortcut, I was soon back at the nurses' station where I had started. Turning down the corridor toward Jack's room, I saw both Wilson and Wachowski standing outside the door. With a small nod and a quiet "excuse me," I slipped between them and into Jack's room.

Kate met my return with a small smile and an outstretched hand. I handed her the coffee. After taking a sip, she asked if the police were still there. Acknowledging that they were, I asked Kate if there was anything I could do for her.

"Actually, Erick, there is. Go talk to the cops and see if you can find out anything more about what happened."

Doubting that they knew any more, I nevertheless agreed to see what I could learn.

Wilson was gone, but Wachowski's hulking bulk lurked right outside the door. I idly speculated on the intimidating effect it would have on a would-be lawbreaker to see him unfold from a squad car.

"Officer, do we know anything more about how this might have happened to Jack?"

"No, sir; that's why I'm waiting to get his statement. I told you all we know. I just need to wait for the detectives who are going to follow up on this."

"I'm a little surprised to see you still here. Shouldn't you be out on the street by now?"

"Normally, yes, but we've been asked to stay on top of this one."

I was surprised. On the surface, it must have looked like a run-of-the-mill mugging. Why was CPD so interested? I asked Wachowski this question.

"All I can say, sir, is that we have some conflicting statements from witnesses that have the bosses interested. And it wasn't a robbery. His watch, signet ring, and wallet were still on him when he got to the hospital. But we can't find his phone. Anyway, I've been told to sit tight until the detectives get here."

"Is Jack in danger? Is that why you're here?"

"Sir, I was told to stay right here. That's all I know."

Realizing that I wasn't going to get anything more from the cop, I went back into the room. Nothing had changed. Kate was on the edge of the big recliner, and Jack was silent and still, his chest rising and falling slowly.

"He didn't know anything more—just that he's been told to wait here until the detectives arrive."

Kate looked almost relieved by my report, although I wasn't sure what there could have been in those few words that would make her feel better.

"Thanks for trying, Erick. Why don't you go? I'll be fine here. One of the staff from the marathon office is coming over with some paperwork for me. I'm going to be here for a while and might as well use the time. I also have to call Jack's parents before they hear about this from someone else. The poor dears have been in ill health, and they don't need a shock like this. So, go on. I insist."

Hoping my relief didn't show, I left with Kate's promise to call me if she needed me or if Jack's condition changed.

As I left the room, I felt Wachowski's eyes on me as I walked down the hall, even as I waited for the elevator. I couldn't help but glance back toward Jack's room. Sure enough, the cop was watching every move I made. I've never been especially paranoid, but there were too many unanswered questions and too many people getting hurt. I didn't know what was happening, but it wasn't good.

25

A few days later, while I was continuing to do research, my phone rang. Caller ID said it was my ex-wife.

"Hello, Kate. How's Jack?"

"He's recovering pretty quickly, although it'll be a long haul. He'll have to do physical therapy for his leg. They don't think he'll ever be able to competitively race again."

The unkind person in me (the one I rarely let come out in public) thought, *no great loss for the world of competitive running.* Jack had slowed considerably over the years.

"That's rough for him. What will that do to his endorsement deals?"

"Just like you, Erick. Maybe you could think of Jack's pain instead of the dollars involved."

"Sorry. Just a gut reaction, I guess."

"If you can be a little more sympathetic, you need to come by and see Jack. He's been pretty insistent on seeing you, and I told him I'd pass the message along, even though I think it's a bad idea."

"Then why tell me?"

"Because he's adamant that he needs to talk to you before he talks to the cops again."

That was disturbing. "What did he tell them the first time?"

"Not much. He was pretty groggy. But they're coming back tomorrow afternoon for what they call a 'more exhaustive' interview."

"Kate, I wanted to ask you something."

"What is it? I need to get back to Jack."

"Why are you carrying a gun?"

"What? What are you talking about?"

"I know you have a gun. I saw it in your bag at the hospital."

"Whether I do or don't carry a gun is no business of yours. Now, are you coming to see Jack or not?"

I wasn't sure which troubled me more: Kate's gun or Jack's insistence on seeing me before he talked to the cops. Reluctantly, I told Kate I would be right over and grabbed a cab. This was a conversation that I was not looking forward to having. Little did I know that it would be even worse than I anticipated.

. . .

Working my way back through the maze that was Northwestern Hospital, I found Jack's room and approached cautiously. As I gently knocked on his door, I realized that I was holding my breath. In a surprisingly clear voice, I heard "Yes?" from Jack.

Pushing the door open, I was a little shocked to see how good Jack looked. Mind you, there were still bruises and bandages everywhere, and his leg was in a cast. But he was sitting up, bright eyed and freshly shaved. His surfer blond hair was clean and covered much of the damage to his forehead. As I walked in, those bright baby blue eyes seemed to lose a bit of their brightness.

"Hello, Erick."

"Jack, you're looking much better."

"Yeah, they say I'm getting out tomorrow and starting rehab."

"That's great. So what's up? Kate made it seem like an emergency. Like you simply had to see me right away."

"Erick, when I first woke up I couldn't remember much of the night. For some reason, all I could remember was you—seeing your face and hearing someone shout your name. Everything else was a blank."

"You were in pretty bad shape, Jack. It's completely understandable that you don't remember everything. You probably remembered me because we had just talked at the bar."

"As things started to come together, that's what I thought too," said Jack. "But over the weekend, my memory has been coming back. And now it all makes sense."

"How so?"

"Erick, I wasn't robbed. And I wasn't beat up by some random thugs. They thought I was you. They wanted you."

"What? But why?"

"How the hell should I know?" Jack was visibly angry, and I couldn't blame him. He got the shit kicked out of him by somebody who thought he was me. I'd be pissed too.

Jack continued, "As soon as some metal pipe or something like that hit my leg, I heard this man say, 'Anderssen, mind your own fucking business. And this is just the start unless you stay out of things that don't concern you.' That's when he started kicking me, first in the ribs, then on my head. I guess the slash across the throat was just for added emphasis. So that I—you—would get the point."

I didn't know what to say. Who wanted me beat up? And why?

"Jack, I feel terrible about this. I just don't know what to say."

"I don't know what you're messed up in, but you'd better watch your back from now on. The guy didn't seem like an amateur at breaking legs."

I could feel myself start to sweat with guilt.

"Jack, what can I do to help? How can I make this up to you?"

"You can't. Plain and simple. I've been running competitively since high school. Running has given me more than I could have ever hoped for. And now that's gone. I'll never compete again, and nothing you can say or do is going to change that."

"So what are you going to tell the cops?"

"Exactly what I told you. And I'm going to make sure they believe it."

"Why wouldn't they believe it?"

He didn't respond.

"Jack, I wish I knew what the hell is going on. Why would someone—"

"I don't want your apologies or your sympathy, Erick. I wanted to make sure you knew what I was going to tell the cops. Now I've done that, so get out."

"Does Kate know?"

"Of course she does. Now, get out."

Not having anything else to say, I mumbled something about Jack calling me if he needed anything, and then I made my escape. I paused outside Jack's door for a moment, wondering if anywhere I went was safe anymore, and then hurried out of the hospital.

26

After feeding Max and letting him out one more time, I was getting ready for bed when the phone rang. Caller ID said GrandHotel Chicago. I couldn't think of who I knew that would be staying at the hotel so I let voice mail pick it up. After listening to the message, I was glad I had.

"Mr. Anderssen? This is Ashley. I just got into town, and I'm excited that you've signed up for our Chicago Marathon project and can't wait to meet you. Can you stop by the hotel sometime tomorrow morning—say around 10—so we can start planning the book?"

Our project? So we can start planning the book? I would certainly stop by the hotel tomorrow morning, if for no other reason than to set this pop diva's mind straight on whose book and whose project this was going to be.

27

Before leaving for the hotel, I reviewed the research I'd done on Ashley and did a quick Google News search. The most recent pictures they had were of a young woman who had been to one too many Hollywood parties and enjoyed two too many celebrity buffets. There was no way that this little blond butterball could get whipped into shape for a marathon in a few short months. Maybe I could talk her out of this so that I had one less challenge to deal with. Shutting down my PowerBook and throwing it into my Coach bag (a gift from Kate that I loved long after I stopped loving her), I headed out the door to grab a cab.

Sunday mornings in Chicago are magnificent. The entire city is out enjoying the day, not caring that tomorrow starts another week of the real world. Of course, I'm hardly one to talk. I haven't had a nine-to-five day since leaving the *Tribune*, and I considered myself incredibly fortunate to have escaped that grind. My lucky star again!

Tempering the day, however, was the deepening puzzle of my life. I felt like I wasn't getting any closer to answers while the questions just kept piling up.

Lost in thought, I looked up just as the cab pulled up in front of the hotel. Built in the 1920s, the classic beauty and magnificence of an historic hotel is never lost on me. People may turn on you, but architecture is rooted in stone. The hotel's details started with a gorgeous façade and carried through to each and every room, public and private. The builders and workers took pride in the character they gave these great gems. Not like today's glass boxes of cookie-cutter rooms piled on top of each other with little or no thought toward creating a character for the property. Put a big flat screen in the room and no one cares that it looks like crap.

Setting that rant aside, I smiled as the doorman greeted me and held the big bronze door wide open. The GrandHotel Chicago was known not just for its classic art deco design but also for having the best staff in the city. Its doormen, from their prominent spot in front of those big doors right on Michigan Avenue, were especially well known for their outgoing personalities and season-changing wardrobe. From their tall faux fur hats in winter to August's tropical pith helmets, the GrandHotel makes a statement.

I swept through the huge vaulted lobby (one always sweeps through vaulted lobbies) and headed to the front desk, where I asked for Ashley. The staffer very politely asked for ID before even admitting she had ever heard of Ashley.

"Ah, yes, Mr. Anderssen, welcome to the GrandHotel Chicago. Miss Ashley is waiting for you in her suite on the forty-second floor."

Thanking the very attractive young lady, I headed for the elevators. Why did hotels hide their elevator banks as if they were embarrassed to have them?

I pushed 42 and watched the doors close slowly and elegantly. I was especially pleased to see no media screen in the elevator and to hear no canned music. The GrandHotel grasped that I did not need to be entertained for the eleven seconds it would take me to get to my floor of choice.

The doors glided open and I stepped out into a beautifully designed foyer with a conical ceiling, carved and gilded. An enormous bouquet of pink, purple, and white lilacs on a small deco table (which looked like an original Ruhlmann) dominated the room, as did the enormous blond man in a black suit standing next to that single door. He didn't have the telltale earpiece of security guards everywhere, but he didn't have to. His shoulders would barely fit through the door behind him, and his suit was stretched to its limits across the chest and arms. No one was going into that room without his approval.

As I walked closer, he gave me a thin smile of welcome, and in a deep voice that seemed to fit his bulk, he asked for a photo ID. He examined my license closely, even holding it up at an angle to see the holographic image of the Great Seal of the State of Illinois.

Keeping the thin but oh-so-polite smile on his face, he asked me to wait for a moment and then slipped into the room. As I waited, I wondered how many layers of staff and hangers-on I'd have to go through before meeting Herself. I encouraged myself to be patient and settled in for a long-drawn-out process.

28

Before I could even get myself all riled up, the door opened and the big blond guard came out.

"Please come in, Mr. Anderssen."

As he held the door open, I stepped into the suite. And what a suite it was.

I went through a small, elegant foyer and into a gorgeous art deco gem. The main room had twenty-foot ceilings and was highlighted by a huge black marble fireplace at the far end. Centered on the fireplace were several sitting areas, all in white and shades of gray with throw pillows in varying shades of blue and side tables that reflected the glow of a stunning deco cut glass chandelier. I was so taken by the room that I didn't see the person coming down a gracefully curved staircase until she called out to me.

"Mr. Anderssen, I am so glad you agreed to meet me here. I'm Ashley."

As she quickly came down the last few steps, she finished her sentence by stretching out her hand to take mine. I took one look at her and decided that perhaps they were right: You can't trust everything you read on the Internet.

The plumpish girl I thought I'd see was, instead, a beautiful young woman who was in much better shape than I had expected. She was dressed simply in what appeared to be exercise clothing with a light scarf around her neck. I knew that the scarf was one of her signature looks, but this one served to highlight her fitness rather than hide a double chin. Her blond hair was pulled back into a simple ponytail. Her handshake was firm, and the look in her emerald eyes was determined yet friendly. A modest smile—vastly different than the overdone, toothy grin I'd seen from red carpet photos—added to her appeal. I wondered what else I had gotten wrong in my rush to judge.

The guard had slipped back out into the exterior lobby, leaving Ashley and me seemingly alone in the suite.

"Could I offer you something to drink? A bottle of water or some fruit juice?"

I don't know what I expected, but it certainly wasn't fruit juice. I mumbled something about juice sounding nice.

"I have a few fruit trees in my backyard in LA, so I've been experimenting with fresh juices. I got this great juicer at Target and made this pomegranate-orange mixture that I think you might like. I pop in a little club soda to give it a little bit of fizz."

She makes her own juice and shops at Target. I was batting zero when it came to preconceived notions. I was also strangely (especially for me) non-communicative. She handed me a small juice glass that was beading with condensation and offered me a seat at one of the groupings nearest the fireplace. I sat down, still clutching my bag and the glass of juice. Ashley smiled at my discomfort, and then she reached over, took my bag from me, and set it on the floor by my chair. She pulled a small table up, found a coaster, and took my juice glass, setting it on the table near me.

"There, all settled in."

"Thank you. I'm not usually this awkward, but I seem to be having one of those days."

"Not to worry; we all have those days. Can I get you anything else?"

"No, thank you. I'm all set."

"Good." She paused. "I have to admit, I'm a bit starstuck. So, as I said, I'm so glad you agreed to do your next book on marathoning. I think your readers will enjoy your experience and be motivated to run a marathon themselves."

"Have you ever run a marathon, Ashley?" I was dreading the answer. Just because you're cute and fit doesn't mean you can handle 26.2 miles.

"Oh, never! I usually run a half marathon or two every year, but it's gotten harder with touring, and my new projects take up so much of my time. That's why I built my summer schedule around training for the Chicago Marathon. My trainer in LA said that it's perfect for first-time marathoners—a flat course, well organized, and logistically easy. So here I am, ready to start serious training."

"I have to say I'm a bit surprised to hear that you run half marathons. I haven't seen anything about that online. How do you avoid the publicity?"

She laughed a simple, honest laugh. "Actually, that's part of the fun. I built myself a secret identity that I use for training and running. I use another name and my cousin's address in San Diego for all my running stuff. With a cap on my head and no makeup, I've never been recognized. It's been great—but I'm not going incognito for Chicago. Raising money for my foundation is more important than my privacy."

"That's amazing. I can't believe you've gotten away with it." I took a drink of juice to settle my brain. "So what's your foundation about?"

"It's brand new, but I have big plans for it. The John and Monica Frederick Foundation for Inner City Schools. Part of everything I'm involved in—my music, the Lagerfeld collection—goes toward building an endowment and finding a great staff. I'm hoping to start funding programs as early as next year."

"I'm sorry, but who are the Fredericks?"

"My parents. We were very poor. They sacrificed everything so that my brother and I could get a good education. I want to honor them by helping other disadvantaged kids break the cycle of their own poverty. I studied secondary education and psychology at Michigan State so that I could help kids. Who knew then that I'd be helping them in this way?"

I was more and more impressed by Miss Frederick as our conversation progressed.

She continued, "It'll be awhile before I catch up to your Alex Project, Mr. Anderssen. I really believe in this and want it to make a huge impact on kids as soon as possible."

So she had done some checking of her own. Good for her. Hopefully she got a better impression of me than I did of her, but I was rapidly learning how wrong my flimsy research had been.

"First, please call me Erick. Now, I heard about your project with GrandHotel. Is that related at all to your decision to run the Grand-Hotel Chicago Marathon?" I felt a little snarky asking that question right after she had told me of her good intentions, but I figured that if we were going to be spending time together, I might as well let her see my snarky side.

"Actually, it is related. GrandHotel has offered to make a sizable contribution to the foundation if I run and finish their marathon. That'll be part of the media story, and it'll give me additional motivation to finish."

Up front and honest. Okay: I was going to throw out everything I thought I knew about this woman and just appreciate her for who she seemed to be. Interesting notion, I know.

"So, Erick, since I never trust what I read on the Internet, tell me all about you." The irony was not lost on me.

I spent the next fifteen minutes telling her an abbreviated and slightly cleaned up life story. I told her about Alex, about our parents, the marriage and divorce, how I got into writing, and even squeezed Max into the story. She laughed at the right spots and teared up a little when I told her about Alex's final days. I think I did too.

"Erick, you haven't said anything about running. How many marathons have you run?"

"I have to say that I am a recreational runner at best. I've done a 10K and some neighborhood fun runs, but running for me is a way to keep enjoying my food and drink while staying in somewhat reasonable shape. Nothing more than that."

"Well, don't worry. We have the most incredible trainer and a training program that is guaranteed to succeed, so we'll get you through this and set your book up for success."

She was encouraging me. Not quite how I thought this was going to go, but maybe she was right. Maybe it was me that would be the issue. Of course, my more-than-healthy male ego wouldn't permit me even to think of not keeping up with Ashley.

Sometimes I shouldn't listen to my ego.

. . .

We chatted for a minute or two more, and then we agreed to meet the next morning at 9:00 a.m. for the beginning of our training regime. GrandHotel was rolling out new fitness centers in all their properties, and the as-yet-unfinished Chicago center was to be our home base for the next couple of months.

I cabbed home and immediately changed into my running gear.

Catching a glimpse of myself in the hallway mirror, I wondered how Ashley was going to feel about faded mesh shorts and t-shirts with faded rock bands. I decided she'd have to get used to my look. Leaving a sad-eyed Max behind (his speed was impressive over a short distance, but he didn't have the endurance for the distance I hoped to achieve), I headed across the park to the running trail and, turning left, started working my way up the lakefront. I'll admit that I was looking over my shoulder for the first mile or so, wondering if the leg breaker who'd attacked Jack would pop out from behind a bush.

A few minutes later, I was passing several slower runners (some younger and in much better shape than I) and feeling pretty good about myself. I had a good pace going, and all the moving parts were running smoothly. I passed the 4-mile marker and wondered if I should turn back, but I decided to go a bit further. Before I knew it, I saw the 5-mile marker and decided to make my turn for home there. Just as I was turning, I felt a twitch in my hamstring that seemed to go away if I slowed down. I could tell that my breathing was getting more labored and my pace was slowing significantly. Looking ahead, the next 3 or 4 miles were going to be tough, but I was determined to stick it out.

With about 2 miles to go, discretion triumphed over ego, and I veered off the trail to find a cab. Suddenly, running 26 miles in October seemed like a much more daunting challenge than it had just a few short hours ago.

Unfortunately, the challenges of a marathon seemed to have a simple solution: train. The other challenges I faced were much more complex: understanding what Lord Greene was up to, uncovering the source of Kate and Jack's newfound wealth (and gun), and, of course, solving Barbara's murder.

29

Monday morning came early. I took Max out for a quick walk and then showered and dressed. Yes, I showered to go work out. I may not be able to run 10 miles, but I still have my pride. That same pride had me agonizing over which of my many heavily worn t-shirts would make the best first impression on Ashley. Being a musician herself, I wanted to find a band that she would appreciate, true artists that a connoisseur would acknowledge. Almost at the bottom of my drawer was the one I knew was right: Springsteen and the E Street Band. Realizing that my search for the perfect T was about to make me late, I hurried out the front door and quickly found a cab for the short drive to the GrandHotel.

Bypassing the front desk, I arrived at the suite door a few minutes after nine. My large, imposing friend from the day before greeted me with no more warmth, but with an acknowledgment that he knew who I was. He again went in to announce me, and only a minute or two later he returned to escort me into the living room of the suite. I didn't need to be a mind reader to know what he thought of my running gear. He actually curled his lip in disdain. It literally curled. Impressive.

Even more impressive was my first sight of Ashley. She came in from the kitchen of the suite wearing a beautiful pale blue running ensemble. Yes, I know ensemble seems a bit much for something you sweat in, but outfit is too common of a word for what she was wearing. She gave me quick kiss on the cheek (I was again dumbstruck) and went to sit down by the marble fireplace.

"Have a seat, Erick. Our trainer just arrived in the lobby and is on his way up."

"I meant to ask you about this trainer. Do we really need someone to tell us how to run? I've been putting one foot in front of another for almost forty years now."

"Erick, don't underestimate the marathon; 26.2 miles of nonstop running challenges even the strongest athlete. Remember, you'll be running for several hours without a break. That is incredibly taxing, and if it's a warm day—well, it can be downright dangerous. Several people have died running the Chicago Marathon, and I don't want either of us to be added to that sad toll. And this guy is the best. He's an Olympian and one of the most respected trainers in the country."

I was actually staring at her so intently that I didn't hear the door open, and I didn't know that anyone else was in the room until Ashley jumped to her feet. "There you are! We're so excited that you are going to be part of our team. Jack, I think you know Erick—"

Jack. As I stood and slowly turned, I kept thinking, *what are the odds? There have to be a lot of Jacks that are athletic and runners. It couldn't be Jackson Clark. That would be just impossible.*

They say the impossible happens every day. It certainly happened that day, because standing in front of me, leaning on two crutches, was none other than my old buddy Jackson.

My pause was clearly measurable because Ashley had to call my name again to shake me out of my stupor. Trying to recover from my surprise, I walked over and shook Jack's hand.

"Jack, it's great to see you already up and about. How are you feeling?"

His response was as cool as I feared it would be.

"I'm fine, Erick. Just fine."

After yet another uncomfortable pause, Ashley threw herself into the breach.

"Jack, I'm so happy that you weren't more seriously injured. I was just horrified when I heard you were attacked. I'm glad you're still willing to train us, even if you can't run with us anymore."

"Thanks. I appreciate you sticking with me."

Ashley smiled. "Let's get Jack off his feet and sit here at the table and talk about the marathon."

Eyeing each other with mutual skepticism, Jack and I took seats on either side of the suite's big dining room table, with Ashley taking the head of the table. I moved yet another massive bouquet, this time of yellow and pink tulips, off to the side so that I could keep an eye on Jack.

We stared across the table as Ashley made what seemed to be opening remarks. Maybe she was just trying to stall, or perhaps cut the tension that suddenly had filled the room.

She said how happy she was to be running the Chicago Marathon, how happy she was to be working with both of us, yada, yada . . . I could tell that Jack was paying less attention to her than I was (if that's possible). He seemed to alternate between glowering at me and staring off into the distance, as if he was looking for something that wasn't quite there. I knew he had had a really ugly experience that still wasn't fully behind him, but I really hoped we weren't going to have five months of angry glares between us. I wanted to close the gap, even if it meant getting Ashley involved as an intermediary.

Finally, Ashley seemed to be winding down and leaving a gap open for one of us to speak. I stepped into the momentary void.

"Jack, you're the expert here. Why don't you tell us what we're getting ourselves into."

Jack looked at me as if he was expecting a dig or snide retort. When one didn't come, he gave me a half-smile and started to speak.

"Running a marathon is a very exciting experience and one you'll never forget. But it's also an enormous amount of work, and it's really, really hard. So hard that you'll want to quit many times. It's an enormous time commitment as well. You'll be running six days out of seven for the next five months, and you'll learn to treasure that one-day a week off. By the time you hit race day in October, you'll have run more than 750 miles and invested more than 150 hours of your life in getting ready. You'll change your diet, your sleep habits, and your social life. You'll have blisters, you'll bleed, your toenails may fall off, and you'll wake up some days feeling like you can't even move.

"But, despite all the challenges, you'll be glad you did it, because at the end of that Sunday in October, you'll be able to say that you are a marathoner. You ran the most challenging distance in road racing and conquered it. You ran the marathon distance."

Despite my natural skeptical state, I was actually inspired by Jack's remarks. He'd been there; he knew what he was talking about. He knew the ups and downs, knew the hard work and the pain. He also knew the high that must come from finishing a marathon.

Ashley sounded equally inspired by Jack's remarks. She gave him a brief round of applause.

"So, Jack, let's go. We're ready to start right now."

Jack held up a hand. "Not today. We need to talk about the schedule and how this is all going to work. We'll start running tomorrow."

I was disappointed that I wouldn't get a chance to start running with Ashley, but Jack wasn't going to have that happen yet.

Ashley asked, "So when do we start training? What's the schedule?"

"We're going to base your training on the classic Hal Higdon model, modified a little to work around Ashley's schedule. Normally, we wouldn't start training until the middle of June, but because we're going to have some gaps in the coming months, we'll start this week and slowly work up to Hal's schedule."

Ashley asked, "Who is Hal?"

"Hal Higdon is the best known authority on marathon training in the world. He's written more than three dozen books and also writes for *Runner's World*. He's run more than one hundred marathons. You'll meet him at the GrandHotel Marathon expo."

I felt like I wasn't contributing. "Sounds like Higdon's plan is a great place to start, Jack. And if you endorse it, then I'm sure it's the right way to go."

Still looking skeptical—and who could blame him?—Jack nodded and moved on. "I'll give you your schedule for the month a week or two in advance so you can plan ahead. Ashley, your manager gave me your summer engagement calendar, and I've already built around that. Erick, do you have any summer commitments?"

"No, not really. I was hoping to keep the summer open for whatever my next book was going to be—and now this is it!"

"Great. Now let's talk about Ashley's security during training runs."

Ashley nodded at the question, but it struck me as odd.

"Security during training runs?"

Ashley turned to me with a troubled expression on her face. "We've had some issues with stalkers over the last several months. There are two in particular that have my management really concerned. That explains Charlie at the door here and the security team that travels with me."

"With all due respect to Charlie, there is no way he's keeping up with us on a training run, and you certainly can't either, Jack. I'm no bodyguard. So what do we do?"

"I've been working with Ashley's people on this. They have a couple of people who are serious runners—very qualified people—who will run with you on your longer runs, or if you're running in the park, where there is a greater risk of Ashley being recognized. We'll use alternate exits and entrances from the hotel and use some less frequented running trails as well. We're pretty comfortable that we have security covered. But Erick, we need you to help us out by keeping an eye on the people around Ashley and letting security know if you see anyone who looks like they could be a threat."

"Sure. I'll be that extra set of eyes for you and the team." I paused. "It sounds like you've been working on this for a while. How was all of this affected by your injuries?"

I knew I was getting into dangerous territory by bringing up the incident, but I needed to know how long Jack had been working with Ashley and her people. Okay, call me paranoid, but it seemed as if a lot of people were involved in me and Ashley running the marathon long before I knew this was going to happen.

Jack didn't hesitate. "I've been talking to Ashley's people for several months about working with the two of you on the race. I just thought I'd be running with you instead of standing on the sidelines. But it's all good. I can get you two in shape and ready and feel like I'm part of the event, even if I'll never run the race myself again." He generously avoided my gaze as he said that. Kind of him. I guess.

"Jack, we're incredibly fortunate to have a world champion runner like you in our corner. I know you'll make all the difference. So what's next?" Ashley asked.

"Here's your schedule for the next several weeks through the end of May." Jack pulled some sheets from a folder he had brought with him.

"A typical week early on will have you run for thirty minutes on Tuesday, an hour on Wednesday, cross train for an hour on Thursday, run again on Friday, and then take Saturday off. Sunday will be your long run of the week. We'll start out slowly at 5 miles. Within a few weeks, however, your Sunday run will be up to 10 miles. Which explains Mondays."

"Mondays?" I asked.

"You get Monday off every week. And you'll need it."

Huh. Didn't look too bad to me, despite my disastrous run in the park the other day. Ashley certainly seemed comfortable, and Jack sensed our confidence level.

"You both think this is going to be easy, right? Well, it won't be easy, but the training program is designed to ease a novice runner into the longer distances. You'll start out slow, gradually increasing your distances and endurance. And then it gets tough. Really tough. Puking on the side of the path tough."

Accepting what Jack said without much thought, I moved on.

"I've been promised unfettered access to the behind-the-scenes action of the Chicago Marathon. How will that work?"

"Kate asked me to talk about that with you. Since she's so completely immersed in the planning and organizing of the event, she asked me to introduce you to the marathon staff. You and I should sit down and talk about how this is all going to work. And Kate confirmed it: no holds barred, nothing hidden behind the curtain. You get to see it all."

"Dinner tomorrow?"

"You got it. But not at O'Shaughnessy's."

Jack said the last part with a small smile. I wondered if this was the beginning of a thaw between us.

. . .

Jack, Ashley, and I agreed to meet at the staff entrance at the back of the hotel at 9:00 a.m. the next day, hoping to make a covert exit. We'd be only a block or two from the running path in Grant Park.

I headed home, feeling much more confident about Ashley's capabilities, how it would be to work with Jack, and my own ability to run the marathon.

As I walked into the house, I immediately saw a small cardboard box sitting in the middle of the foyer. I knew it wasn't there when I left, and the only people who had keys to the house were Ted and my cleaning lady. I picked the box up, took it into the kitchen and sliced open the tape holding it shut.

Inside was an old-fashioned alarm clock with two sticks of what appeared to be Play-Doh and some random wires sticking out here and there. And a note.

Anderssen: this one is fake but the next one will be real. Stop asking questions about things you don't understand or you'll regret it for the rest of your life. Which won't be very long.

The note appeared to be from a computer printer on plain white paper. My hands shaking, I put the note back into the box and called 911.

. . .

Using the word "bomb" when calling the Chicago Police Department clearly warrants a rapid response, even when the word "fake" is included. Three patrol cars, an ambulance, and a bomb squad van appeared in just a few short minutes, followed soon thereafter by Detective Hanson. Once the bomb technicians determined that it was, in fact, a fake, the place cleared out except for Hanson and me. The fake bomb went with the technicians.

"Mr. Anderssen, you seem to have an admirer."

"Sarcasm isn't really becoming of you, Detective. I'm really not in the mood."

"I can understand that. So what have you been digging into that would result in a threat of this kind?"

I wasn't ready to share my work with anyone, much less Hanson, so I talked around it the best I could.

"I honestly don't know, Detective. It could be some research I'm doing on any number of subjects."

"I thought you did action adventures. Not normally something that would attract this level of threat."

"I agree. That's why I'm so confused by the whole thing."

"How did the package get into the house?"

"No clue. The front door was locked and I don't think any of the windows were broken."

"That's correct; our guys checked everything out. There are no signs of a break-in."

"Then I can't help you. It was just here when I walked in."

"And no fingerprints other than yours. Professionals."

"Maybe I pissed off a neighbor. Seriously, I have no idea who it could be."

He looked at me skeptically.

"I'm sure you can appreciate that I don't find that to be believable. You'll be safer in the long run if you just tell me what's going on."

"Believe me, if I had something concrete I'd share it with you. But I don't. And it's been a long day. You need to leave now."

"Very well. But remember: we can't help you if you won't tell us what's going on. I hope you don't forget that." And he was out the door.

30

Morning came quickly after a restless night of sleep. A cab got me to the GrandHotel quickly. Receipt in hand (business expense!), I walked through the lobby, wondering how I could get to the staff entrance without being perceived as a kook or a threat. Fortunately, Ashley's Charlie was waiting for me in the lobby and ready to escort me to where Ashley was waiting.

Like every hotel backroom space I'd been in, the decorating budget had clearly been spent on the front-of-house, with the staff area of the hotel lit by fluorescent and featuring concrete and floor tile. Winding our way through back corridors, we reached the staff entrance. Motivational posters and legal disclaimers on a massive bulletin board let me know that I was in the right place. Seeing Ashley and Jack both check their watches pointed out that I was late.

"Good morning, Erick," Ashley chirped. Way too chipper for a 9:00 a.m. run. I guess I should have expected chipper.

"Good morning, all," was my effort to maintain a positive attitude for our fledgling team.

"We're going to take it easy this morning," said Jack. "Just a quick thirty minutes along the lakefront, but try to keep it strong. We'll stay off the main paths and see if any issues arise with Ashley's security. There'll be a security person a bit behind you just in case."

Trying to find a bit of humor in the situation, I joked, "We? What's this 'we' stuff? You're not headed out to pound out a thirty minute run."

"You don't have to remind me, Erick. You know how much I wish I was out there running today," said Jack, with no trace of that almost half smile I saw fleetingly yesterday. I had blown it. Tried to use humor to make things better but ended up losing any of the progress I might have made. I vowed to keep a closer watch on my words going forward.

"Anyway, head out the back of the hotel, then to your left to Randolph Street, then out to the lakefront. Head south along Columbus to Museum Campus, turn, and come back."

Deciding to stick with my new rule of watching what I said, I kept quiet and headed out with Ashley. Our first run together. As I was enjoying the moment, Ashley took off and left me almost standing still. I hustled to catch up.

. . .

The run went well, I guess. At least I didn't embarrass myself any further. We kept up a steady, respectable pace down Columbus to the beautifully landscaped Museum Campus. Home to the Field Museum of Natural History, the Adler Planetarium, and the Shedd Aquarium, the Campus pulled together these three great venues. Just south of the Campus is Soldier Field (again, not Soldier's or Soldiers Field, Soldier singular), with the heavily trafficked running paths going parallel to the attractions. We stayed along the sidewalk, and no one seemed to recognize Ashley, who was reasonably well disguised in a baseball hat (Cubs, somewhat worn) and Oakleys. Reaching the turnaround point that Jack had designated, we kept up our steady pace and returned to the back of the hotel. Jack was waiting for us.

"Not bad," he said, clicking on a small stopwatch that I would learn to hate over the next several months. "You'll pick up the pace over the next few weeks, but not bad for a start."

"Thanks, Jack," chirped Ashley. I wasn't about to show it, but the run had taken a lot more out of me than I cared to admit, and certainly more than it seemed to affect Ashley, who looked as if she hadn't broken a sweat.

Jack remained serious.

"Tomorrow we'll do this again, but double the time you spend running. I'll give you a couple of distance markers to use to make sure you are picking up your pace. While you're doing so, you'll start building endurance. Remember, we've got lots of time to get the training in, so don't be too intimidated. Erick, I'll see you at Gibsons at 7:00."

I went out the front entrance and got in the cab line in front of the hotel so that I could get home, shower, and take care of Max. Dinner that evening was my first chance to talk to Jack about how I wanted to do my behind-the-scenes research on the marathon and meet the key members of the staff.

After a nice walk with Max, which included guilt-inspired extra time to sniff every bush and lamppost along the way, I caught up on email, did some additional research on the business of marathoning, and cleaned up to go to Gibsons, one of Chicago's great steak palaces.

I carefully selected my wardrobe to balance that fine line between casual and business. I'd heard from Kate that the marathon staff was pretty informal, and I like to have a good time, so I tried to dress to fit Gibson's class and the marathon team's style. Glen plaid blazer from Paul Stuart, crisply starched white dress shirt from Polo (the outlet, but who's asking?), and jeans I paid way too much for at Top Shop in London.

I was a few minutes early arriving at Gibsons, but somehow I wasn't surprised to see Jack and company already at the bar. Ordering a Grey Goose and tonic from James, one of Gibson's long-tenured bartenders, I joined the group at one end of the bar.

Jack introduced me to the people who made Kate look so good. There were four, and I had done my homework on each.

Carlos Ramirez was a tall, dark-haired man with a runner's build and a too-big grin. He had been a collegiate distance runner and would-be business tycoon who couldn't make a go of it in the real world, so he went back to the only thing he knew: running. He turned a middling successful running history into a job as the elite athlete coordinator for the Chicago Marathon. With a nearly unlimited budget for world-class runners, it was almost impossible for Carlos to screw up, but somehow he did. Over the last several years, I read, Carlos had invested huge sums of money in a series of flame-out rookies and has-beens with an occasional burst of brilliance. Hey, even a blind squirrel can find a nut now and then. The best days—the world record setting days—of the race seemed to be behind it. A shame. $3 million in elite athlete fees used to get the race a couple of world record contenders. I heard from a number of runners that Carlos was desperately trying to hold on to his job after several years of plodding race results and one nameless Kenyan winning year after year. He seemed to never appreciate the value of the huge budget dropped at his feet by the sponsors. But through it all, he continued to see himself as the brains behind the outfit.

Martin Michaels was Ramirez's right hand man and the person who really made the race succeed. As operations manager, Michaels was responsible for making the race actually happen. He measures and marks the course, works with the City of Chicago for police support and street closings, orders hundreds of ambulances, runs the medical program, coordinates the work of 10,000 volunteers, and handles a million other details. An almost reclusive micromanager with obsessive-compulsive tendencies, Michaels manages his very complex world with an iron fist and an enormous series of microscopically detailed spreadsheets that control his world in ten-minute increments. He found the perfect job for his personality and was more than happy to fade into the background and let Ramirez and Kate take the spotlight. Even his size—perhaps five-six, thin, and pale—made him fade into the background, especially around the more vibrant Ramirez.

The source of much of Kate's media coverage was Sarah Peters, the race's marketing director. She and her staff, the largest team within the marathon's thirty-plus employee group, kept the race in the media spotlight twelve months a year, a major coup for an event that literally lasted six hours on one Sunday. Peters was young for her job, having come to the marathon from the PR department of a big bank, and before that, one of Chicago's thoroughbred horse tracks. Not a traditional media background, but not a traditional person either. It appeared that Peters combined a natural, smarmy gift for schmoozing with a keen talent for knowing whom to suck up to. She was a slave to fashion and showed up at every event in something new, with makeup and hair all perfectly in place and styled to match the event. Not a natural beauty, rumor had it that she spent the bulk of her salary just looking good. She was the antithesis of the blue-jeaned, t-shirt wearing event crew one normally associated with operations like the marathon. Rumor also had it that she could drink a sailor under the table, with language to match.

Finally, there was Paul O'Bannon, the sales director for the event. O'Bannon's name matched his appearance: You could see the old country in his wavy red-brown hair, bright blue eyes, and big happy grin. With a long history of sponsorship sales for the City of Chicago's various events, and known throughout the city for his family's deep roots with South Side Democratic politics, O'Bannon brought in an eight-figure stream of revenue for the event despite his seemingly never putting in a full day's work. His time was being spent elsewhere, but no one was exactly sure where. There was quite a bit of speculation that a certain tavern in Beverly saw more than its share of Paul. Would it ever catch up to him? Inquiring minds want to know.

Almost as if to prove the rumors I had heard about them, each responded to my presence in line with their reputations. Ramirez was blustery and overly friendly, clearly seeking a primary role in my upcoming book. Michaels was reserved, looking up only briefly from his ever-present iPhone and messages. Peters was openly flirtatious, offering me "anything I wanted or needed," while O'Bannon nodded briefly and then went back to his beer.

Jack had told me earlier that the team knew the directive from Kate to give me total access and that she had been quite clear, as only Kate can be, that there were no options other than full disclosure. Knowing Kate all too well, I knew there would be secrets that I'd have to work hard to ferret out, but ferret them out I would. I couldn't quite decide where best to start, but Ramirez and Peters seemed to be the most open to conversation, while Michaels and O'Bannon lived in their own worlds, although living in a spreadsheet is quite different from living in a neighborhood pub.

Once everyone had a drink, Jack made yet another inspiring speech (it was by now obvious to me that I had underestimated Mr. Clark), and then we all toasted the success of the event and my book. Ramirez tried to pull off a second toast, but everyone essentially ignored him.

I was getting the impression that, like a child, Ramirez lived in his own world and was oblivious to everyone around him. As Ramirez continued to talk about himself and his gloried days of running, the rest of the team went back to what they apparently were doing before I arrived: Michaels texting, Peters flirting, and O'Bannon drinking. When Ramirez paused to take a sip, I used the opportunity to break in and ask the group a question.

"Your race has been around for more than thirty years and you haven't changed the course much. Why do so many people keep coming back to run Chicago? Why do you sell out every year?"

Before Ramirez could answer, Peters jumped in. I could tell she was launching one of her canned responses but let her start anyway.

"Erick, we sell out every year for three basic reasons. One, the operations of the race are top-notch. Nothing ever goes wrong, and people appreciate that. Two, the course is flat and easy, and runners like a loop course. And three, people love to come to Chicago. It's the greatest city in the world!"

Reason number one was a lie. Things go wrong every year at every race. Just nothing catastrophic. The first part of number two made sense: Flat seemed better than hilly. I made a note to ask what a loop course was and why that was great. And three, well, I loved Chicago as much as any other local, but there are other great cities with great marathons: New York, Boston, and London, to name just three. But following my "don't say stupid things" rule, I kept my mouth shut and just nodded and smiled. Smiled and nodded. I did a lot of that during drinks, watching the interplay between the four of them—what little there was—and seeing how Jack fit—or more appropriately, didn't fit—into the mix.

Drinks were meant to be just an introduction, and when our reservation was called, the four staff members knew that was their sign to exit. And exit they did, with nary a look back at the check with which they stuck Jack and me. Another business expense for Anderssen, Inc.

Jack and I followed Phillip to the table, a nice, relatively quiet one in the corner. I vowed to be on my best behavior for the evening so as to not further antagonize the person who was to be my gatekeeper and trainer for the next many months. I needed Jack. And he knew it.

31

Dinner was pleasant and delicious. We kept the conversation business like, talking schedules and key dates, and access and the like. The only awkward moment came when I was describing Barbara's role in my life and original pressure on me to write the marathon book. Although I couldn't figure out why, Jack couldn't wait to change the subject.

Meanwhile, we kept the food coming. Hey, it's important to fuel your body when training, right? Lots of protein, carbohydrates, enough servings of fruits and vegetables? I had it all covered. Lovely filet with béarnaise for protein, double baked potato for the carbs, and enough cabernet to satisfy the fruit and vegetable needs of a small village. It was a very nice evening.

And when I looked at my credit card receipt the next morning, I realized that I perhaps shouldn't have fought so hard to pick up the check. It was going to be a real treat explaining all my business expenses this month to my accountant, Amy. She's creative and always up to date on the latest tax news but an absolute bear when it comes to "supporting documentation and appropriate accounting" as she called it. I called them receipts. Potato, po-tah-tow.

. . .

And it wasn't just the expense I came to regret. All of that rich food and even richer cabernet came to haunt me during our first day of cross training. The fact that I would have to get up and be out the door before 9:00 a.m. clearly wasn't front of mind during dinner. I stumbled into the GrandHotel lobby only a few minutes late. I hoped I didn't look as bad as I felt, but one look from Charlie convinced me that I probably did. He at least had the courtesy to wait to tell me my Dire Straits t-shirt was inside out until we got into the elevator. As I was straightening out that fashion faux pas, Charlie punched a code of some kind into the elevator keypad and then pushed an unmarked button toward the top of the panel. Seconds later, the doors opened, and Charlie gestured for me to step out. What I saw literally took my breath away.

It was as if someone had peeled off the roof of the hotel and put a giant glass bubble in its place. I'm not sure how the illusion was created, but it felt like the walls and the ceiling of the new GrandHotel health club were made of one seamless piece of glass. Enhancing the illusion was what appeared to be a glass ledge surrounding the entire space and jutting out several feet from the body of the hotel. As I stepped closer to one of these ledges, I could look down and see traffic some fifty stories below me. My fear of heights kicked in and I fell backward into the bulk that was Charlie. He straightened me out and turned me around to face the main part of the club where I saw Ashley, Jack, and a young, very fit woman waiting for me. Trying to recover some dignity, I walked over to them just as Jack and the woman were finishing what seemed like a heated discussion.

"Erick, I'd like you to meet Margaret Newman, my trainer," said Ashley. "She flew in from LA this morning to get us started on cross training. She'll be running that part of our training regimen while Jack focuses on the running work."

"Margaret, I'm pleased to meet you," I said, noticing that this very fit woman was even more fit close up. Scary fit. I was clearly the least fit person in the room, including Charlie, who stood implacably nearby in his ever-present black suit.

"Erick, I've read so much about you. It's a pleasure to meet you in person." Margaret's voice was low and raspy, sort of the whiskey and cigarette kind of voice, but I seriously doubted she got hers from Jack Daniels and Marlboros.

Jack interrupted. "Ashley, I've said this several times. I can handle both parts of training. We don't need to fly someone in from the left coast just to show you how to ride a stationary bike a couple of times a week."

"I know you feel that way. But it's my race, and I want to train in my way. Margaret got me into shape for my first tour, and I've worked with her ever since. This is not a discussion, Jack; it's a decision, so just accept it so that we can get started."

With a curt nod, Jack turned and walked over to a sitting area where he rested his crutches against a chair and flopped down onto a silvery couch. He pulled out his iPod and headphones.

We all turned to face Margaret as if to say, let's go.

"Okay, here's what I have in mind. We'll start out cross training for forty-five minutes once a week, and then after a few weeks, we'll move that to a full hour twice a week. We're going to avoid anything that might damage the tissues and muscle you're building for running, so no tennis, no aerobic dance, no basketball until after the marathon. Instead, we'll use a rotating schedule with one day devoted to the rowing machine, cycling, and the elliptical, the other day swimming and deep-water running. Any questions?"

Just one. Can I swim in my t-shirt? Maybe a sweatshirt? My casual running kept me in reasonably good shape, but at nearly forty, I certainly didn't have the muscle definition of my earlier days, and it was clearly not in line with what these two women had. I also was suffering from the Chicago pales, that anemic look fostered by five months of gray skies and cold temperatures. Not wanting to appear vain, I avoided asking that question and just smiled and shook my head no. See, I can learn from my mistakes.

"Great. So, let's just spend today checking out all the equipment in this facility, and then we'll start seriously next week." My hangover and I breathed a sigh of relief, hopefully not in the direction of anyone who hadn't enjoyed Gibson's béarnaise sauce on their steak the night before.

As if summoned, a young man suddenly appeared at Margaret's side. With the body of a gymnast and well-tailored warm-ups with the GrandHotel Spa logo, Brian was one of the club's personal trainers, and he gave us the full tour of what was an almost-but-not-quite finished facility. The huge expanse of the machine room dominated the floor, but cleverly placed mirrors and free weight units disguised the entrance to the rest of the club, which turned out to be nearly as expansive as the machine room. A snack bar (looking dangerously healthy), lounge areas, shower and dressing rooms, and a gift shop were at varying stages of construction. As we finished walking through the area, Brian turned to a large piece of plastic covering one interior wall.

"Watch your step, everyone; there's a stairway right behind the plastic."

As we stepped through, we saw a gracefully winding stairway that led to the floor below, which contained a full European spa with dozens of treatment and massage rooms, makeup, nail, and hair salons, and a very high-end tearoom that looked as if it were straight out of London. As with the floor above, there was significant work to be done, but it appeared like it would be beautifully appointed with a hushed elegance to it. GrandHotel was sparing no expense in building out its new facility. I mentioned that to Brian.

"This is the first installation of the new GrandHotel Spa concept that we're rolling out this summer to all the GrandHotel properties. It's very exciting for all of us," said Brian.

Very exciting and very expensive. A multimillion-dollar spa renovation, all new Ashley-themed restaurants, and Ashley's endorsement deal. How was GrandHotel able to gamble on high-end spas and a young talent like Ashley? I needed to get to the bottom of this and hoped that Bruce had made more progress on his research.

As Brian went on with a list of the locations for the new spas, I wandered the floor. I came upon an old, painted door that seemed out of place within the glitz of the new spa. Curious, I opened the door to find several large wooden crates piled up. Printed on the side of each box was a large "Regency Suppliers" label. Regency. Impossible that they weren't connected, but what would a real estate company, my publisher, and a supply company of some kind have in common?

Seconds later, Brian came around me and closed the door firmly, pushing me back out into the main room.

"That's our construction office. We're not allowed in there—it's highly confidential."

His attitude was somewhere between anger and fear, and it was clear that the tour was now over.

. . .

I took my leave of Ashley, Jack, and Margaret and headed back to street level. It was another beautiful April day in Chicago, and since we hadn't worked out, I thought I'd walk home and sweat out a little of last night's excess.

Heading north on Michigan Avenue, I went back to pondering some of the many open questions still in front of me. Who had killed Barbara and why? What were the connections between Lord Greene, GrandHotel, and Regency? And where were Kate and Jack coming up with the money to afford their lifestyle? Even Barbara seemed to have more money than I had ever thought she had. Could I make a compelling book out of the Chicago Marathon?

And there was a new question: Could I actually run a marathon?

32

Recognizing that I had to start getting serious about the race, I used the rest of the day to make some changes. After giving Max a little exercise, I headed over to Whole Foods to stock up on the things I'd need for a healthy training diet. I'd seen on Hal Higdon's website that I needed a lot of complex carbohydrates—fruits, vegetables, bread, pasta, and cereal—which would have to make up 60 percent or more of my diet for the next few months. I stocked up on chicken and fish for protein and loaded up on sports drinks. Staying hydrated had never been a problem for me, but I knew Stella Artois and cabernet weren't exactly what the sports medicine doctors recommend for training. I added a couple of six packs of Amstel Light—hey, there's a lot of good stuff in beer.

Unloading all of this in the kitchen presented a challenge: where to store it all? I soon realized that the only way to make this work was to throw away all the things that I shouldn't be eating anyway, thus making room for my new healthy choices. Out went the frozen dinners, ice cream, pudding, and that lovely box of pastries from Nellie's. Ditto for the Fruit Loops, the bacon, and the potato chips (and the nacho chips and the Tostitos and the Fritos and the . . .) Not surprisingly, I suddenly had plenty of room for my new acquisitions. Oh, and I bought a scale. First scale I've owned since the twelve-function, voice-activated scale that Kate brought to the marriage. And took with her. Good riddance. I don't need a guy with a British accent telling me I've put on two pounds.

Healthy food in the house, some great low-fat, high-carb recipes culled from the Internet, and I was set. Since I was starving, I grilled a nice piece of skinless chicken, cooked up some broccoli and rice, and cracked open one of my Amstel Lights. This healthy living thing was going to be a snap.

33

Two hours later, I was ready to go through the trash to see if the ice cream I had thrown away was completely melted. I was starving. Bound and determined to last at least twelve hours on my new training diet, I went online to see what snack could tide me over until morning. Found some great suggestions: a handful of nuts (with no added salt), or perhaps a hard-boiled egg with the yolk removed. I really wish I had enjoyed that Gibson's meal a little bit more. I missed food already.

Since the night before hadn't been my best rest ever, I decided that an early bedtime would help me catch up on my rest and make me forget that I was as hungry as I was. So I let Max out back for a few minutes and then checked my email before heading up to bed. Besides the usual rubbish, I noticed a message from Martha. It was odd to see it coming from the publisher's email address instead of BronfmanRepresents.com, but it was pretty low on the list of things I was now getting used to.

In her message, Martha told me of her new position within Greene's publishing empire and that she would be handling my next book, which she understood would be on marathon running. She was pleased to hear that I was well underway with my research (she knew this how?) and wished me luck (didn't believe a word of it). She also asked for a two or three page précis of the book so that she could begin circulating it to the editorial staff. I was used to this request and had actually started outlining the précis in my head. Knowing that there was no time like the present, I closed my email and started to move the outline from my head to the screen. An hour later, most of the work was done, and I must say that the narrative was compelling. I highlighted the hard work, the dedication, the time commitment, and the sheer willpower required to train for and complete a marathon. I talked about the huge organizational challenges involved in putting on a 26.2 mile circus in the heart of one of the world's largest and busiest cities. I spoke of the stories that runners had to tell—why they ran, for whom they ran. The millions raised for hundreds of charities both large and small. The big money involved: elite athlete payments, prize and bonus money, sponsorship payments, apparel purchases, and even the underground economy of buying and selling bib numbers for a closed out race. And, of course, I talked about the drama. The photo finishes, the runners crawling across the finish line, desperate to say they completed the race. Marriage proposals and long-standing training partner breakups both happened under the pressure of the marathon distance. And the deaths. While no one liked to talk about it, runners tragically die, usually due to a previously undiagnosed health issue. I wondered if that kind of death would be a part of the marathon I'd be running.

If I'd only known. Could I have stopped what was going to happen?

34

I sent the précis to Martha, who responded quickly and positively. It was exactly what she was looking for. Since it was her first book to manage, I wasn't sure how she knew it was right, but I had a long-standing rule never to argue with "Yes."

I still hadn't figured out how all the Regency companies were connected to this mess, so I dropped Bruce Mays a quick note to find out why I hadn't heard from him.

Later than I had planned, I finally went up to bed, Max following closely behind. He was a little clingy these days, and I wasn't sure why. That was a trait he normally had only when I'd been on the road and he was with the sitters.

. . .

I woke just before the alarm, rested and refreshed. Or that's what I'd claim. I was actually stiff, sore, and starving. I had a feeling that those three adjectives would be with me for the next several months.

I went down, again followed closely by Max, and boiled an egg to have with my dry toast. I hate boiled eggs.

Slipping into a Pearl Jam t-shirt and my best pair of running shorts, I headed again to the GrandHotel and my daily date with Ashley and Jack.

Two hours later, after a quick run and some weight training, I was back home, showered, and ready to start the rest of my day. My goal for the day was to outline the book and set deadlines for each section. Although I worked best under pressure (the habit of finishing assignments the night before they were due had stuck with me since college), I knew this book had too many moving parts to crank out in the last few weeks before it was due.

While the ending, of course, had to wait for October and the real thing, there was quite a bit of the book that I could write now. To do so, I had several background interviews scheduled with runners, a nutritionist, an exercise physiologist, a cardiologist, and my own doctor. Before I got too far into this process, I wanted to make sure I didn't have any ticking time bombs in my chest that the marathon would trigger.

35

As the next few weeks progressed and spring suddenly morphed into summer, my days settled into a rhythm. Training in the morning, interviews, meetings, and research in the afternoon. I'd started turning some of my notes into sections of the book, and I was pretty pleased with how it was shaping up. The stories I was hearing from the runners were truly inspirational, even to a cynic like me.

Like the woman who was diagnosed with invasive Stage 3 breast cancer on her fortieth birthday. She was a survivor, but her success came only after years of painful chemotherapy and radiation. Her husband left her, but she had built an amazing support group of runners who'd experienced cancer and survived. She ran three or four marathons a year now, raising money for breast cancer awareness.

Or the young man whose brother was killed by an IED in Afghanistan. The soldier was due to go home after his final tour of duty, but he volunteered for one last mission. He left behind a beautiful young wife and two small daughters. The young man I interviewed runs nearly every month in one race or another, raising money to help military families who have lost a husband, a wife, a brother, or a sister to war.

I was getting great background from the fitness specialists, and I had a clean bill of health from my own doctor. Training was going well. That is, I hadn't embarrassed myself too badly. I had a feeling that Jack was going to turn up the heat on us when the July schedule came out, but for now we were slowly building strength and endurance. Jack's recovery was coming along well; he had moved to a cane, and I knew he was working hard with a physical therapist. I hadn't seen my charming ex-wife in some time. I assumed she was with her team, working on the millions of details that make up an event as big as the Chicago Marathon. Jack warned me that I needed to get much of my behind-the-scenes research into the marathon done by the end of August, since the marathon staff went into overdrive in September, often working twenty-hour days just to get everything done in time for the race. The last thing they needed was me trailing along, asking questions.

"How is your research going? Finding any skeletons in the marathon closet?" Jack asked.

"Nary a one," I replied.

"No hidden agendas, no deep dark secrets?"

"Nothing like that—but if you have something to tell me . . . ?"

Jack glanced over at me.

"Who, me? I'm just the help. No one tells me anything."

He slowly moved away, leaning more on the cane than he had just a few minutes earlier.

. . .

Bruce and I finally connected. Turned out he had been on a new business trip to Asia. A likely story. After regaling me with stories of his trip, he finally got around to reporting on his findings.

"There isn't much there, Erick, but one interesting thing has popped up. I told you before that Regency doesn't have very many shares out on the market for daily trading since so many big blocks are held by institutional investors. I tracked the volume and share price, and I saw that there's almost always a big increase in trading volume right before the company announces some piece of news or another. It looks like insiders may be taking advantage of news they've learned before it's announced to the market. I know that can't be—the SEC would have figured something like that out long before I did. But it is curious."

"You're right—if you could have figured that out, surely the Feds would have too. Have you found any connections between the Regency companies and the GrandGroup and GrandHotel?"

"I've been looking, but I haven't had much luck."

About as much luck as the police had in investigating Jack's beating and my bomb threat. There were lots of loose ends waiting to be tied together, but no common threads with which to do so.

36

As we wrapped up June and got ready for July, Jack sat us down in Ashley's suite to review our progress and talk about the month to come.

"You've both making good progress and are close to being where you should be, given the modified schedule I've put you on. Ashley, you're actually a little ahead of schedule, which is good given the distractions you have coming up with your summer tour. Erick, you might be a little behind, but you have the advantage of nothing much else to do but train over the next month."

While I didn't appreciate hearing Jack remind me that I was behind in his goals for me, I knew it to be true. I was doing everything he wanted me to do, but I was having an extremely hard time building endurance and speed at the same time. I was able to complete every run he set us off on, but my times were disappointingly slow and—even worse for my machismo—well behind Ashley's. I had expected to be leading and guiding Ashley, not the other way around.

While my running wasn't up to anyone expectations, a few things were going well. I was making good progress on the early part of the book, and it was great working with Ted to plan the photography that would accompany my story. The difficulties we had faced seemed to be behind us, and our friendship was as strong as ever. My working relationship with Martha as my contact at the publisher was steady, if not close or warm. I was perfectly content with steady, given how Martha felt about me. And we had received a six-month reprieve on the Alex Project space. Ken told me that the new owner was involved in some serious issues in New York and couldn't be bothered with making big changes on a small piece of real estate in Chicago. I thought the timing was suspicious. Just as I started to dig deeper into Regency, they pulled back. Had I hit on an open nerve? Ken claimed to have no knowledge of Regency's issues.

Meanwhile, Jack gave us our schedules and goals for July, and I saw Ashley's tour schedule for the first time. Knowing how important the marathon was to her, her manager, Johnny K, had designed a mini-summer tour with a two-week East Coast block in July that started off in College Park, Maryland, as well as a Midwest and West Coast series in August capped off with a week of campus concerts in September. I met this mysterious Mr. K the week earlier. He even called himself "Johnny K." When I asked Ashley about this, she laughed and said that his last name was Serbian and so difficult to pronounce that he'd given up trying to explain it to people and just called himself "Johnny K." Kind of like Cher, I guess, but with an initial.

As we were going over plans, I commented that this was a pretty short tour for a rising pop star. She told me that her original plan was for a six-month US and European tour with an Asian tour in the winter. Now she'd do a limited summer tour and ramp up the big international tour starting in January. She'd been working on new material since late last year and had been recording at a studio in Chicago's West Loop since late spring. She had started tour rehearsals in March. I was surprised to hear all of this, but I realized that we never really spoke about what we did with our lives outside the early morning hours we spent training. I did see some of the work she was doing for GrandHotel, as it was front and center in her suite and the upstairs health club. I asked her when the first rollout would happen.

"They tell me that they want Chicago to be first to take advantage of the buzz from the marathon," she said, "but they still haven't put the finishing touches on the health club or closed the old restaurant downstairs to start renovating. I've given them all my designs and drawings, but they seem to be moving very slowly. I'd be surprised if they can pull off the opening much before New Year's."

I agreed with her about the progress on the Chicago hotel. Work on the health club seemed to have come to a complete halt. Nearly every morning, Jack, Ashley, and I were the only people there other than a skeleton staff of way too fit young people waiting around for the club to be finished and open to hotel guests. Most of the time they just worked out for most of their shift. Not that any of them needed the exercise. Neither did Ashley's trainer, Margaret, who came in from Los Angeles every other week to check on our progress.

As we were leaving the pseudo health club one morning, I realized I had left my phone and wallet by the weight bench. Walking into the now-empty club, I saw again the old beat-up door I had noticed earlier. Since I had the place to myself, I was compelled to check the door. Finding it open, I slid in, shutting the door behind me.

Not much had changed in the intervening weeks. The "Regency Suppliers" boxes were still there, seemingly undisturbed. I couldn't resist the temptation to look into one of the partially opened boxes. On the outside, a packing slip indicated that the contents were intended for the spa's tearoom. Inside there were small, delicate lamps that I could see perfectly fitting that elegant room.

On further inspection, though, I realized that the lamps were incredibly cheap and shoddy, with flimsy material and poor workmanship. They in no way matched GrandHotel's elegance and well-earned reputation for high quality. Was this another sign that the money was running out for GrandHotel?

37

Kate had suggested that I start my marathon office stint on a Wednesday, which was when she held her big weekly team meeting. All her direct reports would be there, as well as most of their staffs and some of the senior volunteers and reps from GrandHotel as title sponsors of the event. For what GrandHotel was paying for the title sponsorship—a rumored world record of $4 million per year for three years—theirs was the most expensive seat at the table.

Kate loved the big open space office concept, so her West Loop loft space was perfect for the marathon staff. Aside from her huge office and two or three conference rooms, everyone else worked at open desks, grouped around Kate's direct reports in work pods. I'm sure it was terribly efficient, but the noise level was something else. Perhaps it was due to my solitary life as a writer with just my MacBook Pro to accompany me (and an occasional whine from Max when he needed to go out), but the sound of twenty or more people in intense work mode was more than I could handle. I headed for Kate's office to check in before the team meeting.

"Erick, good to see you. Thanks for coming in for our meeting."

"A pleasure to be here. I promise I'll keep quiet during the meeting and save my questions for the one-on-one interviews with your team. Everyone is all set for those interviews this week, right?"

"Of course. I booked one of the small conference rooms for you for the rest of this week and next week. I asked Sarah Peters, our marketing director, to coordinate scheduling everyone—there are a couple of small issues, but it looks like you'll get everyone in by the end of next week."

"And they know that they need to be open and honest with me, right? No holding back, no keeping secrets from me?"

"Absolutely. I'll remind everyone at today's meeting. And speaking of which, we'd better move over to the conference room. We don't want to be late."

"Of course not."

As we were getting ready to leave Kate's office, I wondered if Kate had turned over a new leaf. She was notoriously late for everything and had been for years. She was late for our wedding, her graduation, her first day at her first job, and countless times since. I think the only time she was on time for something was the first time Jimmy Choo came to town for a private trunk show. She was twenty minutes early for that.

We were almost in the conference room when Kate stopped and turned back to her office.

"Erick, I just remembered a phone call I need to make. Go ahead and grab a seat in the conference room and tell them to wait until I get there to start."

So much for the new leaf.

I walked into a packed conference room with every seat taken (except for Kate's chair at the head of the table) and people sitting on the credenza and on the floor.

Suddenly, it was a scene right out of an old Western movie. You know the scene: guy walks into a bar (through those cool swinging half doors) and suddenly all sound ceases. The piano player stops, the poker guys put down their cards, the bartender stops wiping the bar with a greasy cloth and just stares.

The conference room sounded just like that bar; you could have heard a pin drop. After a beat or two passed, two of Erin's directs jumped into action. Sarah Peters, the PR schmooze, came up, gave me one of those fake air kisses, and started introducing me to everyone in the room. Meanwhile, Carlos Ramirez, the elite athlete coordinator, grabbed one of the younger guys by the back of his shirt and pulled him out of the chair. I guess that was going to be my seat, provided to me in the showboat way that was Ramirez's well-known style.

I was halfway around the room, remembering no one's name but trying to at least remember who did what, when Kate came in. Suddenly the meeting was under way. Someone—likely someone other than Kate—had a printed agenda on the table. Given the high level of detail it contained, I guessed that was the meticulous ops guy, Martin Michaels.

The two-page agenda had a section for each major group: Elite Athletes (first, of course, but more on that later), Operations, Sales, and Public Relations, with sub-subjects and projects interspersed based on the topic. Some of those seemed more important (registration, the timing system, and police coordination) than others (visiting race director hospitality, merchandise inventories, and deciding who was going to hold the finish line tape), but I assumed decisions had to be made on the great and small.

True to her word, Kate opened the meeting by introducing me, explaining why I was at the meeting, and giving clear instructions that I was to be treated as a member of the team, openly, honestly, and with no holds barred. I saw a number of nods and smiles around the table, people excited that they might appear in my book. Or were they smiling because they knew that Kate had already instructed key people on what to say and not to say? I'm guessing it was some of both.

38

After Kate's opening remarks, she turned to Ramirez.

"Carlos, give us an update on the elites for this year's marathon. Since this will all be new to Erick, why don't you give us a rundown of the field you've assembled?"

From the self-satisfied grin on Ramirez's face and the rolling of eyes around the table, I could tell that this was going to be the Carlos show. And it was. He went on for close to twenty minutes, listing a series of names (mostly African) I had never heard of, their splits and half marathon times (seemingly to the nanosecond), and how they had performed at races that I had never heard of. Each and every one seemed to be a champion in the making. As he began to wind down, Sarah Peters interrupted him.

"Carlos, I keep coming back to the same issue with you. While you and the other marathons' race directors may be drooling over the latest Kenyan hot shot, bringing in a field of Third World nobodies does nothing for the media or the public. They can't tell them apart, they don't speak English, and they will never be seen here again. You've got to bring in runners who can actually speak to the media without a translator. That Japanese girl last year was horrific. Even with a translator she was unintelligible. Get me some Americans, even a Brit or two. What about that beautiful woman from England who set a world record a few years ago? She ran great here—we even got her on Oprah the next day."

From the expression on Carlos' face, I could tell this was a conversation he'd had with Sarah many times over. And from the looks around the room, the Sarah-Carlos battle was a source of entertainment to the staff.

"As I keep telling you, Sarah, the Kenyans are the royalty of marathoning. They keep winning for a reason. And we need to keep bringing the fastest runners to Chicago. We have the flattest and fastest course in the world, a course made for records. And the Kenyans and the Ethiopians and the Russians—they'll get us the world record back."

And there it was. As my research told me, Ramirez—like his counterparts at all the other big races—was obsessed with records. Breaking a record of any time seemingly justified his existence. Budget be damned; let's break a record. Who cares if it's by a nobody that nobody will ever hear from again? Breaking the record was what mattered. Some of the running media were beginning to question the budgets of the big city races, wondering if the millions they were spending on elites couldn't be used for better purposes. I certainly knew that the rumored $3 million that Carlos was spending on his pampered greyhounds could certainly sustain the Alex Project for years to come.

Kate watched as Carlos and Sarah continued to bicker, but she finally had enough and brought their argument to a close.

"Sarah, we've been through this too many times already. Carlos always brings one of the best fields in the business to race day, and you'll just have to figure out how to promote them better. He has his job; you have yours."

Sarah and Carlos both sat back in their chairs, neither surprised by Kate's backing of Carlos, who seemingly could do no wrong in Kate's eyes. A look passed between Carlos and Kate, but it came and went so quickly I didn't have a chance to assess it. But I did file it away for a later pondering.

Kate continued, "So, let's move on. Martin, you're next. How are things with operations?"

Michaels leaned forward, putting his iPad aside for the first time since I had entered the room. He opened up one of the four-inch binders in front of him and pulled out an enormous spreadsheet, done in what appeared to be a four-point font. My first thought was that he was going to read the entire thing to us. Instead, he glanced down the columns quickly and turned to Kate with a serene expression.

"We're good."

"Could you perhaps amplify that for Erick?"

"Tell you what—he and I are meeting later; I'll give him all the details then. No reason to bore everyone here. The ops team is on schedule and under budget. What more do you need to know?"

The Chicago Marathon has an outstanding reputation among runners for its top-notch operations. Novice runners are drawn to Chicago partly due to the flat, easy course, but also for the word-of-mouth spread stories of the smooth and efficient organization of the race. Other than a small problem with water during an unseasonably hot Sunday a few years back, no one could ever really find fault with the organization of the race. And that was all attributable to the maniacal obsessions of Martin Michaels. While Sarah and Carlos were the face of the event, their success lay entirely on the diminutive Michaels. I wondered if either of those egotists would ever admit that fact. Another mental note: pursue that with both and see what I get.

Kate sighed. "Fine, Martin. You've never let us down before, and I'm sure you won't this year."

A small, knowing smile came to Michaels' face.

"You got that right."

With that, he picked his iPad back up and began typing. Kate was dismissed.

"Okay, then. Sarah, how is this year's marketing campaign coming along?"

Sarah leaned over and pulled several poster-sized pieces of paper from a big leather portfolio next to her chair.

"We're all very excited about the campaign. Our agency came up with an absolutely brilliant concept and gave us a few preliminary ads, as well as a couple of TV and radio executions." Sarah walked over to one of the conference room walls that was essentially one big corkboard. She pinned each of the big sheets of paper to the wall and stepped back.

As she began to talk through the proposal for the ad campaign, I could see that Kate and the others liked what they saw. Using a mix of humor and drama, the ads sought to humanize the event. Sarah read the scripts for the proposed TV and radio ads, using changes in her voice to bring life to the stories they told. While I didn't really know how much advertising cost, it seemed to me that what Sarah was proposing would be costly. And for what reason? The race sold out months ago, and whether there were more or less spectators along the racecourse didn't affect anything other than further inflating the made up crowd counts that the race bragged about every year. So why spend all this money on advertising?

As the group began discussing the concepts, I could see that Sarah was looking for approval, not input. As more and more people began tweaking this and that in the ads, her frustration grew and the charm slipped away. Meanwhile, Kate remained silent.

"Look, people," Sarah fumed, "this is an outstanding campaign that hits the right demographics and pushes all the right buttons. It tested very well with our focus groups. I'm not really looking to make a bunch of changes so late in the calendar. We're scheduled to start shooting the TV spots this weekend so we can get them on air in September."

Kate nodded. "Sarah's right. I said earlier that everyone has his or her job to do, and this is Sarah's. We need to defer to her judgment and experience on this one. Sarah, go ahead and start production."

Sarah smiled, said thank you, and sat down. See, don't argue with "yes." Smart woman.

Paul O'Bannon, the sponsorship sales guy, spoke up.

"Look, this meeting is running way long. And I have a lunch with a prospect at noon, so I gotta run. I'll send out the latest sales report by Friday, but for now, just know that we're a little behind budget. I think we'll be able to make it up by race day, but it'll be tight."

Kate looked surprised. "Paul, this is the first I've heard of any shortfall. This is serious. Tell me what's happening."

"Like I said, Kate, I gotta run. I'll stop by your office this afternoon and fill you in on where we are."

Kate didn't appear happy about it but she nodded her agreement. O'Bannon, with a relieved look on his doughy face, hoisted himself out of his chair and headed for the door.

"Paul's right, we are running long, but I think the extra time has been a good investment for us to make for the sake of the wonderful book that Erick is going to write about our incredible event. Don't you all agree?"

The room was suddenly full of bobble head dolls as everyone vigorously nodded his or her agreement. Even I felt like nodding.

As the meeting ended and everyone was filing out, Kate pulled me aside and asked me to stay in the room. When we were alone, she sat back down with a sigh.

"That really wasn't what I wanted you to see. The team is much better than that. Sarah should have found a better time and place to talk to Carlos about the elites, but God knows they've had that same conversation enough times that you think she would have learned by now. And Martin was essentially rude. But so was Sarah when she shut down input from the team. Paul, well, I assume I'll only get anything out of him in the mornings. Once he goes to his daily lunch meeting with prospects, I know he'll either not come back or come back so boozed up he can't really function."

"So why do you put up with them if they have all of these issues? Especially with someone who appears to be a barely functioning alcoholic?"

"Why? Because despite their faults, they are some of the best in the business."

"Then your business has incredibly low standards. The few minutes I've spent with them says dysfunctional."

"You'll see. Once you get to know them, they really are a talented group. Just a little quirky."

I've seen quirky. This group went way beyond quirky, but I wasn't going into that with Kate right then.

I asked Kate about Jack.

"His recovery is going well, but I'm a little concerned about him."

"What's making you concerned? Do you want me to talk to Jack?"

"No, no . . . that's the last thing you should do. Just let us be. Stop meddling!"

I wasn't sure where Kate's hostility was coming from or how to respond, so I mouthed some platitudes about the hard time he'd been through and got up to leave.

As we walked out, I saw a bright spotlight shining down from the ceiling on an acrylic case at the far end of the offices. I asked Kate what that was.

"Oh, Erick, come and see!"

Getting closer, I saw what it was and why Kate was so excited to show me. Nearly four-feet tall and gleaming in the light was the marathon champion's trophy. I'd seen pictures in my event research, but they really didn't do it justice.

"This is really a very special icon of the event, Erick. It was designed and crafted for us by Tiffany, and it's sterling silver. It took Tiffany months and months to make. Isn't it beautiful?"

For once, I had to agree with Kate. The trophy was spectacular. The top was a stylized Chicago skyline, and the lake and parks decorated the base, which had each year's winners' names and times engraved. Kate told me that Tiffany's staff did the engraving by hand, with the trophy shipped to Tiffany's New Jersey workshop each year.

"Can I touch it?" I asked.

"No, actually, you can't. The case is locked and on a timer. We have to call the security firm ahead of time to schedule an opening. Plus, once it's out, we handle it with white cloth gloves. Silver is very susceptible to damage, both from dents and from the oil in your skin."

"Don't the marathon champions touch it? Do they damage it?"

"Don't be ridiculous. They don't touch it either. Can you imagine what those sweaty hands would do to the finish? We give them a replica, which they don't really want. They only want the check. A few years ago, one of the champions gave the replica trophy as a tip to the hotel maid. He said he didn't want to haul it home."

"So essentially, this is a prop. A very expensive prop."

Kate was clearly upset with my characterization.

"No, it's an icon. People all over the world have their pictures taken with the trophy at the marathon expo. Plus, it has an important place at our kickoff press conference and in our VIP hospitality tent. It's the symbol of the race."

"So how much did it cost, this icon of yours?"

"That's confidential. Let's just say that neither Tiffany nor silver comes cheap."

I looked at my watch and realized that I was about to be late for a meeting back at my place with Ted. I thanked Kate for the morning and went for the elevators.

. . .

As I got out of the cab, I saw Ted again sitting on my front steps, waiting for me. This time, though, he wasn't waiting alone. He had Detective Hanson sitting next to him. This couldn't be good.

39

"Ted, sorry I'm late. Detective Hanson, did we have something scheduled?"

"Mr. Anderssen. No, we didn't have anything scheduled. I was talking to your friend Ted here, and he said you two were meeting this afternoon. So I thought I could kill two birds with one stone, so to speak, and talk to the two of you together."

"Talk to us? About what?"

"The investigation into Ms. Bronfman's death is still open. As is the investigation into what happened to Mr. Clark. We have good reason to believe that the two incidents are connected."

"How could they be connected?"

"Were you aware that your agent and Mr. Clark had been in a pretty intense series of conversations for the last few months?"

"Jack and Barbara were talking? About what?"

"Apparently, Mr. Clark wanted to write another book—his second, I believe—on marathoning. And he wanted Ms. Bronfman to be his agent. She declined the opportunity, but he kept pursuing it. It became a bit of an issue."

"Who told you all of this? I've heard nothing about it!" I protested.

"Ms. Johnson, Ms. Bronfman's assistant. She gave us copies of the emails and phone logs."

It was clear that Barbara was involved in a lot more than I thought she was. Striking a carrot-laden book deal with Ted, turning down Jack. But neither made much sense. Ted was a talented photographer, but I still couldn't figure out how he was going to turn that gift into a book that was any better than every other coffee table book and that would be one day destined for the $3.00 sale table at whatever bookstores were still open. And a book by America's gold medal marathoner should have been an easy sell. Why did Barbara encourage—even enable—me to take on the book instead of Jack? And why, then, was Jack helping me to complete the book he wanted to write?

"Detective, this is all news to me. I don't know how we can help."

"You can help by telling me why so many people connected to your agent have gotten killed or hurt. According to Mr. Clark, he may have been an innocent victim of mistaken identity. Mistakenly believed to be you, Mr. Anderssen. The killer was out to get you, wasn't he?"

Ted looked at me in confusion. I hadn't told him the full story behind Jack's injuries.

"I don't know, Detective. I know what Jack said, and I believe him, but I can't connect any of these dots of yours. I wish I could. I want Barbara's killer brought to justice. But I only know what I know. I don't know what connects these crimes."

"I don't know anything about this either, Detective," Ted stammered. He looked awful, pale and shaking. I could only wonder what the detective was thinking. Ted looked like he was hiding something, even to me. And if a friend thought he looked guilty, what would someone trained to ferret out guilt think?

The detective stood up. "You know what I think? I think you are both lying to me. I can't prove it, but that's what I believe. And I'm going to keep on this—and so is the FBI. We're going to get to the bottom of this and soon. If you two are smart, you'll start helping me."

The detective walked away, leaving a fair amount of damage behind.

40

I knew it was coming. "Erick, what did he mean about a mistaken identity? Jack's attacker thought he was beating you up? Why? And if you knew, why didn't you tell me?"

"Ted, I guess I forgot. With all the confusion—"

"That's just bullshit. You found out before we went to New York. And I thought we were going to be honest with each other. No more lies. Isn't that what you said? What else are you lying to me about?"

"What else am I lying about? What about you? You looked like death when that cop asked about what might connect Barbara and Jack. Why? What are you hiding?"

"Nothing, I don't know anything," Ted cried, almost in tears. "I just know that everything has turned to shit, ever since Barbara came to me about the stupid book deal. Ever since I gave in to my fucking jealousy. I shouldn't have ever thought that I could win at something. I should have just accepted my role as a bit player in someone else's life. That's the story of my life. Second-class roles, second-class jobs, and second-class lovers. I shouldn't have ever reached for anything higher. I should just take what I deserve."

With that, Ted jumped up and headed for the door. I went after him, reaching for him to tell him how wrong he was. As I did so, he shoved back, harder than I thought he could, catching me off balance and sending me careening to the floor. I sat there, a bit dazed, as Ted headed out the front door.

By the time I could get up and tear open the door, he was gone. And I knew my friendship was damaged, perhaps broken forever. And it was my fault. Again.

Not knowing what to do, I paced the front hallway. Even Max sensed my unease and stayed in the living room, watching me carefully, not knowing whether he should come to me or stay away. I wondered if I should rush to Ted's place, call his cell phone, or give him some distance. In the end, I decided that he needed space and time. I'd find him in the morning and do whatever it took to repair our relationship. I only had one best friend in the world, and I couldn't afford to lose him. I knew that Ted would come around. I knew that our friendship was important to him. I knew that he just needed some time. I just knew.

41

The phone woke me. I looked over at the clock. 3:32. The dead of night. The time that tests men's souls. I suddenly thought of the William Demint quote, "Dreams permit each and every one of us to be quietly and safely insane every night of our lives." Something told me that before the night was over, I would be desperate for this to be a dream. Or a nightmare. Anything but real.

I answered the phone even after the caller ID said CHGO PD. I knew it would be Hanson.

"Hello."

"Mr. Anderssen? Detective Hanson."

"Yes, Detective. How can I help you at 3:30 in the morning?"

"I need to talk to your friend Ted McCormick. He called me fifteen minutes ago and left a very confusing message. I need to talk to him. Now."

"As you might have guessed, Detective, I was sound asleep when you called, as are most people at this time of night. I haven't seen Ted since he left my place a few minutes after you dropped your shit bombs and left."

"Was he upset when he left you?"

"Yes, I'd say so. And with good cause. You dumped on us both and basically threatened us. We were both upset."

"Mr. McCormick was very emotional when he called me. He said he knew all about the problem and wanted to give me proof of what was going on. He said he had Ms. Bronfman's file and couldn't wait to get rid of it. He said that he was sorry that he had been a part of something so hurtful, so damaging. He hoped that everyone would forgive him. And he told me to call him to set up a time and place for him to hand it over—*get rid of it forever*, were his words. Now I can't reach him. We sent uniforms to his place, but he's not there, and he doesn't appear to have been there tonight. Mr. Anderssen, we need to find him."

"Can't you track his cell phone? That's what they always do on TV."

"We tried that. The cell phone appears to have been deactivated. Perhaps the phone is broken or someone pulled the battery."

I was stunned. What was happening here? Just when I thought all the tragedy was behind me, suddenly my best friend was deeply involved in all of this mystery, obviously into something that was driving him to despair. I knew I had to help Hanson find Ted, but I didn't know where to turn. Where would Ted have gone? Not to me, I saw. Whatever it was, he couldn't share it with me, couldn't—wouldn't—allow me to help.

"Detective, I have no idea where he could be. If he's in trouble, or troubled, he always comes to me. But he's not here. I haven't heard from him since he left here hours ago."

"I seem to continually have a problem with one or both of you not being responsive to my calls. Makes me think the two of you are involved in all of this. Don't bother answering; I know you'll just deny it. Stay near a phone. I'll call you if we find Mr. McCormick."

With that, the detective hung up, leaving me with my middle-of-the-night fears. Fears for my friend, fears for all of us.

42

I woke up a few hours later, feeling like crap from the stress and a poor night's sleep. Training was in front of me, so I quickly dressed and headed to the hotel to meet Ashley. In my head, I went over how I was going to confront Jack about the marathon book and his conversations with Barbara, but Ashley was alone with a security guy, another young, buff guy in black.

"Good morning, Erick; how are you today?"

"Fine, Ashley, just fine. Maybe a little tired."

"Well, we'll run that tiredness out of you so you'll have energy for the rest of the day!"

I was seriously contemplating going straight home for a nap, but I avoided that conversation with Ashley.

"Where's Jack?" I asked.

"He left a message with my service saying he had to go to New York for a couple of days and to stay on our training schedule without him. I have to say, he was very abrupt with the service—rude even."

With that, Ashley headed out the door, with me already behind. We hadn't dramatically increased our distance over the last few weeks, but at 15 miles, it was going to be a struggle. Making matters worse was an early July heat-and-humidity wave that had hit Chicago like a warm, wet bar rag. The air even smelled a little like stale beer.

As we headed down the park, Chicago was in full-bore tourist season. Even this early in the morning, the park was crowded with families and groups taking pictures and looking at the world-class skyline or the incredibly diverse collection of sculpture in the park. Seeing all of those people, I was reminded of how lucky we had been that no one so far had recognized Ashley or hassled her. The guard that ran with us was well in back, I was sure out of diplomacy rather than fitness level. As I looked over at Ashley, I saw a young, very fit, and attractive woman who looked light-years away from the glamorous singer and performer known to the world. I had seen Ashley's performances on YouTube and appreciated her talent, but I liked my running companion version so much better.

As we finished up our run and re-entered the hotel service entrance, Ashley asked if I had plans for the evening. A little taken aback, I said no.

"I was supposed to have dinner with my agent, but he's stuck in LA—one of his clients who had his own sitcom just got fired by the network and he's in major disaster mode. How about dinner?"

"Dinner would be lovely. Do you want to stay in the hotel or go out?"

"I would love to go out. As nice as the hotel is, I feel like I'm in a gilded cage. Let's go somewhere casual and fun, jeans and t-shirts. Maybe a burger and a beer. Is that okay with you?"

"Ashley, beef and brews? Jack will kill us."

"He'll never find out. Pick me up at 8:00 and take me to Chicago's best burger. Until then!"

She blew me a kiss as she headed toward the elevators, sweaty guard in tow. I stood there for a second, wondering if our relationship had just changed. Or was I imagining things? Maybe I'd find out later today.

43

I spent far too much time getting ready, going through a number of combinations, trying to get the mood right. Maybe a date, maybe not. Should I be trying to impress her, or was this just running buddies out for a drink?

I settled on my True Religion jeans, Kenneth Cole loafers (no socks), and a very crisp, very pink Thomas Pink dress shirt, cuffs rolled up to the elbows. I was in the lobby at the stroke of eight.

I saw one of Ashley's security people by the elevator but no Ashley in sight. I was about to ask the guard when the nearest elevator doors opened and she came out.

She was neither the glam rock star nor the fresh-faced athlete I ran with every day. She was yet another Ashley, simple makeup and a simple outfit of jeans and a blouse, but in a way that very few women can emulate. She carried herself with such confidence, such poise. She was clearly comfortable in her skin, maybe more so in this persona than in the others I had witnessed.

"Erick, I am so happy to see you!" She came up to me and gave my cheek a kiss.

"I'm just as happy. You look awesome."

Awesome. Was I twelve? Wow, I really needed to work on my dialogue.

"Thanks, you look very handsome. Pink becomes you."

Not sure what that meant, I offered her my arm and led us toward the Michigan Avenue entrance of the hotel.

As we walked out into the warm summer night, I wondered whether this new look for Ashley would draw any attention. My question was answered almost immediately.

"OMG! It's Ashley!" The squeal came from nearby. I looked to my left and saw two teenage girls and an older woman, all staring with amazement at Ashley. They rushed up to her.

"Ashley, you are my absolute favorite! I was at your concert in Grand Rapids last year. Can I take a picture with you?"

Ashley was gracious. "Of course. Come stand by me."

As the two girls approached Ashley, the mom pulled out her iPhone and began to take pictures. I stepped back as quickly as I could. Absolutely nothing to be gained by me and Ashley ending up in the same photo.

Ashley's security guy got a cab for us, but he asked her, "Are you sure you don't want us to drive you? These people have a habit of showing up at the worst times."

She shook her head, "No, but thanks. I'm sure Erick can take care of me just fine."

Of course, she had no idea that I was having trouble taking care of myself, but this didn't seem the time to bring that up.

The guard nodded once and opened the door. I slid in after Ashley as the Michigan schoolgirls continued to shout and take pictures.

She was smiling as she got into the cab.

"I know this sounds so egotistical of me, but I still enjoy being recognized. I'm new enough at this to find it exciting that people want to meet me."

Having no experience at being recognized except at O'Shaughnessy's, I smiled and gave the driver the address of our destination.

Like every great city, Chicago had its contenders for the best of everything—best steak, best restaurant, best baseball team (Cubs, hands down). But best hot dog and best burger were perennial shooting matches. Everyone had their favorites, and the burger empires were ruled by a dozen favorites. Classics like Beinlich's, Billy Goat, and Hackney's. Epic. David Burke. But I had my favorite. And I knew Ashley would love it.

Lincoln Square is a charming residential neighborhood on the city's North Side. A bit of an enclave, it is home to lots of families with small children, young people, and long-time residents. Old Town School and the last building Louis Sullivan was to build call it home. As does Jury's.

Jury's is a smallish local favorite perched on a corner of Lincoln Avenue. Full of locals, it boasts a great little bar and delicious menu. I loved their burgers. As we walked in, the locals looked up to see who was joining them but quickly returned to their food and drink. There were two seats at the bar, and I figured, why not? Ashley wanted to see Chicago and have a beer and a burger.

Dave, the tall lean bartender who if given the chance will talk your ear off about alternative energy or the Wisconsin Badgers, quickly came up and placed cocktail napkins in front of us.

"Evening, Erick. Hello, ma'am. What can I get for you?"

"Dave, this is my friend Ashley."

"Nice to meet you, Dave."

"The pleasure is mine. Erick, your usual?"

"Yes, Dave, please. Ashley, what would you like?"

"Whatever Erick's having."

"All right then. Two Stella Artois it is."

I cautiously looked around. No one was paying special attention to us, so I was comfortable that we could enjoy dinner without being bothered.

And enjoy dinner we did. A couple of Stellas, Jury's fantastic burgers (rare and medium rare), crispy fries, and laughter. We each told stories about growing up, stories that we normally wouldn't share. First dates, first rejections. Times of great joy and great sorrow. The ups and downs of dating and growing up.

At one point, I shook my head slowly. "I'm still amazed that you've read my books. You're not exactly my target audience."

"Okay, full confession."

"Ah ha! You haven't read them."

"No, really, I have. But they were recommended to me. By my mother."

"By your mother."

"Yes, at least the first one was. And like I said when we first met, I loved how each one took me to a new and exciting place. A place I probably will never go to except in the pages of your books. But there's more."

"More?"

"Your books make me want to achieve more, to live more, to take more chances. You have no idea how inspirational your stories can be, far beyond the travels themselves. I can only imagine how many lives they've touched."

I didn't know what to say. Fortunately, Dave saved me by showing up just then with the check. I insisted on paying, and we found a cab almost immediately. The evening had been perfection.

If only I didn't have one friend dead and people around me getting hurt. And a lot of unanswered questions.

44

Perfection didn't last long. We were so engrossed in conversation that we weren't paying attention as we pulled up to the hotel. As I paid the driver and got out of the cab, there was a sudden rush toward us. Photographers, fans, passersby were all shouting Ashley's name. There must have been more than fifty people pushing each other to get closer to Ashley. Just as I was near panic, one of her security people came through the crowd and leaned toward us.

"Ashley, you know you should have had one of us go with you. And you certainly should have let us know you were on your way back here. We'll discuss this more tomorrow. In the meantime, let's get you inside."

With that, the guard grabbed Ashley by the elbow and, leading the way, pushed through the crowd. The hotel doorman was waiting with a side entrance held open, which they slipped through just before he closed it and turned toward the crowd.

"Okay, she's inside and not coming back out. Just leave now, please."

Caught in the back of the crowd, I didn't know what to do. Should I go inside and try to catch up with Ashley? Or was she too upset by the crowd to continue our evening?

Suddenly, a couple of the photographers realized that I had been in the cab with Ashley. Flashes started going off as questions were shouted at me. Not knowing what to do, I quickly ran into Michigan Avenue, waved down a cab, and got in. Just as we pulled away from the curb, my mobile phone rang. Caller ID said it was Ashley.

"Ashley, are you all right?"

"I'm fine, Erick. I had such a wonderful night and am so sorry you had to put up with that crowd. I feel just terrible—and after saying how much I enjoyed the fans."

"No worries, Ashley. I had a great time too. Do you want me to come up?"

"Not tonight, Erick. I'm exhausted, and the security people want to go over some new issues. I'll see you at our run tomorrow. Good night."

And so the night ended.

45

As I neared the hotel the next morning, I remembered what Ashley had said during our brief call. New issues—I wondered what that could mean. I wasn't sure how to breach a sensitive subject like her personal security, but I figured if I was going to be with her nearly every day from now until October, I needed to know if there was something that could affect her.

I needn't have worried. As I entered the hotel lobby, Charlie, the big blond security guy lurking outside Ashley's room the day we met, walked up to me.

"Mr. Anderssen, I need a few minutes of your time. Ashley knows you'll be a few minutes late for your run. Let's find a couple of seats over in the corner of the lobby where we won't be disturbed."

Seeing that I had little choice, I followed Charlie to a secluded corner of the art deco lobby—a corner made for assignations, it seemed. I hope no one assumed that's why the big young blond and I were there.

"Mr. Anderssen, I understand Ashley mentioned a new security issue to you last night."

"She did, but didn't share with me what it was."

"Ashley's agent authorized me to tell you what we are facing. Your morning runs with Ashley aren't something that any of us support. The risks are too high. But Ashley is insistent that she trains out of doors, not in the safety of the health club. She's the boss, but it is becoming increasingly dangerous for her to be out in public in an unsecured area."

"Charlie, what's happened?"

"Ever since Ashley first started touring, she's had an issue with stalkers. We've had two restraining orders granted by the court against the more aggressive ones, but more seem to pop up. Yesterday, her website was hacked by someone who said that they were going to be with Ashley if it was the last thing they ever do. They included some personal information about Ashley that very few people know about, and even included candid photos of the two of you running that Ashley thinks were taken two days ago. So this technologically adept person is here in Chicago, watching Ashley."

"Watching us?" I felt like the center of a very large target.

"Ashley says she's not worried about it, but she does seem to be taking this one more seriously than previous issues."

"So what are you doing about it?"

"We have taken several measures, none of which concern you. What you will see, however, is a doubling of the running team that accompanies you every day. We'll have one runner in front, one in back, and they'll be much closer to you and Ashley than the single runner has been before. We're also going to vary your path each day, some days taking you out to the suburbs to run."

That all made sense to me, and I didn't think it would affect our training. I wondered if Ashley was as calm as Charlie claimed.

"Two other things, Mr. Anderssen. No more going out in public with Ashley without security involvement. We need to know where you are going at least twenty-four hours before an event, and we will accompany you from start to finish. We'll provide a car and driver."

I wasn't wild about the idea of a chaperone, especially if last night's wonderful evening was going to be repeated, but I figured Ashley and I could work that out rather than me trying to argue with someone whose job it was to protect Ashley.

"Charlie, you said two things."

"Yes. Now that the media has published pictures of you and Ashley together, you need to take some precautions regarding your own security. We'll send someone to your house later today to do a security audit. We'll also give you numbers where you can reach us if anything goes wrong. I suggest you immediately begin to vary your routine. Change grocery stores, go to the dry cleaners at different times, take the dog with you as often as possible."

"Dog? How do you know I have a dog?"

"Mr. Anderssen, we are professionals. We do background checks and basic investigations on anyone who is going to be close to Ashley. You were thoroughly vetted before you walked into her hotel room for the first time. I hope you understand why we did so."

I actually didn't understand, and I was disturbed by the fact that all of this had happened without my knowledge. I was trying to figure out how they knew about Max when Charlie stood up, towering over me.

"Ashley is waiting by the service entrance to the hotel. There was a man waiting there earlier that we've identified as one of the people stalking Ashley. Hotel security moved him away. Ashley is in a black Lincoln Town Car. We've moved your run for today as a precaution. The driver knows where to go and will give you a map of the trails. After your run, he'll return Ashley to the hotel and then bring you home. Going forward, anytime we move the runs out of the lakefront parks, we'll follow that routine. Now, if you don't have any more questions, Ashley is ready."

I had a lot more questions, but I didn't think I'd get much more from Charlie. I followed his black-clad back to the rear of the hotel. As I stepped out into the July heat, I saw the Town Car with a Charlie-like figure standing by the door. As I approached, he opened the door and I slipped in. As soon as the door clicked shut, the driver took off.

I looked over at Ashley. For all her claims that she was fine, she looked shaken by this new threat.

. . .

As I started to say something, Ashley shook her head and gently touched my lips with her fingers.

"Erick, I am so sorry that this has gotten so complicated—maybe even dangerous. I had such a wonderful time last night. You are such a great person and great running partner, and I just know that we can both make it through the marathon—and hopefully get to know each other better."

At that last phrase, she looked down and blushed ever so slightly. I was completely smitten. She continued, "But this isn't what you signed up for. You never agreed to be running surrounded by security guards, being rushed away from scenes, having to worry about your own security just because you were photographed with me. I will completely understand it if you want to back out of our arrangement and drop the book. No one will blame you. No one."

"Stop right there. I'm not going anywhere. I'm having a great time running with you and spending time with you. If there are any issues, your security guys have it covered. I'm not at all worried. I had a great time last night too. I hope we can do it again soon."

Ashley smiled. "I hope we can too. It was terrific. It was so nice just to be sitting in that bar with you, loving the food and talking and laughing. I don't get to do that too often." She sounded a bit sad.

"We'll go out as often as you want to. How about tonight?"

She laughed. "I want to, but my agent is coming in for dinner. Room service, I hear. Sounds like more of a business meeting, doesn't it? Oh well, I'll just remember how much fun we had last night and soldier my way through it."

She leaned back into the upholstery. "I thought you looked awfully cute in the paper."

"Paper? What paper?"

"You didn't see the *Tribune* this morning?"

"No, should I have?"

She leaned forward toward the driver. "Paul, do you have today's *Trib*?"

For the first time since we got in the car, the driver spoke. "Yes, ma'am. Here you go."

Ashley took the paper and opened it to the Arts section. She folded the paper open at the second page and handed it to me.

There we were, Ashley and I, getting out of the cab at the hotel. Ashley looked terrific, smiling at the fans. I looked somewhere between stunned and terrified. Not my best look. But I have to say that all that running and eating twigs and seeds had me back in pretty good shape. All in all, not a bad shot.

What was a little surprising was that the paper had identified me by name. I certainly hadn't reached the type of literary fame whereby I was a household name, and I didn't do the Chicago party circuit. The only thing I can think was that one of my former *Trib* colleagues had recognized me. And seeing my name there associated with Ashley's reinforced what Charlie had said: I needed to pay a little more attention to my own security.

A few minutes later and we were in the parking lot of the Baha'i temple in north suburban Wilmette. A leafy, family focused community on Lake Michigan, it seemed to be an odd location for one of only seven Baha'i temples in the world. A nine-sided white edifice just off the lake, it has a soaring, white dome more than 135-feet tall and lace-like ornamentation. I'd been inside once or twice, so I showed Ashley the serene, soaring interior before we headed north on the lakefront path.

True to Charlie's promise, the driver met us an hour later and took us back to Chicago. I think one or two people may have recognized Ashley along the way, but no one bothered us, a fact that I think both of us appreciated.

After dropping Ashley off at the hotel, the driver headed into Lincoln Park and my place. Max was, of course, grateful to see me and sorely in need of exercise, so I thought I'd give him a good walk around the neighborhood before I showered.

Before leaving the house, I checked both my phone and email for word from Ted. No word from Ted, but also no word from Detective Hanson, which I took as good news. Still, I was increasingly worried about my friend, and I wondered if I needed to head back up to Wrigleyville to check on him. I decided that if I hadn't heard from him by the end of the day I would go in person to explain and apologize.

With a sudden sharp bark, Max reminded me that he was anxious to go so I hooked him up to his leash and followed him out the front door. As we were going down the steps, the Singhs were walking up their front steps.

"Erick, we didn't know you were dating a superstar," said Minu. "Yeah, nice job, buddy," added Amar. I stopped briefly, smiled, and said, "Thanks, but it's not like that. We're training for the marathon together and just had gone out for dinner."

"Of course you had," said Minu, "Everyone just goes out and grabs a quick bite with international celebrities. You aren't moving to Hollywood, are you? Maybe your next book will be about how baby boomers can deal with celebrity spouses!"

I think I might have actually blushed. "Nothing like that, really. Hey, I gotta get this big guy out for some exercise. I'll see you soon."

With that, Max and I left the Singhs. Forty-five minutes and many blocks later, exhausted, we returned to the house.

Not too long ago during a much happier time, I came home and found Ted sitting on my front steps, a bucket of iced beer at his side. Today, Max and I found Detective Hanson on those same front steps. And instead of chilled Heineken, he had a tall man in a dark suit with him. I knew that I was about to get yet more bad news. And I was right.

46

Hanson stood at the top of the stairs with the other man as Max and I made our way up the steps. Not saying a word, I stepped between them and unlocked the front door, releasing Max from his leash as I did so. The big dog bounded into the house, oblivious to the tension out front. At that moment, I wanted to follow him and not have to hear what these men had to say. But that wasn't to be.

"Mr. Anderssen, this is Special Agent Drury of the FBI."

Drury flipped open his credentials as Hanson introduced him. Since I had only seen FBI credentials on TV, I assumed they were legit. And if the credentials didn't look real, Drury certainly did. He could have walked right out of central casting. Tall and lean, with one of those chiseled jaws. The high and tight haircut said serious as much as the jet black suit, crisp white shirt and dark, somber tie. This was not a man to be trifled with.

"Mr. Anderssen, may we come in?"

"Let's go sit in the living room," was about all I could say.

Drury spoke for the first time, as formal in speech as he was in appearance. "Thank you, Mr. Anderssen. We appreciate you permitting us into your home."

"Hanson, is this about Ted?" I just blurted it out.

"I'm afraid so. We just came from his apartment. He wasn't there, but the place has been ransacked—almost destroyed, really. Everything emptied from the drawers, cabinets tipped over, furniture ripped open. Someone was obviously looking for something important."

"But Ted wasn't there?"

"No, he wasn't. But I'm afraid to say that there was a great deal of blood on the bedroom carpet. Someone was seriously injured there."

Part of my mind worried about how upset Ted was going to be when he found his place destroyed. He had spent so much time getting it just right and was so proud of his home. Then a vision of the blood-soaked carpet pushed the rest out of my way. I sat down heavily on the sofa.

"Do you know when all of this happened?"

"Very recently, apparently. One of the neighbors called 911 just after midnight, reporting a disturbance, so we sent out a patrol car. I heard about it first thing this morning as Mr. McCormick's name went into the system. I talked to the rest of the building tenants and one of them saw Mr. McCormick come home yesterday evening with another man. The neighbor hadn't seen the other man before, but he did give us a reasonably good description."

"What did he look like?"

"That's partially why we're here, Mr. Anderssen. From the description, he looked an awful lot like you."

"Like me? I've been looking for Ted as much as you have been, Detective. I haven't been to his place in quite a while."

"Mr. Anderssen, you were home alone the night Ms. Bronfman was killed, you were at the bar with Mr. Clark when he was attacked, and I'm guessing you're going to say that you were home alone again last night. True?"

"Yes, all of that is true. But I had nothing to do with any of this. Why would I want to hurt any of these people?"

"I don't know, Mr. Anderssen. Maybe we should talk about that down at the station."

After standing silent through this entire exchange, Drury finally spoke. "As Detective Hanson said, we're here to talk about Mr. McCormick's disappearance and how it might be tied to these other crimes. But we're also here to talk about the message that Mr. McCormick left on the detective's phone. If you'll recall, Mr. McCormick said that he had Ms. Bronfman's file. We need to find Mr. McCormick, and we need to find that file."

"You know that I don't know anything about the file. Barbara never had a chance to tell me what she was so upset about. That's why she was coming to Chicago. To tell me what was going on. There are a lot of people who seem to know more than I do about this file. Why do you keep coming back to me?"

Hanson answered, "Because everything in this case keeps coming back to you. You are the hub of a series of violent crimes for which we have no motive and very few suspects."

"Am I a suspect?"

"Right now, I'd say you were a person of interest to our investigation. Would you agree, Agent Drury?"

Nodding slowly, Drury replied. "I would, Detective Hanson."

I asked, "Do I need a lawyer?"

"We aren't arresting you, if that's what you are asking. Do you think you need a lawyer?"

"It certainly feels like it."

"We can't tell you what to do, Mr. Anderssen. But I strongly advise you to start telling us everything you know about Ms. Bronfman and Mr. McCormick and their relationship. Lying to us will ensure that you need that lawyer sooner rather than later."

"I didn't know Barbara and Ted even had a relationship until a little while ago. And why does the FBI care about this? Since when did the FBI investigate murders?"

Drury and Hanson exchanged glances. Hanson gave an almost imperceptible nod. After a pause, Drury nodded back, sat down in one of my wing chairs, and, with an intense look, began to speak.

"The FBI has jurisdiction over more than two hundred categories of federal law. We divide our work into two major groups: national security and criminal matters. Criminal law priorities include corruption, civil rights, organized crime, violent crime, and my division, white-collar crime. Money laundering, insurance fraud, antitrust, and—my area of focus—securities fraud are all part of our ever-growing white-collar division."

Securities fraud. Something like an alarm bell started ringing in my head. Drury's voice broke through my thoughts.

"Working with the Securities and Exchange Commission and other parts of the US Treasury such as the IRS, we've spent millions on sophisticated computer models that look for unexpected patterns of securities-related activity. Once those patterns are detected, we analyze the activity and parties involved. Oftentimes there is a rational explanation for these activities. But when there isn't, we escalate the issue and begin a full-scale investigation. I'm here today as part of one of those investigations. We have been looking at a series of insider trading transactions involving a small group of people who have one and only one connection in common. Barbara Bronfman."

"You think Barbara was in on some insider trading scam?"

"No, Mr. Anderssen, we don't think she was. We know she was. We have evidence that she bought or sold stocks more than a dozen times over the past year, each time just days before a major corporate announcement that affected the stock price. In the last twelve months, she made nearly $2 million from these trades. And—almost always on the same day—a handful of other people made the exact same trades, usually with smaller gains, but gains nevertheless. And each of these people has a connection to Ms. Bronfman. All in all, we're talking about nearly a dozen people and more than $10 million in illegal gains."

"Who else was involved?"

"We can't give out that information. But I can say that besides Ms. Bronfman, at least two of the other investors are dead, and Mr. McCormick is missing."

"Ted was in on this scheme? No way."

"I'm afraid so. He was the newest investor in the group and had made a number of trades. But it's clear that he benefited from the same insider information that Ms. Bronfman was sharing with the other investors."

"But Ted had no money. He wouldn't know how to make trades. He was barely able to pay for his apartment."

"That may have been what he wanted you to believe, but he had substantial assets," said Drury. "We found more than $200,000 in a bank account and believe that there is more hidden elsewhere. Illegal trade proceeds, primarily, but also a $50,000 deposit in May that we haven't been able to trace. And Ms. Bronfman had the same so-far-untraceable deposit made to her account on the same day in May."

"So you think someone was paying them for something?"

"We don't know yet, Mr. Anderssen. Do you know what it could be for?"

"I don't. But I do remember something that Barbara said to me on the phone the day she was killed. It didn't make sense at the time, but it does now."

"What did she say?" Hanson asked.

"She reminded me that I once said she'd be the next Martha Stewart. She sounded sad and said that I didn't know how right I was about that. Wasn't Stewart jailed for insider trading?"

"She was," said Drury. "Either the guilt was getting to Ms. Bronfman, or she sensed that someone was onto her scheme. We think that the missing file contains evidence both of her crimes and key information about whomever was feeding her the information. Frankly, at this point we're really after the insider more than anyone in Ms. Bronfman's circle. Now that she's dead, the rest of the schemers are too small to warrant a full-scale investigation. But we do want the tipster."

"How would Ted have gotten his hands on the file if she brought it with her to Chicago? She was killed before Ted could pick her up. Doesn't the killer likely have the file?"

"From our investigation thus far, it appears that the only people who knew she was coming to Chicago were you and Mr. McCormick. One of you may have met her at the airport, taken the file, and eliminated the problem by killing Ms. Bronfman."

"Why would I want the file? I didn't even know any of this was going on."

Drury responded, "That's why we need to find Mr. McCormick and get his side of the story. But the ransacked apartment and blood in the bedroom have us concerned for his safety. Are you certain you haven't heard from him? You aren't protecting him."

"He's my best friend, and I'm terribly worried about him. But I'm not protecting him or hiding him. I've been looking for him, and I'll continue to look for him until he's found."

"Don't get in our way, Anderssen. You'll only make things worse," growled Hanson.

"The detective is right, Mr. Anderssen. The best thing you can do is to stay close to your phone and let us know the minute you hear from Mr. McCormick. Of course, if you think of where he might have gone, tell us that too. And we'll make sure that you are kept up to speed on any progress we make in finding him."

Leaving me his card, Drury walked out with Hanson following close behind. They were barely out the door before I was on the phone, leaving a message for the one person I thought might help me get to the bottom of Ted's problem.

"Bruce, it's Erick Anderssen. I still haven't heard from you, and now I really need your help."

47

I knew I couldn't just sit there. I had to find Ted.

I spent the rest of that day and most of the evening traveling across the city. Talking to Ted's neighbors, visiting his favorite bars, calling our mutual friends once again. No one had seen Ted for days. I left phone messages and hastily scrawled notes anywhere I thought Ted might show up.

Exhausted after hours of searching, I collapsed into a sleep filled with nightmares about what might have happened to my friend.

48

I had a pair of veteran marathoners scheduled for an interview over lunch the next day, so I had to put my search for Ted on hold temporarily.

We were scheduled to meet at Four Farthings, a neighborhood gem just between the Lincoln Park Zoo and Oz Park (one of my favorites). I couldn't decide between the beautiful outdoor seating area or the high ceilinged, wood paneled main room with its beautiful wood back bar. The entire place was in a gorgeous brownstone and felt like it had been there since the days of Old Chicago.

Steve and Shellee were veteran runners. Both had served on the Chicago Distance Runners board of directors and were instrumental in getting the city to rebuild the lakefront running paths. They each had run more than fifty marathons, including several Chicago marathons and most of the other big city races. Steve and Shellee were incredibly well connected in the local running community and could, I hoped, offer insights into Kate's organization, sponsors, and how the race was perceived.

Going into lunch, I wondered how religious Steve and Shellee were about their training diets. Four Farthings has wonderful grilled shrimp and Andouille pasta with a spicy Cajun cream sauce that I really wanted but knew I shouldn't have. I vowed to stall and let them order first. Please let them not get the lettuce leaves with a squeeze of lemon juice.

I needn't have worried. After a round of outstanding Bloody Marys, Steve got the half chicken Vesuvio and Shellee the chicken and bow tie pasta. I was delighted, so I ordered the salmon (healthy), which came with a delicious dill cream sauce (did I say delicious?) But I had to ask.

"Everything I read says you have to stay on this very strict diet. I've been eating protein, leaves, and twigs for months. What's your secret?" I asked.

Shellee was quick to answer. "We decided a long time ago that we enjoy food way too much to give it up for running. So, we let ourselves splurge once in a while and enjoy a meal like this, then go back to a good training diet. I'd say we are spot on with our diets for six days out of seven when we're ramping up for a race."

"I don't know about six out of seven, honey. This week we're more like four out of seven," responded Steve.

"Well, what the hell? Life's too short anyway," replied Shellee with a grin.

We chatted more about their training regime, pre-race and recovery meal planning, and the best liquid fuels (we agreed on beer). Suddenly I was starving, but with perfect timing, all that wonderful guilt-laden food arrived just then.

As we started to eat, I began to dig into their perceptions of the Chicago Marathon.

"You guys have been running for a long time. And you've run Chicago lots of times. How does the race stack up against the other great races today? And has it kept its standards as high as in the past?"

Steve and Shellee looked at each other for a moment, and then

Steve said, "Funny you should ask, Erick. We were out to dinner just last night with some friends who are about as crazy about running as we are. And this very question came up: was Chicago as good as it used to be?"

He continued, "We decided that technically, it is. It's still one of the top races in the world from a production perspective. But something seems to have gone out of the race—some of the excitement, the energy. It's like when a small company gets acquired by a big one. The charm, the personality that the race used to have is gone. Now they seem to only care about getting the race done and keeping the big money happy."

"It's all about the money now, isn't it?" Shellee said. "Start time is dictated by the TV contract. There are so many banners and signs advertising sponsors that it's hard to see where the next aid station is. We used to look forward to seeing what was new each year, what changes they had made. Now the only thing different from one year to the next is the weather, which seems to have gotten progressively worse. But I guess we can't blame that on the event, can we?" she finished with a smile.

"What's caused the changes? Has it been sudden or gradual?"

"Very gradual, I think," Steve said. Shellee nodded agreement.

"They kept the small, local race feeling for as long as they could, but the big money just proved to be too much. Sponsors want more every year to justify the big price tags. And I don't think the race organizers are strong enough to resist the temptation. I think the GrandHotel deal was the last straw. Too much money to resist."

"$4 million, I heard," I said.

"Check your sources. The $4 million was just to get in the door. They spend another $2 million or more on advertising their involvement, hospitality the week before—they fly in celebrity guests from around the world every year for their big Friday night party. Get yourself invited to that party, and you'll see what we're talking about."

Shellee added, "And it's not just the Chicago Marathon. GrandHotel is doing the same thing with the GrandHotel Tokyo and GrandHotel Dubai marathons: big money, big celebrities."

We went on to talk about race strategy ("Don't start out too fast; your adrenalin will be flowing and you'll want to rush the start, but you'll burn out early") and apparel ("Even if it's chilly, don't overdress. You'll get warm as the race progresses, so wear layers of clothes you don't care about and can ditch as it warms up.") Tips for running and perhaps a lead to follow regarding yet more GrandHotel spending. Definitely a worthwhile lunch, and I was happy to pick up the tab. We all promised to keep in touch and look for each other at the race in October.

49

A couple of calls came in during lunch, but none of the ones I was looking for: no Ted, no Bruce. On the other hand, neither the cops nor the FBI had called. Max was eager to get out, so I hooked up his leash and took him on a long walk through the park.

As we walked, I pondered the news I had heard in the last day. Barbara and Ted were involved in a big money insider trading scheme. Now one of them was dead, and it didn't look good for the other. GrandHotel was spending enormous amounts of money on its hotels and events like the Chicago Marathon at a time when the hotel business essentially sucked.

As Max and I walked up to the house, Minu was just getting home as well. I teased her about the state's attorney adopting bankers' hours. In return, she gave me a thin smile and walked in the house. Quite unlike Minu's normal friendly demeanor. I wondered briefly what I could have done to offend her, but the big dog was pulling me toward his water bowl, and my neighbor's frosty mood slipped my mind.

. . .

As I was locking the house up for the night, my phone rang. Caller ID said it was Bruce.

I grabbed the phone. "Bruce, where the hell have you been?"

"If you have to know, I've been fostering a new relationship with a leading Asian investment banker that I think can be very helpful in the years to come."

"You didn't have a minute to call me?"

"Let's just say that I wasn't in a position to make phone calls, if you get my drift."

"How pretty is she?"

"Man, she's freaking gorgeous. And brighter than a shiny new dime. Harvard MBA. She's got one of the hottest boutique firms in Shanghai."

"I'm happy for you, Bruce. But I have a problem and need your help."

"Man, that means you've got two problems. Because that Grand-Hotel deal you asked me to check on is coming back to bite me in the ass."

"How so?"

"One of my best sources at the SEC called and told me that he was getting his ass fried for asking questions about Regency and Grand-Hotel. He told me to never call him again. He cost me a fucking fortune over the years, and now he's completely burned. Same thing happened with a guy I use at the IRS. Who the hell are these people?"

"That question is still open, but put it on the back burner for now. I have a friend in trouble."

"You seem to be surrounded by trouble these days, my friend, so that shouldn't come as a surprise. What's the latest crisis?"

I told Bruce what the detective and FBI agent had told me about the insider trading scheme that Ted and Barbara were involved in.

"Bruce, can you find out how deep Ted is in this? I can't find him, and I think he may have been killed."

"How does me finding out what happened help your friend?"

"If I can understand what he's involved in, maybe I can find a way to help. I really don't know, but there isn't much else I can do."

"At the risk of burning another bridge, I'll make one call to an old friend at the FBI in DC. And that's it. No more after this. I can't afford to help you anymore."

"You got it, Bruce; I understand."

"Okay, I'll get back to you after I talk to him. It'll be sometime tomorrow."

I thanked Bruce and hung up. I checked my messages and email, but there was no word from Ted. Knowing I had to get up early in the morning to run, I got ready for another restless night's sleep.

50

As I walked into the hotel lobby the next morning, I was surprised to see Jack sitting in one of the big, overstuffed chairs that made up the main section of the lobby. He looked remarkably comfortable with the *Trib*'s sports section open in front of him.

"Jack."

"Erick, good morning. Ashley is finishing up a fitting for her concert wardrobe and will be down in about ten minutes. We're heading out to one of the north suburban forest preserves for your long run today. After the run, we need to talk about whether or not you're going with Ashley on the first short leg of her tour."

I was ready to confront Jack about his conversations with Barbara about the marathon book, but I was so taken aback by the thought of going with Ashley on the tour that my book questions went out the window.

"Go on the tour? Why?"

"It's only a few days, but I think it would be best for both of you to be able to continue training and running together. If you can get away, I think you should go for at least part of the trip."

"I'm sure I can. When and where?"

"We'll go over all of that after your run. Here's Ashley. The car is waiting outside."

"Good morning, Erick! You look terrific this morning!" As Ashley hurried up to me, she reached up and gave me a quick kiss on the cheek. Any thought I had of not going on the tour was gone. I was going where she was going.

51

As happy as I was with the news that I would be joining Ashley for even a brief leg of her tour, the message waiting for me when I got home ruined any pleasure the day might have had for me.

"Erick, it's Bruce. I don't know a lot about your missing friend except that he's in a world of trouble—serious trouble. And so, it seems, are you. I'll call you tonight with details. Until then, don't talk to the cops, and definitely don't talk to the FBI. If you have a good attorney—one that deals with big-boy financial issues—now's the time to call him."

I sat down, shaken by Bruce's message. I knew that Ted was in trouble and that he had been working with Barbara on something, but how did that extend to me? I knew nothing about their schemes.

Not knowing where else to turn, I went next door. Minu was a prosecutor in the Cook County State's Attorney's office. She'd know who I could call for help.

As I rang the doorbell, I realized that I didn't know the Singhs terribly well. I knew that they both had stressful jobs—her as a prosecutor, him heading up neurosurgery at Northwestern Hospital—and I knew that we all enjoyed simple food served with great wine. I knew they were second-generation Asian Americans who both came from huge, overachieving families. We really hadn't gotten much deeper than that in our conversations.

The big oak door opened. It was Amar, clearly headed out.

"Erick, how good to see you. But I'm sorry; I was just called in to the hospital for emergency surgery. Can I help you with something? Do you need us to watch Max for the day?"

"Amar, no, I'm fine. I just had a question for Minu. Is she home?"

"She just walked in the door. Come in, come in."

As he ushered me into the house, Amar shouted toward the kitchen.

"Minu, Erick from next door is here. He wants to talk to you. I'm leaving now. Love you."

Amar walked out, closing the door behind him. It seemed like minutes passed. Quiet, still minutes with me standing in the front hallway of the Singh's home. Wondering where Minu could be.

When she finally emerged from the back of the house, Minu had that same cold look on her face that I had seen the other day.

"Erick, hello."

"Hello, Minu. I'm sorry to bother you. I won't take too much of your time but I need your help."

"Erick, before you say anything else, I need to tell you that I can't help. I can't talk to you; I can't be seen with you. You really need to leave."

"You can't be seen with me? We're next-door neighbors. We've known each other for years. How can you say you can't talk to me?"

She gave a small, cold laugh. "Funny thing is: I can't tell you that. I've been warned by my office to stay away from you. So I'm sorry, but you need to leave. Now."

I was shocked into silence. I heard her words, but I didn't know how to respond. My friends were dying, missing—criminals. People I had trusted were betraying me. And now my next-door neighbor was told by the state's attorney's office not to be seen with me? How the hell could this be happening?

. . .

Returning home, I simply sat in the living room, mindlessly scratching Max behind his big ears. I couldn't think, didn't know where to turn. I was rapidly running out of people I could count on.

As my mind was churning, my phone rang. I grabbed it like a drowning man. It was Bruce.

"Bruce!" I croaked.

"Wow, buddy, you sound terrible."

"I have good reasons for it."

"Sorry, but I'm afraid I'm not going to make things any better."

"Let's get it over with. Tell me what you found out."

"As you know, Ted is being investigated by the FBI and the SEC for securities fraud. They seem to have convincing evidence that he was part of a group—one that included your friend Barbara—that's been trading on insider information for the last couple of years. The US attorney's office and the state's attorney"—that explained my next-door neighbor's icy demeanor—"have been working on tying up loose ends and getting ready to go for indictments over the last couple of weeks, but they're completely off course now that many of the major players are dead or have disappeared. Speaking of which, no one has seen or heard from Ted since you last spoke with him. His cell phone is off, and his credit cards haven't been used—he's completely dropped off the grid. The good news is that no one has found a body that might be his—and believe me, they're looking."

"That's good news?"

"In this case, Erick, it is. Now, you."

"Me?"

"The Feds are convinced that there are too many connections to you and the conspirators, so they've been doing some serious digging into your life, especially your finances."

"Well, they won't find anything wrong, I can tell you that."

"And so far, they haven't. They've even gone into the Alex Project, but that seems to be clean as well."

"*Seems* to be clean?"

"Yeah, they've got a couple of issues to resolve, so it's still open. But so far, so good. And that's all my source could tell me."

"I can't believe this."

"I know, buddy, I know. You have a good attorney?"

"Not this kind. You know somebody?"

"Of course I do. I'll send you her contact info. She's really good."

"The sooner the better, Bruce. I'm starting to feel really, really paranoid about all of this."

"Don't blame you. Call her first thing in the morning." With that, Bruce hung up.

A minute later, Bruce's email showed up with the name and address of a lawyer at one of the big Loop law firms. Feeling that I was at least on the track to getting some help, I told myself things would be better in the morning and went to bed.

52

For the first time since we had started training, I just couldn't motivate myself to get up the next morning. I left a voice mail for Jack and sent a text to Ashley. No response from Jack, but there was a quick text from Ashley: *Sorry to hear, let me know if I can help.* I didn't respond to Ashley, but if I had, it would have been along the lines of, "I wish you could help, but I don't think you can raise the dead."

By 9:00 a.m., I was feeling sufficiently guilty to get out of bed, throw on some clothes, and take Max out for a walk. While it wasn't the 12 miles plus weights I would have put in at Jack's direction, at least Max finally got some attention from me. I showered when we got back, made myself a pot of strong Jamaican Blue Mountain coffee, and treated myself to a bagel with chive and onion cream cheese. Marathon training be damned.

Feeling more human, I dug out Bruce's email and checked the information again. Cynthia Ingwalson of Butcher & Benson was Bruce's recommendation. I knew the firm; multinational and incredibly expensive immediately came to mind. Given the depth of Bruce's contacts, I knew he'd only send me the best.

Ms. Ingwalson's office told me that she'd be happy to meet with a friend of Mr. Mays' and would tomorrow at 2:00 p.m. work? Of course it would work, unless I'd already been arrested and put in the

Metropolitan Correctional Center, a charmless concrete South Loop high-rise with slits for windows. Many of Chicago's most distinguished citizens had spent time as involuntary guests there.

In an attempt to take my mind off my problems, I turned back to my book and wrote up the chapters from my latest runner interviews and did a section on the lucrative business that was marathoning. I also had an email full of edits from Martha, who was turning out to be a much more valuable asset than I had expected. The years she had spent at Barbara's side gave her a good education on both the theoretical and practical sides of writing. Of course, she still hated me for what she saw as my role in Barbara's death, but I was getting used to it.

I spent some time recalling Ted's friends and his favorite hangouts. Still no sightings, no calls, no late-night appearances. I didn't know what else to do, but I swore I'd keep looking until I found him.

After missing morning training, I promised myself I'd be up and at 'em in the morning, so after a light dinner of grilled chicken with a small frisee salad, I took Max out for a stroll and then went to bed. And for once, I was able to fall asleep and stay asleep. A big shout out to the guy who invented Ambien.

53

As we were wrapping up our run in the morning, Ashley told me how excited she was that I would be able to join her for part of the tour.

"I know it's only a quick trip, but I'm so happy that you can come along. It's really quite a circus. I think you'll enjoy the behind-the-scenes stuff, and we can run together. And I hope you'll enjoy the concerts, too."

She actually blushed when she said that. Who blushes anymore? I was falling for this girl.

We chatted about the trip and her love of live performances for a few minutes after we cooled off. Ashley was obviously excited to leave the struggles of the last few weeks behind and return to the audiences she loved. As we approached the back door of the hotel, I watched one of the hotel maintenance men take down a small folding ladder and carry it into the service entrance. I was about to call out to him to hold the door when, out of the corner of my eye, I saw a flurry of activity just behind us. A heavyset man in what appeared to be a dirty navy jumpsuit came running out of the shadows of a neighboring high rise. He didn't look like Ashley's typical fan, but I put my arm around her just in case, thinking I could pull her into the hotel service entrance quickly if he got aggressive. Then, and just then, I saw the gun in his hand. It was small, I irrationally thought, but very, very shiny.

As he raised his arm to fire, I pushed Ashley to one side as I jumped the other way. His shot flew between us with a crack, hitting the concrete side of the building. Like the linebacker he must have been in his youth, Charlie came from out of nowhere and tackled the man before he had a chance to fire again. I grabbed Ashley and pulled her into the building as one of the hotel security people ran out to help Charlie subdue the gunman.

Just inside the building entrance, I stood, holding Ashley as we both trembled. What the hell was going on? I'd been shot at. Ashley had been shot at. She seemed okay . . . was she? Who was he? Did someone send him?

After quickly making sure she wasn't injured, I handed Ashley over to another hotel security guard and went outside. Charlie had the man flat on the ground, gun kicked off to the side. Seconds later, I heard the now familiar siren of a police car. Charlie's crisp white shirt had a large crimson stain of blood on the chest. As I drew nearer, Charlie shook his head. "It's not mine. Is Ashley all right?"

. . .

Less than a half hour later, Charlie was upstairs with us in Ashley's suite.

"Ma'am, I am so sorry this happened. It's entirely my fault, and I intend to resign and let someone else take over your protection."

"Charlie, that's ridiculous. You saved my life. You and Erick."

"But we should have had that entrance better covered. You need someone who won't make mistakes like that."

"Stop it, stop it now! You aren't going anywhere and that's that. Who was he?"

"CPD is investigating, and you'll need to give your statements to the officers in a few minutes. They're giving you the courtesy of coming up here so you don't have to go back down into the lobby. I've given mine already, as have the hotel security people. But you need to know that he isn't one of the people we've been watching for. He doesn't match any of the known stalkers. One thing, though."

"Yes?"

"He had a picture of Mr. Anderssen in his pocket. Maybe he was the target, not you, Ashley."

I sat down abruptly, my hands shaking. Another attempt on my life. And one that might have harmed—even killed—Ashley. When would this end? I knew I had to tell them.

"Ashley, Charlie. I should have told you this earlier, but I was looking for more answers first. Now it looks like I've put Ashley in danger."

I spent the next ten minutes telling them about Barbara's murder, Ted's disappearance, the fake bomb, and most of the rest. I didn't share all my speculation with them, but what I did share was enough. I could see the anger in Charlie's eyes.

"With all due respect, Erick, you're right. You did put Ashley in danger and didn't give me vital information that I needed to protect her. That's just wrong."

"I couldn't agree more, Charlie, and I am so sorry."

I turned to look at Ashley.

"I can't apologize enough to either of you. I'm going to quit the marathon project and get as far away from you as I can. I can't have you in danger anymore. I'll drop the book, I'll drop the research, I'll stop digging into all of these questions. Anything to keep you safe."

She looked at me with a mix of shock and sorrow.

"Erick, you can't quit. You need to keep training, but more importantly, you need to help find who killed Barbara. And you need to find your friend. You can't give up on any of this now. Charlie and his guys will keep us safe. Won't you, Charlie?"

He looked at me, anger still in his eyes, his body tense with it.

"If we're sure we understand all the risks in front of us, we can plan coverage. But Erick, I have to have your word that you've told us everything."

"Charlie, I've told you everything you need to know to protect Ashley. I swear I have."

"All right. Ashley, I don't want you leaving the hotel for the next twenty-four hours while I reconfigure and staff up. Is that acceptable?"

"Yes, of course."

There was a knock at the door. One of the younger security guards opened the door.

"Charlie, CPD is here for Ashley and Mr. Anderssen."

"Thanks, Brian. Show them in."

54

An hour later, we were done with our statements, and the police had left. We didn't get much useful information from the officers, but I suspected another visit from Detective Hanson was in my future. Ashley was shaken but supportive, knowing how the attempt had affected me.

"Charlie is working on an enhanced security program for us both. I'm in the hotel for the day, so he'll take you home, and we'll talk through all of this tomorrow."

I tore myself away and headed home with Charlie. I could feel Max glaring at me as I walked in. I'd been ignoring the poor boy. I gave him one of his favorite treats from the doggie bakery (yes, I go to the doggie bakery for Max) and promised him a good outing after my meeting with the law firm.

I knew I couldn't get away with my usual author chic-shabby. I settled on a classic navy blazer, linen slacks, and a shirt and tie combo from Thomas Pink.

I arrived at Butcher & Benson's Wacker Drive office building a few minutes before 2:00. Most of the big-name firms had deserted the canyons of LaSalle Street for the newer buildings coming up along Wacker, and Butcher & Benson had one of the prime locations. The architects had won a Pritzker Architecture Prize for the design. It was at once intimate and sweeping, with a grand lobby that both welcomed and intimidated. Or at least that's how I felt waiting at the marbled security desk to be vetted before being allowed upstairs.

Security was expecting me, and a name badge popped out of a tiny printer next to the security person's console. Suitably authorized, I was directed to the forty-eighth floor, where another receptionist was waiting for me. Sitting at an ultramodern slice of a desk and with her back to a stunning view of Lake Michigan, she gave me a smile as she touched her cordless headset. "Ms. Ingwalson, Mr. Anderssen is here. Yes, that's correct. Of course, ma'am."

With another touch to her headset, the receptionist rose with an easy grace. I could tell that what she wore was expensive.

"Hello, I'm Megan. Let me show you the way to Ms. Ingwalson's office."

Since she already knew who I was and since she was already halfway down the long wood-and-stone hallway, I simply said I was glad to meet her and followed a few steps behind.

As we turned a few corners on our voyage, I noticed conference space and sitting rooms on either side, all beautifully decorated and filled with fresh flowers and art. One last turn found us in a luxuriously carpeted foyer with a huge glass-and-steel staircase winding its way up to the floor above. Megan, with me following, headed up. One other thought on Megan's dress: whoever designed it knew what he was doing when it came to movement. I've never seen anyone look so good climbing stairs.

We navigated another long hallway, this one filled with small open spaces for administrative assistants and much larger offices for attorneys. Of course, the attorneys enjoyed the glass wall overlooking the city and the lake, while the admins enjoyed the overhead lights.

Megan knocked on the semi-closed door to an office and waited for admission. A voice, surprisingly deep, acknowledged the knock and requested entry.

I wasn't sure what to expect from a Cynthia Ingwalson, but the woman standing behind the desk wasn't it. Instead of the Nordic blond ice princess that was Bruce's normal stock in trade, I saw a clearly middle-aged woman whose grandparents more likely came from Nigeria than Norway.

"Mr. Anderssen, so nice to meet you. Please, have a seat. Thank you, Megan."

"Please, call me Erick."

"Then you must call me Cynthia."

"I was initially thinking that we could compare our Scandinavian roots, Cynthia. Ingwalson and Anderssen clearly sound like they came from the same neighborhood."

She gave a deep chuckle. Her voice had the classic whiskey and cigarettes rasp, tinged with a bit of the old South.

"I'm afraid we won't have much to talk about. If you want to talk genealogy, you'll have to find my husband. Anders is somewhere in Brazil looking for undiscovered plants that might be the source of new medicines someday. He's a curator at the Field Museum, so he appreciates family histories. Perhaps when he gets back in the fall, we can all get together and swap family stories."

"Of course, I'd like that."

"Now, Bruce gave me a little background on why you are here, but I find it so much more useful to hear the story from the involved parties directly. Why don't you tell me what's been happening to you. It sounds dreadful."

Her charm and confident demeanor immediately gave me comfort, so I sat back and started my story, beginning with Barbara's call about the marathon book and ending with Ted's disappearance and Bruce's concerns about the Feds looking into my life.

When I finished, I realized that my telling of the story had taken more than thirty minutes, with little input from Cynthia other than a few pointed questions here and there. I also realized that I had spent most of the half hour on the edge of my chair, leaning forward as if to convince Cynthia of the merits of my concerns. I sat back, feeling a sense of relief that I now had someone who knew all that had been happening to me, someone I could trust to help me get past this crisis.

"So, Cynthia, that's my story. Can you help me?"

"Erick, I'll do everything I can for you. It sounds like you've been through a terrible time, and I'm sorry for your troubles. Let me make a few phone calls to see what kind of a case—if any—they are building against you. I'll get back to you in a few days. In the meantime, don't talk to anyone about this, especially the FBI or CPD. If they do call you or show up, immediately tell them you want to talk to me. Here's my card with my office and cell phone numbers. Call anytime, day or night."

"Thank you, Cynthia, I really appreciate your help."

"That's why I'm here. Stop and see Megan on your way out. She'll give you our standard retainer agreement to sign and let you know how much you need to give us up front."

I must have looked surprised to hear her mention the money. She looked at me with a set smile.

"I didn't starve my way through law school and five years as an associate for nothing. We're here to help our clients and make a nice profit for the firm. Don't look so surprised."

"I'm not," I hastened to respond. "I'll take care of it right away."

"Terrific, Erick. Talk to you soon."

With that, another attractive young woman was at Cynthia's open door, escorting me back to Megan. After filling out the forms and getting information on where to wire transfer the $10,000 retainer (you get what you pay for, I guess), I was back on Wacker Drive. It looked like one of Chicago's summer thunderstorms was about to hit, so I grabbed the first cab I could find and headed home. I beat the storm just in time to get Max out and back inside.

55

The next few days passed quickly. Suddenly, Ashley and I were on our last run before she left on the first leg of her tour. We ran up the lakefront with security in front and in back. As the PR machine was now cranking in earnest, Ashley couldn't get away with a baseball cap and shades anymore; she was just too recognizable. Rather than give up our outdoor runs, Ashley's manager brought in extra security to discourage anything more than a wave and smile from fellow runners. For the most part, it was working. And I must say, Charlie and the other security guys weren't just steroid-jacked sides of beef. Any one of them could keep up with us, even though our runs continued to get longer. Just the Sunday before we had put in a 30K run (almost 19 miles), and the guards were with us every step of the way. One, a very young, very fit guy they had just brought in from LA for the tour, didn't seem to even be breathing hard, but I attributed that to him trying to show off for the pretty boss and her friend, the old guy.

As we finished, we cooled down with a leisurely stroll back to the hotel. Approaching the staff entrance, I wondered aloud about the lack of progress the management had made in finishing the penthouse health club. I hadn't told Ashley about my little visit to the locked room. She looked concerned by my question.

"It's not just the spa, Erick. The plans for the clubs and restaurants in the hotels have been done for over a month, and there's still no word from GrandHotel on when they're going to start rolling them out. I've asked a number of times, but no one can seem to tell me anything."

Maybe the significant expense of the project was finally hitting home with GrandHotel. But they must have known what they were getting into before they started work. Had something changed?

But for now, it was time to say good bye to Ashley until I could join her in Miami. Since I knew she had a million things to do before leaving, I didn't want to keep her long, but I also didn't want to let her go. We found a secluded spot in one of the back rooms of the hotel.

"Ashley, I'm really going to miss you. I know it's only a few days, but I can't wait to get to Miami."

"I'll call every night. We'll have a wonderful time in Miami, and then I'll be right back here in Chicago before you know it."

With that, she reached up and touched my face with her hands. I leaned over, and we kissed for what seemed like a moment or forever. I'm not sure which. A knock at the door interrupted us.

"Ashley, it's Charlie. We're scheduled to leave for O'Hare in an hour, and you really can't be late."

We stared into each other's eyes for a moment or two, and then she looked away and walked out the door.

56

If there was a silver lining to Ashley's absence, it was that I wouldn't be distracted from necessary work on the book. As we were getting into late July, marathon preparations were heating up. I had scheduled time with each of Kate's direct reports so that I could shadow them for a day or two to see what went into producing a major city marathon.

I had already spent two days with Paul O'Bannon. I was surprised to see the level of detail involved in the sponsorship deals he worked out, as sponsors were increasingly finding ways to get value out of the money they spent on the marathon. For some, it was the old-fashioned approach. Write a check and have your logo slapped on a few signs at the marathon. Increasingly, however, companies were demanding more for their investments. Greater levels of website and social media interaction, more client and prospect hospitality opportunities, more access to the runners and their families: all ways of getting a bigger bang for their very expensive sponsorships. And, of course, more complexity and follow-through for the event staff.

O'Bannon surprised me. He was more than just a glad-hander. He ran a tight ship, tracking entitlements and ensuring that the marathon delivered on every promise. As we were slogging through a particularly complex deal with a major local grocery chain, Paul told me stories of missing shipments, stolen merchandise, and, in one especially embarrassing case, four hundred signs printed and ready to go up when a summer intern at the marathon office noticed that the sponsor's logo had been printed upside down.

This week, I'd be spending time with Sarah Peters, the marathon marketing and PR maven. I wondered why PR people were always called mavens. I'll have to Google that at some point.

As I was leaving for the marathon offices, my phone rang and caller ID said it was Cynthia Ingwalson.

"Hello, Cynthia."

"Hello, Erick. How are you on this fine, humid Chicago day?"

"I don't know, Cynthia, you tell me. How am I?"

"Not so bad, Erick, not so bad. I've made a few calls, and yes, they are taking a look at you, but so far they haven't found a single thing out of the ordinary. It appears you lead a virtuous life."

"That's great to hear, but let's not go too far. Virtuous I'm not, but basic honesty, yes."

"These days, honesty isn't so basic. I'm still waiting to hear back from my SEC contact and will let you know when I do. Now don't be overly concerned, Erick. So many people you know have gotten caught up in this that it's no wonder they're looking at you. But if they can't find something soon, they'll have to move on."

"Thanks, Cynthia. I appreciate the call and reassurance."

I guess I felt reassured, but Barbara and the others were still dead, Ted was still missing, and mysteries continued with Jack, Kate, and Lord Greene. Until I had answers, I wouldn't rest easy.

57

When I got home, there was a police car, its light bar flashing, and a number of uniformed officers in my front yard. As I rushed toward the front door, my next-door neighbor Pam came out.

"Erick, he's very brave, and he's fine."

"Who's brave and fine? Pam, what the hell is going on?"

"We're not sure what happened, Erick, but it seems like someone broke into your house a little while ago. Your alarm system tripped, and the security company called the police. It looks like Max confronted the burglar, who then must have hit the poor dog and knocked him out. He's doing fine, but he has a cut on his head and he's a little woozy. Leslie took him to the vet a few minutes ago."

I pushed past Pam and tore into the house. Everything was just as I had left it. Nothing was missing anywhere. In fact, everything seemed fine until I got to the study, where there was utter chaos. Paper everywhere, drawers ripped out and tossed aside. I knew this wasn't a simple burglary. They wanted my GrandHotel files. The files that were on my laptop. And that laptop had been with me, and would be with me all the time now until I had this solved.

Pam came in, phone in hand. "Leslie is waiting for you at the vet's. The doctor says Max will be fine. He has stitches and some meds for the pain. He's a very brave dog."

My heart went into my throat at the thought of my big, gorgeous Max defending our home against an intruder. I needed to get him home and give him enough TLC to make the pain go away. And I needed to identify these people who brought their anger into my home.

58

The next morning, Detective Hanson called.

"Mr. Anderssen, I hear you had a little trouble yesterday."

"As a matter of fact, I did."

"The patrol officer who took your statement said that nothing was taken in the break-in."

"That's correct. The only room that was even disturbed was my study."

"What do you think they were looking for?"

"Files. My research files."

"And someone shot at you."

"You're well informed, Detective."

"You've clearly angered some dangerous people."

"And you need to get them off the street."

"As I've told you, we're doing everything we can to apprehend the people behind all your problems."

I was too tired to argue. "I know, Detective, I know."

"The best thing you can do, Mr. Anderssen, is to keep a low profile and be vigilant. You never know where the next threat might come from.

And with those inspiring words, Hanson hung up.

59

Later that morning, mentally and physically exhausted, I walked into the marathon offices and saw that the intensity level had risen even in the few days since I had been to see O'Bannon. Winding my way through a mountain of cardboard shipping boxes, I found Peters on the phone at her desk.

"No, I'm sorry, we don't have any more photo credentials for marathon morning. You should have applied in March when we opened the credentialing process. It's simply too late, and I can't help you. I'm sorry." She hung up.

"An unhappy photographer?"

"Yeah, some stringer who tries to cover every event possible in the hope that someone will buy his mediocre output. We only have space for so many photographers at the start and finish, and those spots go to the major media and our own staff. And, of course, the sponsors and vendors."

"Sponsors and vendors?"

"A couple of our sponsors have a clause in their contracts that gives them the right to have a photographer at the finish to get as many of their logo shots as possible. And we have a vendor who has literally dozens of photographers on the course, taking as many pictures of individual runners as possible. They have a computer program automatically sort them based on the runner's bib and then upload them to a website where the runners can buy copies of themselves running and at the finish line. It's a huge business, incredibly profitable for the vendor, and, of course, we get a commission on every dollar sold."

"Six figures to the marathon?"

"Many six figures," she said with a smile.

"Interesting. So what else are you working on?"

That simple question led me to a very busy next two days. I followed Sarah as she met with the marathon's advertising agency to finalize the last round of newspaper and web ads (TV and radio were done and ready to run), including two major newspaper ads for the Monday after the marathon. One thanked the runners, volunteers, and spectators while the other congratulated the winners. Each had a couple of iterations: the thank-you ad versions covered beautiful weather, challenging weather, horrible weather, and even snow, while the winner ads covered world records, course records, no records at all, repeat winners, and first-time winners. I asked the agency if it wasn't a risky proposition to produce multiple versions of the same ad. Imagine the embarrassment to the race if the newspaper picked up the wrong version.

The agency guy hemmed and hawed: hardly ever happens, controls in place, managed very carefully.

Sarah was a bit more to the point. "Bullshit. It happens all the time. In 2011, the *Miami Herald* ran an ad congratulating the Miami Heat on winning the NBA title. As sports fans know, the Dallas Mavericks won in 2011, so there were definitely some red faces in Miami that day. But that won't happen to us, will it?" she said, glaring at the agency guy. He quickly shook his head. Smart man.

Shooing the agency people out, Sarah spent the rest of the day in meetings with her staff. She gave a quick glance to the latest proof of the marathon program book, which was given to all the participants. The book had a few stories about the elite runners, a brief history of the event, and, most importantly, ads both large and small, all in fulfillment of one deal or another that helped to stoke the marathon's coffers. Most interesting to me was the time Sarah spent with her social media staff. They had crafted a beautiful plan to build excitement via the event's Facebook, Twitter, and YouTube accounts, text messaging, and all the other tools. Much of the content was already written, even though the race was more than two months away. As with the rest of the event's major activities, the team had contingency plans for emergency messages, congratulatory tweets, and all the rest.

I was semi-listening as Sarah met with her public relations team. I was wondering what Ashley was up to and how the previous night's concert in Charlotte had gone. As if they were listening to my thoughts, the group suddenly started discussing Ashley.

"Show me the timeline for the Ashley announcement," barked Sarah.

One of the youngest of a young group of PR folks handed Sarah a couple pages of paper. He started to walk Sarah through the plan when she stopped him with a raised hand and pointed glare.

"I can read. Just be quiet and let me do so."

Risking Sarah's wrath, I turned to the offender and asked for the highlights.

Speaking softly, as if to lessen his offense, he said, "We've been working with Johnny K, Ashley's manager, on the plan for some time now. We're holding a special press event in September to make the big announcement, and then we'll follow that up with a full social and traditional media campaign. You know, a website with a hot link to Ashley's foundation for donations, Facebook page, Twitter support, a

Flickr gallery. Then Ashley will appear at the pre-race press conference the week of the marathon and help award the Champion's Trophy to the winners, be at the post-race press conference at the GrandHotel, and perform at the big post-race party at Navy Pier."

My first thought was if those were the highlights, I'd hate to see the details, but I wisely kept that thought to myself and simply said, "Good plan."

Sarah slowly nodded. "It is a good plan. I have a couple of other ideas for promotions, but we can talk about those as we get closer to the event. Nice job."

The poor young man actually blushed at the compliment from Sarah. Good for him. From what I knew of the PR profession, his blushing days would soon be behind him.

The final meeting of the day was with the operations team and Martin Michaels to talk about one of the event's annual headaches. For many years, all the major races had used electronic timing systems. Each runner had a computer chip assigned to him or her. Sometimes the chip was in a small plastic device that slipped onto the runner's shoelace. Others were woven into the runners' numbered bibs, which were fastened to their shirts. Regardless of the technology, the chip was activated when the runner crossed the start line. The chip would be read at various spots along the course and at the finish. The beauty of this technology was that all 45,000 runners had their own personal timing systems. And that became especially important when you considered that it took nearly thirty minutes for all the runners to cross the start line. The technology had been pretty much perfected over the years, and problems were rare. Of course, the dinosaurs behind the American Track Federation, which governed marathon running in the United States, still used handheld stopwatches to time the elite runners. You could argue that twenty-first century technology had a massive advantage over seventy-year-old men trying to push the button on a stopwatch, but that was an argument that apparently no one was going to win in the near future.

The problem faced by the marathon and its timing system was, frankly, yet another issue fueled by money.

In the never-ending quest for sponsorship dollars, the marathon had figured out a way to make money from the timing system. Runners' friends and family could go to the marathon website and sign up for text messages giving them live updates of their athlete's performance. Since a huge number of fans would frantically cross the city to catch glimpses of their runners at various spots along the course, knowing how quickly (or not) each runner was progressing was critical.

Unfortunately, each year glitches popped up in the system. Communications between the timing system, the marathon's website, and the text messaging software caused delays in the messages going out, incomplete messages, or no messages at all. The local news radio station, which was spending nearly a quarter of a million dollars to be the provider of "the fastest news in town," was sorely disappointed by the technology breakdowns and threatened to pull its sponsorship in a very ugly and public way.

Not surprisingly, the fingers of blame were nearly out of joint from all the pointing they were going through. I sat back, listening to the two teams battle through why the glitches were happening year after year. Sarah and Martin were true to course: Sarah passionately demanding perfection on behalf of the sponsor, Martin using facts and spreadsheets to show that the problems were limited and primarily driven by the volume—and thus the success—of the program. They finally came to some resolution that made no one especially happy, but at least they were able to walk out of the room reasonably content.

With two of my four shadowing experiences behind me, I left the marathon offices and went home to pack for my trip to Miami. I'd see Ashley the next day and that made me happy. At least I was happy until I saw who was standing on the front steps of my house. Why did people keep showing up at my front door?

60

Alone this time, FBI Agent Drury was talking on his BlackBerry as I got out of the cab. He glanced my way, and I could hear his end of the conversation.

"Never mind, he just pulled up. I'll let you know how it goes when I'm done." With that, he hung up and slipped the phone back into the carrier on his right hip. As he did so, I imagined what was sitting on his other hip. Nothing as benign, I was sure.

"Mr. Anderssen, nice to see you."

"Have you found Ted?" I asked curtly.

"No, we haven't. He still hasn't been to his apartment, used his debit or credit cards, or been on a commercial airline. No sign of him whatsoever."

I pushed past him to my front door. "Then I don't think there's much I want to hear about from you."

"Mr. Anderssen, this really is important."

"Agent, I'm going out of town tomorrow, and I have a lot to get done before then."

"You're traveling? We asked you not to leave town. May I ask where you're going?"

"You may ask anything you like. I don't have to tell you." As I said that, I realized that it certainly wouldn't have hurt to tell him and that not doing so made me look like I was hiding something. But the Norwegian stubbornness in me just won't stop.

"Sir, we are genuinely concerned for you. People all around you have been dying and disappearing."

"I, more than anyone, am fully aware of that fact. But if you truly have a genuine concern for me, find the people who are doing this and leave me alone. If you really want to talk to me, here's my attorney's card. Call her."

"You've retained counsel?"

"I have. Now, I really need to pack."

Drury paused, and then he stepped aside and walked down the stairs to the sidewalk. He kept walking, apparently headed toward the large black Suburban that screamed government car. Someone else was in the car waiting, but I couldn't see who it was through the dark smoked glass. As soon as Drury closed the car door behind him, the Suburban pulled away from the curb. And I went inside the house, trying to put all the trouble behind me and look forward to seeing Ashley the next day.

61

I realized as I was walking into the American Airlines Admiral's club the next morning that the last time I was there I was with Ted, enjoying our medicinal glasses of champagne before our flight to New York. As if he was next to me, I toasted Ted with my first glass of the morning, melancholy settling in despite my excitement over seeing Ashley in a few short hours. Smitten? Oh yeah.

The flight was uneventful despite the threat of thunderstorms over Atlanta. As I emerged from the gate area, I saw Charlie waiting for me.

"Mr. Anderssen. How are you today?"

"I'm fine, Charlie. What brings you out to the airport?"

"Ashley asked me to pick you up—she didn't want you to have to take a cab to the hotel."

"Well, that's very nice of both of you. Thanks, Charlie."

"No problem, sir. I assume you didn't check luggage?"

"Nope, this is it."

"Let me take your carry-on. The car is right outside."

And with that, we exited the terminal through sliding-glass doors that felt like the entryway to the world's biggest sauna. In this case, it truly wasn't just the heat; it was the 95 percent humidity that accompanied the oppressive heat. Fortunately, seconds later we were in the back of a big, black Mercedes S-class sedan. I didn't know the driver, so I assumed he was local.

Charlie and I made small talk (weather, sports) as we sped through the city. Less than a half hour later, we pulled up in front of the Delano.

While I hadn't spent much time in Miami, I knew that South Beach was the place to be, and the Delano was the center of it all. Spectacular, hip and seemingly always trendy, the Delano has a well-deserved reputation for exclusivity and, occasionally, snobbishness. I had only been there for dinner, loving every minute of it. As we pulled up to the entrance, Charlie reached into his suit coat pocket and pulled out an envelope.

"We've taken the liberty of checking you in, Mr. Anderssen. Here's your room key and an itinerary for the next day. Ashley regrets she won't see you until just before concert time, but her day is completely taken up by events. She hopes you'll enjoy a late supper with her in the penthouse after the concert."

"Thanks, Charlie. Tell Ashley I'd love to join her for supper."

"I will. The itinerary will tell you when you'll be leaving for the venue, and your ticket for the concert is in the envelope as well. I'll see you this evening."

As I walked into the Delano, an attractive young woman in a blindingly white dress walked up to me.

"Mr. Anderssen, welcome to the Delano. My name is Christine. I'm part of the Delano's guest services team. May I show you to your room?"

"Of course. Thank you, Christine."

"Please, this way."

I wondered how she knew who I was, but I assumed it was Charlie and Ashley's advance team setting things up. As we walked through the hotel, Christine told me about the history of the hotel and all the services offered. Walking poolside, she turned and, using her keycard, opened a door only steps from the pool and ushered me in.

"This is one of our bungalows, Mr. Anderssen. Miss Ashley hopes you are comfortable here."

The Delano's bungalows are famous for their luxury and high style. Two stories high, the room had a marble bath, multiple flat screen televisions, and a spectacular view of the pool from a second-floor terrace. The bungalows are also famous for their price tag, running $2,500 plus in high season. Ashley and I hadn't talked about who was paying for what, but I was afraid I was now stuck with a pricey hotel room. My pride didn't let me show any concern in front of the lovely Christine.

"I know I'll enjoy it."

"Fantastic. I've taken the liberty of making a lunch reservation for you at Casa Tua, and the Delano car will take you there and bring you back. Also, I've made a 3:00 p.m. massage appointment for you at the Agua Spa. I hope those plans are agreeable to you."

How could they not be?

"Of course, that sounds terrific."

She left with a smile.

I unpacked the few things I had brought for the short stay, noticing that the linen blazer didn't particularly enjoy its trip from Chicago. Given the massive humidity of a south Florida summer, I knew that a few minutes hanging outside on the second-floor terrace would do the trick.

As disappointed as I was not to be seeing Ashley until after the concert, I did the best I could to enjoy the wonderful food and exceptional service at Casa Tua (I strongly recommend the truffle risotto). Perhaps I shouldn't have had that last glass of wine, but Marco convinced me that as my server, he would be offended if I finished the risotto without wine. The diver scallops are out of this world, by the way.

Lunch and Inga's deep tissue massage at the Agua Spa on the roof of the Delano had me more relaxed than I had been in months. Arriving back in my room, I checked my itinerary and found that I had just enough time for a quick nap before I had to shower and get dressed for the concert.

I paired my Uomo linen blazer with Citizens of Humanity jeans, a Thomas Pink cotton shirt, and RSVP Scott loafers. I thought I looked pretty good.

The driver, who I learned was Raoul, was waiting for me at the front with the same big Mercedes. Raoul explained that Charlie was with Ashley at the venue, so I'd be traveling solo. The air-conditioning in the car was set to sub-zero, which provided almost a shocking chill compared to the heat and humidity of an early south Florida evening.

As we traveled through Miami, Raoul told me a little about our destination. American Airlines Arena was home to the Miami Heat and the primary venue for Miami's big concerts. Seating just shy of 20,000 for the Heat, I wondered how big tonight's crowd would be. For the first time, I looked at the concert ticket that was in the envelope I had received from Charlie earlier in the day. The ticket simply said the date, venue, Ashley's name, and a three-digit number with a scannable bar code. Frankly, it looked fake. Trusting Charlie, I left the limo and walked up to the entrance that Raoul indicated would be mine. The young Latina at the gate looked at my ticket and, without even looking at me, ran her scanner over the ticket and pointed to the left. As I made my way through the concourse, I was increasingly skeptical about how the night would go. There were a few people around, sure, but nowhere near the crowd necessary to sell out a

20,000-person arena. Even assuming that some of the seating was lost to the stage, Ashley didn't seem to be drawing the crowd her management team must have hoped for. I wondered if this had been the case in her previous shows, and if so, why hadn't I heard about it? This was her first big tour; she'd be just devastated.

As I walked through the concourse, I began to hear more sound. I checked my ticket and reaffirmed that my seat was in section 101. One more turn and I saw a big black curtain blocking access to the concourse ahead of me. Standing in front of the curtain was a big black man in an equally big black suit. As I approached, he visibly stood a bit straighter, his shoulders pulled back to give him an even larger presence. He spoke.

"Sir, may I help you?"

"I have a ticket?" Sounding like I was asking a question rather than making a statement, I lamely held up my simple bit of cardboard.

Reaching for the ticket, he pulled an electronic device out of his pocket and waved it over the ticket. Suddenly, a three-dimensional holographic image of Ashley's tour logo popped from the ticket. So much for the boring bit of cardboard.

He handed the ticket back to me and then held one section of the black curtain aside to allow me to pass through. In doing so, I passed from the quiet of a nearly empty sports arena concourse to complete and total bedlam.

62

People, noise, and light were everywhere. I was clearly in some backstage area for Ashley's concert. Musicians, dancers, and crewmembers hustled from here to there in what seemed to be organized chaos. Guitar players were off in one corner with their instruments, dancers warming up in another, security people surveying both the backstage crowd and a huge food buffet set up against one side wall. As I stood just inside the entryway, Johnny K hurried by. I reached out to grab his arm just as he looked toward me. He pulled me after him. "Come this way."

Still moving quickly, he brought me to one of the entryways into the main arena and handed me off to a young man with a security badge. Without saying another word, the manager disappeared, and the security guard, clearly having done this before, escorted me into the arena. Suddenly I wasn't worried about a disappointing crowd for the concert, as the place was nearly full even though it was an hour until the concert was scheduled to begin.

Following the guard, I went up a series of stairs at the back of the stage. Weaving our way through light arrays, curtains, and miles of cabling, we finally ended up in a small cordoned-off area just off the main stage. Set up like an expensive living room, the area provided a perfect view of the stage while remaining unseen by the main arena's spectators. The space was empty except for an attractive young lady in a form-fitting black dress. Black did seem to be the color of choice for the staff. She greeted me warmly.

"Mr. Anderssen, I'm Renee, and I'm the hostess for the VIP room tonight. Ashley asked me to take special care of you this evening and to tell you that she'll see you at the end of the show. Can I get you a drink?"

As she gestured, I saw the fully stocked bar and buffet at the far end of the space. Not wanting to seem rude, I asked Renee for a scotch. Eyeing the buffet for later, I took the drink Renee made for me and wandered the enclosure. She came with me and pointed out various elements of the set, the band setup, and the spaces where Ashley and the rest of the performers would enter and exit the stage. Everything was black and red, including an enormous crimson curtain that separated the stage from the audience. The curtain featured a monochromatic black version of Ashley's tour logo.

Within a few minutes, the VIP section was full. I didn't know anyone other than Johnny K, but I managed to enjoy several good conversations and another scotch or two before the lights began to dim. I had staked out a big leather chair nearest the stage as my home for the evening and settled in for the show.

Despite all the time Ashley and I had spent together, I had limited experience with her performances. I had seen a few YouTube videos and caught the end of a couple of rehearsals, but neither prepared me for what I was about to experience. For the next two hours, Ashley and the rest of the performers put on an amazing show. Eleven musicians, three backup singers, and half a dozen lean, muscular dancers barely made an impression on me compared to the incredible talent that was Ashley. She moved effortlessly from rock anthems to soulful ballads, drawing out all the emotion she could from each piece. The crowd was loud and adoring, chanting her name, roaring their approval at the end of each song.

Seeing Ashley as a star was an incredible feeling. Despite the hours we had spent together, I felt like I barely knew her. I didn't know this glamorous woman who was adored by millions of fans and who appeared on the cover of magazines. I wasn't experienced with rock stars who had entourages and agents. My Ashley was quiet, smart, and caring; athletic and wholesome. Someone I cared for. Loved, perhaps. And was putting in danger by my sheer presence in her life.

Before I knew it, the concert was nearly over, with the performers leaving the stage as the crowd cried for an encore. Of course, Ashley and her band obliged, having saved Ashley's biggest hit for the finish. With a flash of color and light, the song was over, Ashley was taking her final bows, and the big red curtains closed. As she turned to leave the stage, she looked over at us and blew a kiss. Even though there were any number of people sitting around me, I knew the kiss was for me.

63

As the VIP section guests went for a final drink or plate of food, Renee stepped up to me.

"Mr. Anderssen, if you'll wait a few minutes, Ashley would like you to join her in her dressing room. I'll take you there as soon as the other guests here are settled."

True to her word, Renee made sure that everyone had another drink before leading me back through the maze of the back stage. The main concourse was already less busy as the crew began packing up the equipment and the performers headed to after-parties hosted by local clubs. Past two more layers of security and down a long hallway, I could hear a buzz of conversation ahead.

Renee led me into a large suite clearly built both as a dressing room and for entertaining. The room was full of more people I didn't know. This crowd was younger and hipper than the VIP compound had been. Ashley had already done another quick change, her hair still wet from what must have been an awfully fast shower. She saw me coming through the crowd and, breaking off a conversation with a very earnest young man, ran to me. We kissed.

"Oh, Erick, I am so excited that you're here. Did you enjoy the show?"

"Ashley, it was fantastic. You were fantastic."

"That makes me so happy. I so wanted you to like what we do."

"Everything was incredible. And the crowd loves you!"

Her face grew solemn for a second, and then that fantastic smile came back.

"The crowd was great tonight, wasn't it? That's what gives me energy—hearing them loving our music."

Before I had a chance to ask her what the brief moment of concern was about, she started to get pulled away by her agent.

"Erick, don't forget we have a late supper date at the hotel! I'll call you when I get back."

Like I was going to forget.

Seeing that I wasn't going to get more of Ashley's time here, I made my way through the crowd and left the dressing room. Heading back out to the main concourse, I came across my driver from earlier, patiently waiting for me.

"Raoul, how did you know where I was?"

"Mr. Anderssen, Ashley's team is very well organized. They told me where to wait for you and when to expect you. Shall we go back to the hotel?"

"Yes, Raoul; thanks."

Minutes later, we were pulling up to the hotel, which suddenly looked much different from a few short hours ago. Mobs of people were waiting outside, held back by rope lines and a strong security presence. I asked Raoul if this was typical for the Delano.

"It's always pretty crazy here at night, but the news is out that Ashley is here. Plus two of the Kardashians are supposed to be at Bianca for dinner, so things are wound a little bit tighter than usual."

"I hope I can get in," I joked.

"It wouldn't hurt to have your room card in your hand in case the doormen don't recognize you."

Realizing that Raoul wasn't kidding, I pulled out my card as I exited the car, thanking Raoul for his help.

One of the doormen must have recognized me, because as I approached the main doors they swung open for me. The lobby was a vision with candles scattered on every surface and climbing the walls, the long, white, gauzy curtains were moving as a light breeze came off the ocean. The lobby was full of glamorous people heading toward Bianca, the excellent Italian restaurant in the hotel with its famous Rose Bar. Avoiding those crowds, I headed to my room to wait for Ashley's call.

I must have dozed off for a minute, but I was awakened by my cell phone buzzing. It was Ashley.

"Erick, are you still interested in dinner? I know it's late."

"Of course I am. Are you sure you aren't too tired?"

"Oh, no, not at all. I can't sleep for hours after a show; the adrenalin keeps me going. Erick, I know this is going to sound silly, but to get up here you need to go to the security desk and show them ID. They'll get you up here."

Security precautions didn't seem silly to me at all, having seen the crowds outside the hotel, not to mention the threats that I might not have left behind in Chicago.

I went down to the main lobby, found the security desk, and a few minutes later was headed up in a small, spotlessly white elevator hidden behind the front desk.

As the elevator doors opened, I found myself in a small foyer with, to no one's surprise, Charlie.

"Mr. Anderssen, how are you this evening?"

"Charlie, I'm great. How are you?"

"I'm fine, sir, I'm fine. I'll be better when this tour is over and we're settled back at the GrandHotel in Chicago."

"Problems?"

"Well, since you're part of the family, I guess I can tell you. The stalker incidents are way up, and we had a problem this afternoon here in Miami. Someone rushed up to the car as we were leaving from the hotel's secured VIP lot. Ashley's fine, but she was a little shaken up by the situation."

"Charlie, I'm sure you and the rest of the team will take great care of her. Is she running? We're getting closer to the marathon."

"Not as much as she probably should. But she's getting quite a bit of exercise at each performance, so I think she'll be fine. Now, are you ready to go in?"

"Yes, please."

And with a quiet knock and the opening of another door, I was in Ashley's penthouse suite.

As to be expected from the Delano and from a penthouse suite, the space was elegant. White, silver, and black with not a drop of color to mar the effect. Walls covered with a shimmery silver and white fabric, white leather couches, and a black onyx table highlighted the living room, with a dining area to the side that would seat at least ten. A white-jacketed waiter stepped up to greet me and take my drink order. I turned to look out the suite's windows at the beautifully lit grounds below. In the reflection of the glass, I saw Ashley emerge from one of the suite's bedrooms.

She looked stunning. In sharp contrast to the monochromatic look of the suite, she was in vivid red, a silk sheath that showed every curve of her athletic figure. She had pulled her hair up loosely, held in place by a red lacquered comb. As we came together, I realized that she was nearly my height, brought about by a pair of Louboutins with the classic red sole. We kissed softly at first and then, suddenly, with an urgency that seemed to come out of nowhere. I wasn't sure where we were going, but I was certainly enjoying the ride.

A discreet cough interrupted us. The waiter was waiting at the side of the kitchen with a silver tray complete with two drinks and a small appetizer of some sort. I nodded to him as he came closer, offering Ashley her wine and me my scotch. He held out the small appetizer plate, which held a number of small, one-bite wonders.

"With the chef's compliments," he said. "Dinner will be ready in fifteen minutes if that meets your approval."

"It does, thank you," said Ashley.

"Very good." And he was back to the kitchen.

We made small talk for a minute or two as Ashley showed me the wonders of the suite. I wanted to ask her about the stalker incident, but I didn't want to spoil the exceptionally pleasant atmosphere—Ashley seemed as happy as I'd ever seen her.

We sat on a black-and-white checked loveseat near one of the big suite windows, admiring the night view and talking about the concert. Every night of the tour had been a sellout, and the rest of the summer's events looked to be the same. She shared stories of the dancers, the backup singer who was in love with the drummer, and other tales of the group. All too soon, the waiter returned and told us that dinner was ready.

We had been so absorbed in our conversation that we didn't hear him set the dining room table. Two of the seats at one end were now filled with crystal; large silver chargers with crisp white dinner plates and black starched napkins all complemented the suite's décor and the

Delano's style. Quietly and efficiently, the waiter filled our wine glasses and set out a small bread bowl and other accoutrements of dinner. The meal began with a rocket salad highlighted by the bite of Meyer lemons. Grilled langoustines followed, and then a family-style entrée service with a salt roasted branzino and a veal chop, both expertly set so that we could share them both. We talked nonstop throughout the meal—the concert tour, our marathon training, places we wanted to go when we were both back in Chicago. The waiter moved quietly and efficiently, always there when we needed him. He finished the meal with a beautiful silver coffee service, a small bottle of liqueur with glasses, and a plate of dolcetti misti, little delicacies to share.

Finally, the waiter bid us good night and left through the kitchen service entrance. Without asking, I poured two liqueurs and brought them and the dessert plate back to the oceanfront loveseat.

For the first time that evening, conversation lagged. We both looked out at the ocean and the people moving around the hotel's pool and outdoor bar. At the same time, we both turned from the view and looked at each other.

"Erick, I don't want this night to end."

"Neither do I. And it doesn't have to. At least not right now."

"No, it doesn't. It doesn't have to end for hours. Come with me."

She stood, kicking off her shoes as she did so. She took my hand and led me to the bedroom. Seconds later, our clothes were in a pile and we were on the bed together as if we'd done this many times before. No nerves, no hesitancy, just the coming together of a man and a woman. And it was as perfect as it sounds.

64

Hours later, we were still awake, having explored each other again and again. We talked, we laughed. At some point I found a bottle of champagne in the refrigerator and brought that to bed. We drank from the bottle, and in homage to every sappy movie we'd seen, I poured a bit on Ashley's breasts. Reality set in, and much of it ended up on the bed rather than in my mouth as we had intended. We found that to be hysterically funny.

At some point, we both fell asleep. I woke just as dawn was coming up over the horizon. The new morning's light brought a peachy glow to Ashley's skin as she lay, barely covered, next to me. I leaned over to kiss her, and we made love as the sun rose into the room.

Finally it was time for me to go. I had a flight to catch; Ashley had to get ready to move on to the next venue on her tour. We didn't talk about how this would change things in Chicago. I don't think either one of us wanted to break the magic that we had savored over the last few hours.

I somehow felt better as I was leaving that a different guard—one I didn't know—was in the suite foyer. I wasn't sure I could have faced Charlie, as silly as that sounds.

. . .

Arriving back at my room, I realized that I had to hustle to get showered, packed, and ready to head to the airport. As I was getting out of the shower, the room phone rang. It was the doorman, telling me that Raoul was here to take me to Miami International. I threw my clothes on, packed my bag, and with one last look up at the Delano's penthouse, got in the car and said good morning to Raoul. And it was a good morning.

After my traditional champagne fortification, I was happy to see that the flight was on time. I boarded and was settling in with an additional glass of the bubbly when my phone rang. Hoping it was Ashley, I quickly pulled it out and answered.

"Good morning!" I said.

There was no response. I pulled the phone away and looked at the caller ID. It was Ted. "Ted? Is that you? Where are you, buddy?"

No response. No sound from the phone.

"Ted? Are you okay? Where have you been?"

No response. Without a sound, the phone was cut off. I desperately called back, but no answer. I kept trying until the flight attendant told me I had to shut off my phone. I tried to explain that I needed to find my friend but succeeded only in getting myself cut off from additional champagne.

Where was Ted calling from? Why didn't he talk to me? What the hell was happening?

65

We arrived at O'Hare without delay or incident. I tried Ted again before even leaving the arrival gate, but there was no answer. I checked my voice mail and email, but no Ted.

By early evening, I had succeeded in retrieving Max from the sitter, unpacking, starting laundry, and going through the accumulated junk mail (did anything important ever come in the mail these days?). I'd also tried calling Ted a dozen times or so, but no success there. I shared my news of Ted's attempted call with Detective Hanson, who said he'd try again to have the number traced. He cautioned me that it could have been someone who had found Ted's phone, it could have been someone who had hurt Ted, or it could have been Ted himself. I desperately hoped for the latter.

I returned to my training the next day and returned to work. Today was my day to shadow Carlos Ramirez, the elite athlete coordinator. As much as I had enjoyed my days with Peters and O'Bannon, I had been dreading spending time with Ramirez. His blatant attempts to befriend me were transparent, as was his keen desire to be a primary figure in the book. I'll admit I went into the day expecting the worst and left the day having confirmed it. Everything I had heard and read about Carlos was true.

Cutting through his long-winded stories about his past triumphs and only giving his media kit a cursory review, I told Carlos I had the background I needed, but what I needed was to see him at work—to see how the elite athlete coordinator at one of the world's biggest and most prestigious marathons did his job.

Okay, I piled it on a little thick, but surprise, surprise: it worked. He nodded sagely, complimented me on the depth of my research, and picked up the phone.

What followed were a series of phone calls to elite athletes, their managers, the staff at other big city marathons, and friends throughout the running world. I wasn't exactly sure what the purpose of the calls were; there didn't seem to be anything accomplished by them other than a series of jokes traded, drinks promised, and in one case, an overt attempt to induce an elite athlete to drop his announced commitment to run the competing New York City Marathon and race at Chicago instead. His travel schedule seemed incredibly crowded given the small universe of top athletes in the world. Travel all done at the sponsors' expense, of course.

Ramirez blustered his way through a couple of staff meetings where his input was neither wanted nor needed, and then he headed out for lunch with a race sponsor.

Having been warned by several staff members, I knew that the lunch would turn into a very long, very damp affair, so I begged off, promising to meet Carlos in Millennium Park later that afternoon for a videotaping session. The race was getting ready to announce its elite field, and Ramirez was scheduled for a background piece by one of Peters' video crews. The piece would be given to the media as part of an electronic press kit that hopefully would be run on newspaper and TV station websites as part of the big announcement.

I arrived at the park just before 3:00 to find the video crew nearly done with their setup. The background of the taping was to be *Cloud Gate*, the enormous sculpture that was one of the highlights of the relatively new Millennium Park. More popularly known as the Bean in Chicago, *Cloud Gate* is a stainless steel sculpture with a highly polished surface that reflects the city, the sky, and the millions of tourists who come to admire it. In only a few years, it had become one of the most recognized landmarks in the city. I would have used the $20 million it cost for other purposes, but that's just me.

The Bean's reflective characteristics made it a challenge for the video crew, but they finally worked out an angle whereby Carlos would face slightly away from the sculpture so that the camera and crew wouldn't be seen in the reflection. Now the crew just needed Carlos.

Just before 3:30, Ramirez showed up. As I had been warned, the lunch clearly involved more drinking than eating, and Ramirez was, in a word, dead drunk. Despite his condition, he insisted on going ahead with the video shoot, but it was clear that it just wasn't going to happen. Even with enormous cue cards, Ramirez was unable to complete a thought, much less a cohesive presentation. The director of the video told the drunken Ramirez that they would have to reschedule for technical reasons, and Ramirez blustered about that it wasn't his fault; he was ready to go. As Ramirez stumbled toward Michigan Avenue and a cab, the director and his crewed laughed about the experience.

"I can't believe you aren't more upset," I said. "You wasted an afternoon on this."

"This isn't our first rodeo with Carlos," laughed the director. "We build this into our budget, knowing that he'll miss at least one shoot and we'll have to do it over. Nobody ever really looks at our costs anyway, so we can just include what we call an asshole up-charge for dealing with Ramirez. It's really quite a lucrative experience."

I headed back to the marathon office to see if there was anything to be salvaged from my day of shadowing Ramirez, and I wasn't surprised to find him absent.

One of the office assistants laughed when I asked when he would be back.

"Seriously? It's after four. Carlos is NEVER here this late. I can give you a list of bars where you might find him if you'd like. Or you can just start with the places where the marathon has deals. He drinks at all of those places for free, so he'll be at one of those."

Not wanting anything to do with that prospect, I went home to take Max out and call Ashley. We had only spoken briefly since I left Miami, and I couldn't tell you exactly what we talked about, only that neither one of us wanted to hang up. She was due back from her tour in a few days, but neither of us talked about how this new stage in our relationship would play out when she was back in town. We just enjoyed the moment. If I've learned nothing more from the last few months, I've learned that we need to live in the moment. You never know when you won't have another.

66

On the day that Ashley was returning to Chicago, I got in my last pre-event shadowing day with Martin Michaels. The event operations manager was as compulsively organized as I expected him to be. His day was laid out in fifteen-minute increments, which he never strayed from during the ten hours I spent with him.

It was fascinating to see how he was able to compartmentalize all the pieces of his complex world. He shifted from planning water deliveries to fine-tuning more than a dozen spots on the marathon course to approving the menu for the VIP tent breakfast, and then he pivoted to reviewing the final pre-event communiqué to the various volunteer groups that would staff the aid stations along the marathon course. For each task, his focus would be entirely on that topic, never veering off course or distracted by an external influence. His memory was amazing as he talked about successes and failures from previous events, never wallowing in the first or obsessing about the latter. While he wasn't the most pleasant person to be around, I had to admire his work ethic and deep concern for the event. I knew that he would take any miniscule flaw as a profound personal failure. That trait, in the end, would ensure that his part of the event would be the very best he could possibly make it.

While he wasn't exactly warm, I knew that I had gained at least some measure of respect from him when he invited me on the next big course tour scheduled for the upcoming Sunday morning. Only a small crew was going, so I felt honored to be included. I started to say as much to Michaels, but he basically walked off in the middle of my thanks. I knew he wasn't being rude—at least not intentionally—but rather carrying the weight of the operations solely on his rather thin shoulders.

67

I was waiting in the lobby of the GrandHotel Chicago when Ashley arrived. Charlie came through one of the big brass revolving doors at considerable speed with Ashley right behind him and another security guard close on her heels. I was swept up in their group, Ashley grasping my hand and moving me along.

"Ashley, what's the hurry?"

Charlie answered, "We've got a crowd of paparazzi that's been following us from the airport, and I want Ashley up in the suite before they can get into the lobby. GrandHotel security is stalling them at the front entrance, but it's just a matter of time before one of them breaks through. Ashley doesn't need another camera in her face right now. She had enough of that on tour."

Ashley looked up at me with a small smile as the four of us entered one of the tower elevators that would take us up to the penthouse. Only when we were safely inside the suite did the tension ease.

"Oh, Erick, it is so good to see you! I've missed you so much," said Ashley. She reached up and pulled my head down close to hers, beginning what would be a long and very intense kiss. As we broke from the embrace, I saw that the other guard had taken Charlie's spot outside the suite entrance while Charlie headed up the big staircase with the bags that he and the guard had carried in.

"Ashley," I began, but she stopped me before I could finish my carefully rehearsed welcome home speech.

"Erick, I know, but we'll have plenty of time to talk later. Right now, Jack's on his way so we can get back on our training schedule. I'm so tired of treadmills—I can't wait to get back to running outside again."

"Ashley, like I said before, I don't think that's going to happen," rumbled Charlie. I don't know how someone as big as he is can move so quietly, but somehow he does. He had made it back downstairs and was standing right behind me without me knowing he was there. Trick of the trade, I guess.

Ashley's eyes flared.

"Charlie, we've had this conversation one too many times. I'm not going to be cooped up in an unfinished hotel health club for the next several weeks. I need to be outside, and I need to be outside running. You'll just have to figure out something."

I finally got a word in.

"What's the issue—more stalkers?"

Ashley answered, "No, not really. It's just that the tours are generating a lot of press, and I'm getting noticed a lot more when I'm out. And yes, I know that's the price of being famous, but I never agreed to give up my personal life to sell more records. Charlie, figure it out."

With that and a glare, Charlie nodded and went into the back part of the suite. I was about to start in on my welcome when there was a tap at the door and the guard slipped in.

"Mr. Clark is here, Ashley."

"Thank you, John. Ask him to come in, please."

With a nod, the guard was back outside, and Jack was in. I realized that I hadn't seen Jack since before Ashley's tour began and felt moderately guilty about not keeping in touch with him while Ashley was gone. He gave me a nod and Ashley a quick kiss on the cheek. He had a cool air about him.

"Okay, we have a lot to get done and not much time to do it, so let's get started," he said as he headed toward the dining room table. He sat down at one end, and as tempted as I was to head toward the other end of the nearly fifteen-foot table, I sat down next to him. Ashley took the seat opposite.

"We're down to sixty days to go to the marathon, and your training has to pick up. You're going to run five days a week, cross train one, and take one day to recover. Your long runs on Sundays will now be at least 25K—15 miles—each and every week. It stays very intense from now until race day."

"Jack, I think we're ready for all of that," said Ashley.

"Physically, I don't know. Have you both been keeping up on your training while Ashley was gone? And psychologically, I doubt it. We need to spend time reviewing the course, developing your race day strategy, and talking about logistics. You've got to get used to the fluid replenishment you'll be using on race day. And Ashley, Charlie tells me we have an increased level of security to worry about. He wants you to run upstairs at the health club. And he's right."

Ashley was trying to keep her anger in check.

"Jack, I'm sure Charlie shared with you that I'm not going to do that. I appreciate his concern and don't want to make his job harder, but you and he will have to figure this out. Now that the tour has launched, I have more time available, since the rehearsals and fittings and all the rest are done. I've got my vocal coach coming in for a few days, but that's it. I know we can't run through the city parks anymore; I get that. But find us a place to run."

She stopped and calmly stared at Jack, waiting for a response.

Jack stared right back, clearly angry, but then he nodded. "Okay, I'll see what we can do. In the meantime, tomorrow morning we'll be cross training upstairs with Margaret Newman, who is back from LA. Hopefully by Sunday we'll have a place for you to run."

"Good, thank you Jack," Ashley smiled. "I don't want to be difficult, but this means a lot to me."

Jack nodded, stood up, and left. Ashley and I looked at each other across the enormous table. She smiled, stood, and walked around to my side of the table. She took my hand and led me to the big staircase. As we started up the stairs, without a word, I foolishly thought to myself that it would be the first time I'd see the upstairs of this mini-mansion in the sky. I wondered if they had kept the art deco beauty all through the suite. Then, as the real beauty walking beside me looked up at me, I put all thoughts of architecture out of my mind and marveled that this stunning woman was taking me to her bed.

68

Later, room service cheeseburgers and a bottle of wine from the suite's kitchen made up our dinner, with dessert scrounged from a gift basket delivered from one of the tour sponsors. We talked endlessly about nothing, watched part of a bad movie on the big flat screen in the suite's media room, and then returned to Ashley's big, unmade bed. I don't know how many times we made love, but the last one was as the sun was rising over the lake. Afterward, I pulled on my yesterday clothes, kissed Ashley good-bye, and left the suite, nodding in a terribly embarrassed fashion to the ever-present guard at the door. Again, fortunately, it wasn't Charlie. Adults all, but it would have been hard to look him in the eye.

Poor Max, left alone overnight. He didn't seem too much worse for the wear, but he was very grateful to get out into the backyard. I gave him an extra helping of kibble with some of that vitamin gravy he likes as compensation for his missed dinner, and then I felt even guiltier, so I dredged up a big chew toy that I'd been saving for his birthday. Sappy, yes, of course. The pet store sees me coming and knows they'll have a good week.

I showered and dressed quickly, gave Max a guilt-inspired extra scratch behind the ears, and headed back to the GrandHotel for our workout. I knew it was going to be a tough day: Ashley's trainer,

Margaret, was coming in for the next couple of weeks to get us whipped back into shape. I know that Jack was convinced that we had slipped into slovenly ways without his daily training guidance, but we had been keeping fit in other ways, if you get my drift.

And that tacky remark proves that even thirty-nine-year-old men are actually fifteen-year-old boys in a bigger form. Will we ever grow up? Damn, I hope not.

As I walked into the health club—where no appreciable construction work had been done since the last time I was there—I was surprised to see Kate standing with Jack and the trainer. I hadn't seen Kate lately other than quick hellos during my marathon office visits. Both she and Jack looked tired and out of sorts. Kate was certainly not looking her turned out, cover-of-*Chicago-Social* best. Instead, she was in a simple, sleeveless dress of black linen with her hair pulled back. She looked pale, her complexion made fairer by the severity of the dress. Jack was unshaven and sloppy in a t-shirt and shorts, the scars on his leg red and harsh. They watched me cross the bare expanse of what would become a busy free weights area if GrandHotel ever completed the club. I really needed to get answers about the hotel's finances. Where was Bruce on that?

As I leaned over to give Kate a quick peck on the cheek and Jack a handshake, which he reluctantly returned, Ashley emerged from the elevator that connected her suite to the club. She looked radiant, smiling at all of us. Kate looked at me strangely as I tried to keep a big goofy grin off my face. Knowing me, Kate leaned close and in a conspiratorial whisper said, "Nice t-shirt, Erick. Guns N' Roses—so are you a fighter or a lover these days?"

I turned a bright shade of red, mumbled something about not knowing what she was talking about, and turned to greet Ashley. Of course we tried to keep it semi-professional and failed miserably. Her turned head deflected my attempt at a quick cheek kiss, and I think I ended up kissing her ear.

Forestalling this awkward moment was the arrival of Margaret, Ashley's trainer from hell. Whippet-thin (and that wasn't a compliment to Margaret or whippets), she was in bright pink workout gear, which contrasted nicely with her deep, dark California tan. She had a cold, mean smile on her face, knowing that she had two victims to punish.

And punish she did. It was only an hour workout, but Ashley and I were both exhausted halfway through. At some point along the way, Kate and Jack left together, but not before what appeared to be an angry exchange between them. Or rather, angry hushed words from Jack to Kate, who turned paler yet. Jack had changed into a sports coat and slacks, dark to match his mood.

I momentarily wondered why they had been here at all, but Margaret sweated the thought right out of my mind. Perhaps pulling an all-nighter of any kind wasn't the best idea when we know Margaret is coming to town.

69

Once Margaret was done with us, Ashley and I chatted for a few minutes, and then I left to go home while Ashley returned to her suite. We made plans to have lunch together, so I hurried to get cleaned up, take Max out for a well-deserved walk, and catch up on email.

A brief note from Martha commended me on the most recent chapter drafts I had sent her but in keeping with her new responsibilities, also included a few thoughts on how I could improve my already brilliant prose. I grudgingly admitted that each and every one of her suggestions not only made sense but also improved what I had written. Dammit.

Ashley and I knew that we couldn't go out in public for lunch, at least not without a small battalion of security people and an open invitation for the paparazzi, so we decided to have lunch at my place. Charlie promised to figure out a way to get her there with minimal fuss.

After finishing the emails, I quickly tidied up the place (not too challenging, since I hadn't been around to mess it up), and then went to Pastoral for food. Some rustic flatbread, wild boar salami, chorizo español, and a few cheeses would do us just fine.

I arrived home in time to open a bottle of wine, get out plates and bowls, and set up lunch in my postage-stamp-sized but, I must say, beautifully landscaped back patio. Shaded by a couple of big oak trees and with a brick privacy wall, it made the perfect spot for a quiet luncheon for two. Just as I was finishing the setup, my doorbell rang. Rushing to let Ashley in, I opened the door on FBI Agent Drury instead. Talk about your disappointments.

"Mr. Anderssen, how are you today?"

"Frankly, Agent Drury, I was fine until you rang my doorbell."

"I appreciate that, sir. I just need a few minutes of your time."

"You can have just that. A few minutes."

"May I come in?"

"Is that necessary? I have a guest coming."

"Most people prefer to have these conversations in the privacy of their homes rather than on their front steps. The neighbors ask a lot fewer questions."

"Fine, come in. But I was serious about the few minutes."

I held the door open but stopped in the front hallway. I certainly wasn't going to encourage Drury to stay any longer than necessary by offering him a seat.

"What can I do for you, Agent?"

"A few updates for you, sir. We are continuing to monitor Mr. McCormick's phone and credit cards, but we have seen no activity. We also continue to monitor the financial implications of the insider trading scheme that your agent and others were involved in. We've found several additional parties who benefited in relatively small ways from the scheme. We haven't found the source of the information or the ringleader, but we think we are closing in on both. We just need more hard evidence of the conspiracy and the identity of the ringleader."

"Do you suspect anyone I know?"

"I'm sorry, Mr. Anderssen. I'm not at liberty to share the results of an ongoing investigation with you."

"I understand."

"Finally, we have concluded our investigation into your activities, and we now believe that you had no part in the scheme. We communicated that to your counsel this morning and told her that we'd be letting you know today. Of course, that doesn't forestall any future investigation if new information turns up."

I was surprisingly relieved, even though I knew I had done nothing wrong.

"Thank you, Agent Drury. Of course, I told you that all along."

"Yes, sir, you did. But you can appreciate that everyone claims innocence, especially the guilty."

"Is there anything else?"

"No, just a reminder to let us know if you hear from Mr. McCormick."

"You've told me that several times, Agent. And I will."

"Will you? I wonder. In any case, I'll take my leave."

As he turned and opened the door, a small gray car pulled up in front of my house. Rather the worse for wear, the car's side mirror was held on with duct tape, and a fairly large dent disfigured the passenger side door. The car sat for a minute, and then the driver's door opened and a thin, older man in what appeared to be a maintenance uniform of some kind emerged. He looked up and down the street as if he was looking for someone or something. Apparently satisfied with what he saw (or didn't see), he opened the passenger door and another uniformed person emerged. Even in the blue-gray drab uniform and with a cap pulled down low, I recognized my lunch guest. I tried to hurry

Agent Drury down the sidewalk, but he stalled, interested in my guests. A little dodging and weaving got them around the agent with minimal contact. I let them in the house and closed the door on Drury, who was still standing in the middle of the sidewalk staring at us.

"I've never seen you look more beautiful, Ashley. Is this from your collection?"

"Very funny, Erick. This is Mr. Kaczmarek. He works at the hotel. Charlie came up with the brilliant idea of having Mr. Kaczmarek drive me here in his car. By leaving through the parking garage, nobody noticed us. It was perfect."

"Happy to help, Miss Ashley. Anytime. What time do you want me to pick you up?"

"Let's say four o'clock. I have an *Access Hollywood* interview at six, so I need to get back and get dressed for that."

"Of course, ma'am. I'll see you then."

And with that, we were alone. Max was always delighted to have guests and followed Ashley through the house. As we were sitting down for lunch, with Max wrapped around Ashley's feet (no small feat for a dog of Max's size), I heard the doorbell ring. Excusing myself, I went to open the door and saw my next-door neighbor, Leslie, a bundle tightly wound with rubber bands in her arms.

"Erick, we picked up your mail the other day but forgot to bring it over. Sorry about that, but you know how forgetful Pammie has been lately. Say, do you have company?" Peering over my shoulder, the woman knew full well I had company and was determined to find out who it was.

With all the politeness I could muster, I took the bundled mail from Leslie and closed the door almost literally in her face. I threw the heavier than normal pile onto the big blond table as I passed by on my way back out to Ashley.

Lunch was delicious and the wine even better. After polishing off the bottle, I offered to open a second, but Ashley demurred, given her upcoming TV interview. We enjoyed the backyard for a few more minutes before I took Ashley's hand and, as she had done for me, led her upstairs to my bed. Max wasn't happy at being shut out of the bedroom, but I have never been into audiences.

We had very little time before Mr. Kaczmarek was scheduled to pick Ashley up, but we made the best of it.

I certainly wouldn't have enjoyed that time with Ashley had I known there was a time bomb ticking on my big pine table. Not literally, of course, but it just as well could have been for the impact it would have on us all.

70

The next few days passed quickly. Ashley and I were in a routine of sorts, training in the mornings under Jack's careful eye and then enjoying each other's company in the afternoons and early evenings. Jack and Ashley's management company had found a few places where we could run without being hassled or harassed: a far north suburban forest preserve, a golf course under renovation, even the grounds of a small private college that was so deeply faith-based that they had never heard of Ashley or her music.

I was feeling guilty for not making any progress on the marathon book, guilt that was partially fueled by Martha's almost daily emails and calls looking for the next few chapters. Since I had the research and interviews done, there really was no excuse for getting behind. Oh wait, yes there was. I was in love.

And I'm happy to report it was mutual. We were like two teenagers with our first crush, but with the experience that our years brought us. It was a magnificent combination.

A few days later, Ashley was headed out for the West Coast leg of the tour. Shortened by design, she still had seven concerts over ten days starting in Seattle and ending in San Diego. I desperately wanted to join her, but I knew I needed to get some things done and couldn't justify the time away from home. I had an Alex Project board meeting coming up where we needed to make some tough budget decisions, plus the book was hanging over my head. I had a lot of pages due between now and a week after the marathon, so I committed myself to buckling down and writing while Ashley was out of town.

I had to do something with my pent-up energy.

. . .

The Alex Project board meeting went badly. I had recruited a number of senior business and community people for the board, hoping to get strength both in fundraising and governance. I needed people who would support my vision, raise the money we needed to serve our clients, and ensure the long-term survival of the project with or without me and my money.

Our budget for the upcoming financial year was tight. Our usual aggressive financial goals were now combined with steadily increasing costs for nearly everything we did. Our rent crisis appeared to be on the back burner for now, but health-care costs for our clients were killing our budget. I couldn't tell the board about the quarter-million-dollar donation I was to get for writing the marathon book. I wasn't entirely sure it would actually happen and wasn't ready yet to discuss how it had all come about. Two of the directors with finance backgrounds agreed to develop contingency plans for an emergency fund drive and even a short-term loan if worse came to worst.

I could tell people were disappointed in my lack of a sense of urgency, but I couldn't get too motivated, given that I was pretty confident that we'd have $250,000 in place by the end of the year.

Through all of it, Ken was strangely disengaged. He'd normally have been heavily involved in the discussion, but even the contingency plan discussion got only part of his attention. I wondered what could be bothering him.

The board meeting was on a Saturday morning with the rest of the day taken up with house chores, a quick run with Max, and an early dinner with friends. I was very good at dinner—well, pretty good—since the next morning, I would have an early morning marathon experience. By the end of the morning, I'd have completed the 26.2 miles of the marathon.

And no, not on foot. Inside a Mercedes SUV. One of the big, new ones. Black, of course. Do they even come in another color?

71

Although the marathon course rarely changes much from year to year, there always were tweaks necessary to cover street work, new construction, or a serious deterioration in road conditions. So a few short weeks before the actual race, the senior operations staff does an early Sunday morning course drive to make sure the new course works as it should, to verify the exact distance, and—the most fun of all—to videotape the course. That video is seriously sped up and loaded onto the Chicago Marathon website, and once it's available it becomes the hottest page on the site. First-time runners from all around the world love to see those 26.2 miles fly by in 3.4 minutes, seeing the course they are about to run for the first time. The marathon staff shows it on a big screen at the Health and Fitness Expo, and it is always a big draw. That's why the premier sponsors fight to have their commercials run on the big screen: They have a captive audience.

I met the ops team at the back entrance to the Art Institute at half past dawn. The start line was only a few short yards away, so this is where we'd start the drive. Michaels was behind the wheel and impatient to begin. Holding up progress was Jim Durbin, the marathon videographer. He needed more light to ensure the best possible quality video, and a bank of heavy clouds over Lake Michigan was causing a delayed sunrise. Michaels was understandably anxious to get going: despite best efforts, the city refused to provide the event with a police car to clear traffic ahead of us, so we had to put up with stoplights, traffic, and pedestrians, all of which would be edited out before broadcast. The later we started, the more edits, which would drive up the cost. Michaels was nothing if not frugal with the event's money. At least someone was.

So abruptly that it almost made a sound, the sun emerged from behind the cloudbank, and we were off.

. . .

I hadn't fully appreciated the genius of the marathon course until that morning. I knew it was a bit of a tour through the city, but seeing what a vast section of Chicago was covered by the course was truly impressive. Out of Millennium Park via Columbus, the course headed over to Michigan Avenue, home to Tiffany, Hermes, Armani, and Prada. The street earned its Magnificent Mile nickname. Leaving Michigan Avenue at Oak Street, the course wound its way through Lincoln Park and its beautiful zoo and then headed over to one of my favorite parts of Chicago.

Lake Shore Drive hugs Lake Michigan and the beautiful beaches that have been carefully preserved by the city. Coming over a slight rise at North Avenue, the first clear glimpse of the skyline close up takes my breath away every time I see it.

The course continued down Lake Shore Drive for several miles, a decision that wasn't terribly popular with runners or locals trying to get somewhere on Sunday morning. This was a relatively new development that had been pushed hard by the marketing, PR folks, and, of course, the city tourism people who wanted those spectacular photos of runners along the lakefront. What the photos didn't show was the wind whipping off the lakefront, which dropped the temperature by several degrees from the inland areas where the course used to run.

A final set of turns, and the runners were headed back north again toward the Grant Park finish. The race used to pass US Cellular Field on the South Side (yes, I know—Comiskey it shall always be), but one year the White Sox staff shot off the scoreboard fireworks (which go off for every Sox home run) as the runners passed. Several out-of-town runners thought they were being shot at. Not a pretty PR move, said the city, so the course was moved.

The guys dropped me off back at the Art Institute so I could catch a cab home. Walking in the front door, I was newly motivated to get back to the book. I grabbed the last two folders of research notes from the dining room table and headed toward the den to write.

As I turned from the table, I heard a thud behind me. Looking back, I saw that I had dislodged the rubber-band-wrapped package of mail that I had dropped on the table when Ashley came to visit. The usual junk inside, along with a FedEx envelope. Mildly curious, I brought the envelope to my desk with the notes. I pulled open the tab on the package and pulled out a battered manila file folder. Clipped to the top was a small piece of notepaper with my name on it. I recognized the handwriting immediately. It was Ted's.

72

I ripped open the envelope. There was no covering note, no explanation. Just a bunch of financial information, handwritten notes, and a couple of printed-out emails, all looking like it had been jammed into the folder with no regard for organization. Most of the material was in a cramped handwriting that I immediately recognized as Barbara's—and the rest was in Ted's.

It took me two readings through the material before I could put all the pieces together, but when I did, I sat back in astonishment.

The rumors that Bruce had told me about were true. Insider trading on a massive scale. Cover-ups. Conspiracy. Murder.

While I certainly can't claim credit as a business whiz, I knew enough from my own portfolio to see what was happening from the notes Ted had sent me. The group—which looked to be at least a dozen—had been working in collaboration for years to trade on insider information for a handful of companies. At the direction of a leader, who was referred to in the notes as "Thunder," they would buy a company's stock just before some positive news was announced and then quickly sell and pocket the gains. Not all of them every time, but in some kind of a rotation that the notes only marginally made clear.

What astonished me was this: It was all my friends, all of them involved in something so risky, so illegal. People I thought I knew so well—Ted, Barbara, even the highly respected Ken Hamlar. Felons and frauds surrounded me.

Ken, with his deep and broad financial experience, seemed to be the coordinator, keeping the participants rotating through trades in an apparently so-far successful attempt to stay below the SEC's radar. They used fake names, free email accounts, and a coded messaging process that was only intelligible to me thanks to Ted's poor memory, which forced him to keep the code translations on a sheet of lined notepaper. I wasn't able to follow it all, especially the names of the companies whose stock was being manipulated, but certainly enough.

Enough to feel incredibly sad that I knew these people so well yet knew so little about their moral compasses. People whom I admired and loved had engaged in a crime that would send them to prison for years and ruin their lives.

I suddenly recalled Barbara's sad statement to me the last time we spoke before she died. We talked about her being the next Martha Stewart. But Martha Stewart gone wrong. Insider trading charges, an indictment, trial, and prison time. Was her part of the scheme in her missing bag?

Who was Thunder, the seeming source of the insider information and instigator of the fraud? And who were these other people that were involved? Perhaps people Ted didn't know about. Who else was in on the schemes? Kate and Jack? Is that how they were affording their posh lifestyle?

The last trades noted in the file were from a stock that seemed to be a special favorite of the group. Ted's notes referred to it as Home Base, but that meant nothing to me. Those last trades—the biggest and most profitable that I could find in the file—had happened just before the chain of death started in New York. Barbara was dead, Ted missing. Who knew who else had been silenced to protect the scheme?

I didn't know what Ted's intentions were by sending me the file, but I knew I had little choice. I had to get this to someone who could use the information to stop the deaths and find Ted before it was too late.

Despite the seemingly large number of law enforcement people I had come across in the last few months, I was unsure where to go with this information. Not the Chicago Police Department—out of their depth. Drury at the FBI? Perhaps.

But I knew the answer. It was right next door. I had to find Minu and show her the evidence that would bring down careers and ruin reputations. And hopefully save lives and bring Ted home.

73

I didn't have Minu's direct phone number, so I had to go through a series of what could only be political appointees (due to their incredibly poor phone manners and lack of any professionalism at all) before I could reach her. She was still cool to me and pressed for more information on why I needed to see her right away. I refused to say anything more than that it was critically important and that I would explain when I saw her. She reluctantly agreed.

Clutching Ted's file, I found a cab almost right away and was at the Cook County Administrative Center in a matter of minutes. Part of the city/county government complex surrounding the Loop's Daley Plaza, the 69 West Washington building was surprisingly nondescript for the governmental power held within its walls. Multiple layers of security included metal detectors, bomb- and drug-sniffing dogs, and masses of both Chicago police officers and Cook County sheriff's officers.

Finally, I was at the special prosecutor's section of the complex, waiting for Minu in the central reception area. She came out from a locked section of the floor, serious in a severe black suit and crisp white blouse with a black leather Coach portfolio under her arm. We shook hands in an equally serious manner as she led me back into a conference room immediately behind the secured doorway.

"Okay, Erick, what's this about?"

"I didn't know where else to turn with this information."

"What information?"

"This came to me a few days ago via FedEx. It's from Ted McCormick."

I handed her the file. She opened it slowly, looking up at me as she saw the mess of papers included.

"Just start reading. I sorted the papers by date so that it tells the story. Use this sheet to translate the codes."

Fifteen minutes passed as Minu read through the file once, then started a second read, the translation sheet by her side. This time through, she took extensive notes, organizing her findings.

Completing her second review, she stood up with her portfolio and Ted's file in hand.

"Erick, wait here. I'll be right back."

"But Minu—"

"Erick, please. Just wait here."

She left before I could say anything else. I pulled out my phone to check my email and messages and saw a text from Ashley. Just a sweet little *love you*, but it felt like the sun had broken out from behind the clouds for just a minute.

Then the door opened, and the clouds took over again.

Minu walked in with an older man whom she introduced as her boss, Art Erie, the head of the Special Prosecutions Bureau. Erie was an older, heavyset man who looked like he was carrying the weight of the world on his stooped shoulders. Minu must have told Erie who I was and how I fit into the puzzle since he jumped right in with questions.

"How do you know this came from Mr. McCormick? Was there a

note or anything else in the package other than what you've brought us?"

"No, nothing at all. The box is still at home."

"We'll want that box so we can trace the shipment. We'll have an officer bring you home and get the box from you. So, how do you know this came from Mr. McCormick?"

"Some of the contents are in Ted's handwriting, including the note clipped to the top with my name on it. It's from him."

"Some of it? Who wrote the rest?"

"My agent, Barbara Bronfman."

"And you had no knowledge of this scheme prior to opening the envelope?"

"No clue. I wasn't asked to participate, nor did I have any suspicions that there was something going on prior to Barbara's murder. But since then, everything has gone to hell in a hand basket."

Erie gave me a knowing smile. "Yeah, felony conspiracy tends to get out of hand sooner or later."

At that, Minu asked Erie what else he needed from me.

"We're going to have to take this to the chief deputy state's attorney. It's got interdisciplinary hell written all over it—IRS, SEC, US attorney. Let's let her figure out where we go next. In the meantime, Mr. Anderssen, please don't plan any trips out of town. We'll need to take a formal statement from you in the very near future, and I would guess some of our federal colleagues will want to talk to you as well. And it goes without saying that you cannot discuss this matter with anyone, no one at all. It's especially important that you have no contact with Mr. Hamlar. He can't know that we have this information. Is that clear?"

"I guess so." I got up to leave.

"Mr. Anderssen, you did the right thing in bringing this to us. Thank you."

"Art, I'll see Erick out," said Minu.

She was quiet until we got out to the elevators.

"Erick, thank you for this."

"No problem, Minu. I just really appreciate all your help."

"I think we're going to be seeing a lot of each other in the near future. But remember, we can't discuss this at home. Amar can't know anything about this until it's public."

"Of course, I understand."

"And you have to keep this confidential. You can't tell anyone, even Ashley."

"How do you know about Ashley?"

Minu smiled. "Hey, even prosecutors read the tabloids. I've seen the photos of the two of you. So romantic and exciting! To be dating a star!"

"Trust me, the star part is a major pain. We can't go anywhere without a dozen cameras following us."

Minu smiled broadly. "How about dinner at our house? We'll find a way to sneak her out of the hotel, and the two of you can come over for murgh do pyaaza!"

"I don't know what that is, but it sounds like a wonderful idea. Ashley gets back from her West Coast tour in a few days, so we'll set something up then. Thank you!"

With that, the elevator came, and I headed down to street level. It was certainly easier to get out of a high-security government complex than it was to get in. Unless they didn't want you to leave. Then, I imagine, things get very complicated.

74

One of the sheriff's officers drove me home, took the FedEx box, and left me alone with my thoughts. And poor, ignored Max. The big dog needed much more exercise than I'd been giving him lately and more attention as well. I could feel the guilt vibes pouring off him. I changed into my running gear and took the big lug for a long jog around the neighborhood.

On our way home, we stopped briefly at O'Shaughnessy's. I was sweaty and Max was panting and drooling, but I knew it would still be slow at this hour and that the proprietors always had a big water bowl out back on their patio for the neighborhood dogs. I clipped Max to the fence after he drained the bowl and brought the empty in for refilling. I picked up a Smithwick's from Dennis while I was there. Hey, we both needed a little liquid nourishment.

Sitting alone with my dog on the nearly empty patio, I didn't know how this was all going to turn out. My mind raced from wondering where Ted was to how Ken Hamlar had gotten himself so deeply into this. One of Chicago's most respected business leaders, knee-deep in a multistate felony scheme. Maybe even involved in murder. How could I not go to him and confront him? And with Ashley due back from the West Coast in a few days, how could I keep this from her? And how could all of this have happened without me having a clue?

Ted was right. I am selfish. And self-centered. Sadly, it took momentous loss for me to finally figure that out. But figure it out I did. Lucky me.

75

A week later, things hadn't changed much. Yes, Ashley returned and was full of great stories about her West Coast tour. Sometimes it does seem like California is part of another country (or its own country), and Ashley's stories just reinforced that feeling.

Her excitement over the success of the West Coast tour, planning and tweaking for the late September Midwest college tour, and moving into the last phase of our marathon training made time pass quickly and distracted me from thinking about the insider trading scheme and my missing friend Ted. The only thing that marred the days was Jack's increasing moodiness and sometimes, downright nastiness toward me during our training sessions. He didn't look well, either. His California beach boy looks were fading rapidly, and he seemed to be losing weight. Even his golden blond hair was losing its luster.

At one of our sessions, Ashley tried to approach the issue.

"Jack, are you all right? It looks like you've lost some weight."

"I'm fine."

"No, really, you look thin."

"Ashley, how I look really isn't any of your fucking business. I'm here to train you for the marathon, not to have my looks criticized."

"Jack, I was just . . ."

"I don't care. Leave me alone. Maybe you and your boyfriend

should focus on the task at hand so you don't embarrass yourself—or me—on race day. At the rate you're going, that's pretty likely to happen."

I had to step in at that point.

"Jack, that's uncalled for. Ashley was expressing concern—"

"Erick, you can shut the fuck up too. You know, this all comes back to you in the end. You know that, right?" he snarled.

And with that, Jack stormed out, leaving us to wonder what had set him off—not that this was his first tirade. Our patience with Jack was running out.

During all of this, I was also working hard at finishing the last of the pre-race copy for my marathon book. I was slightly ahead of schedule, which made Martha happy and reduced one source of anxiety for me. I still needed to write the final sections of the book, but since they involved race-day preparations and the race itself, they would have to wait until those achievements were behind me. Assuming, of course, that I actually finished the race in a respectable time and could justify the program to my readers.

Both Ashley and I were increasingly apprehensive about the race. We were in great shape—the best shape of my life—and had finished a 20-mile training run in decent time. But all the stories about the infamous Wall had us nervous.

The Wall. That point in a marathon when you suddenly feel you can't take another step. You've hit The Wall. Your body feels like it's starting to shut down. Your mind goes blank. All you want to do is stop running and lie down. Sometimes it hits at mile 20, others say 22 is the magic number. You can run through it, push through it. But sometimes, runners say, your body just won't let you go on.

Months of training, preparation, and mental hardiness are all for naught if you hit The Wall hard enough. And for me, it would mean a book never published and a default on my contract. And for Ashley—as of tomorrow—not finishing meant a huge public embarrassment.

For the next day was to be the public announcement of Ashley's marathon quest and her efforts to raise money for her foundation.

Over the past fifteen years or so, marathons and other running events had become one of the major fundraising opportunities for charities around the world. From the London Marathon, whose runners raise more than 50 million pounds (more than $80 million) for charity each year, to your neighborhood parish 5K, running for charity was big business.

Add a celebrity to the mix and that business got even bigger. That bigness was reflected in the size and scope of the press conference announcing Ashley's participation in the Chicago Marathon.

Held in the Modern Wing of the Art Institute with its walls of glass overlooking Grant Park, there were more than one hundred media outlets credentialed for the press conference. They were attracted by a simple yet obviously effective tease: America's hottest star. 26.2. October 7. Chicago.

The place was full a good fifteen minutes before the official 10:00 a.m. start time, and you'll know how unusual that is if you've ever worked with the media.

At the stroke of 10:00, Ashley, Kate, and the general manager of the Chicago GrandHotel stepped from a back room and took their places at the dais. Shutters clicked and the TV camera operators focused as the three women sat, smiling in the general direction of the media. They clearly had coordinated their wardrobes, as all three were in the marathon's—and GrandHotel's—signature green and gold color scheme. Ashley looked especially stunning in one of her own creations, a forest green sheath dress shot through with threads of gold. Kate was in her trademark St. John knit, this one kind of a greenish-gray with her jewelry adding the requisite gold. Savvy enough to not try to compete with Kate and a pop superstar, the hotel manager was in a subdued dark green suit with the GrandHotel logo discreetly stitched into the lapel. After a few minutes of posing, Kate began speaking. I hadn't noticed it before, but all three were discreetly set with wireless microphones. Combined with the subtle green linens and small floral bouquets in front of each speaker, the setting was elegant but not overdone, and clearly intended not to overshadow the women or the breathtaking view of the park behind them.

Like her or not, Kate knew how to put on a show.

76

Kate's remarks were simple. She introduced herself and the hotel GM, then used the hackneyed "someone who needs no introduction" to pass the speaking role over to Ashley.

Ashley spoke briefly, almost shyly. She told the assembled media about the roots of her John and Monica Frederick Foundation, its goals and programs. Several minutes into her subdued remarks, she finally got around to saying that she was running the GrandHotel (yes, she got the name right) Chicago Marathon to raise money for the foundation. She said she was getting substantial support from GrandHotel and asked people to go to her website, www.ashleymarathon.org, to make donations to help the foundation achieve its goals. The GrandHotel GM announced that GrandHotel would match the first $250,000 raised between now and the day after the marathon. Polite applause.

As nice as the affair was, I was underwhelmed. I could see that the media were too: several reporters were checking their email, texting away, and generally not paying attention. So far, they hadn't gotten anything they couldn't have picked up from a press release emailed to their editors.

Ashley was speaking again, thanking GrandHotel and Kate for the opportunity and repeating her website address. She then looked directly at me and said she wanted to thank the two people who were making her run possible. She first thanked Jack for his inspiration and all that she had learned from him. When she called on him to stand and be recognized, we all realized for the first time, I think, that Jack was nowhere to be found. The reporters looked uneasily at one another: Everyone knew that Jack and Kate were married, so his absence was a distinct slap in her face.

As the silence grew, Ashley became confused and Kate angry. Finally, Ashley stepped into the silence to thank one more person.

"We haven't known each other very long, but we've been through a lot in the last few months, all of it good. I'd like to thank my training partner and one of the most gifted authors I know, Erick Anderssen. Erick?"

As I stood, blushing from head to toe, the cameras and reporters all turned to me. I gave a quick wave and then sat before anyone could ask me anything. It seemed to work.

Suddenly the lights dimmed to nearly total darkness. Ashley, Kate, and the hotel GM stood up as music began to play. The media suddenly began paying attention.

From what seemed like nowhere, green and gold three-dimensional glowing feet began to appear on the floor of the gallery, running toward the dais in time to the soft beat of the music. Everyone was looking up and around, trying to find the source of the projection and music.

As the music began to increase in volume and tempo, a huge screen began to descend from the vaulted ceiling of the gallery. Even before the screen reached the floor, the highly sped up version of the marathon course began projecting on the screen. But not just the course as we saw it that morning. Suddenly the course was full of runners, all in glowing green and gold gear, running, dancing, laughing, and waving at us as if they were in the room. I didn't recognize the music: it wasn't the marathon's official theme, which resembles the NBC Olympics music combined with an African drumbeat, and which some people unkindly called a track that didn't make the cut for *The Lion King*. Personally, I liked it.

No, this music was different. Definitely a rock tempo, but there were strains of something classical in the background. The volume and tempo were increasing, as was the brightness of the image. Pin lights from the ceiling began to glow across the front of the room, just behind where the screen was still showing the course, now close to reaching the Grant Park finish line.

Suddenly, the screen began to rise at a much faster pace than it had glided down. Doing so, it revealed some of the runners we had just seen on the course, still wearing their green and gold running gear that was still glowing softly. They were now a dance ensemble, their moves choreographed to the music. Everyone in the room was on their feet, some clapping in rhythm, but all fully engaged in the spectacle in front of them. I could hear the TV reporters anxiously ensuring that their camera crews were catching every second.

The runners came together in a group, did one big turn, opened up the group, and revealed Ashley, who had swiftly changed into a one-piece gold metallic running singlet. She was moving in rhythm to the music, leaning back into the spotlight that made her hair and outfit seem like they were on fire.

With a nanosecond pause in the music, she began to sing. I'd never heard the song before, but it was amazing. Incredible beat with a beautiful, inspiring tone. I couldn't make out all the lyrics, but it was a song about believing in yourself and reaching your goals. I was mesmerized, as was everyone in the room.

With a sudden burst of sound and light, the song was over. There was a pause, as if the room was catching its breath. Then a roar of sound, applause from the crowd, questions from the reporters, sound everywhere.

Kate finally gained some semblance of control over the room, pulling Ashley to her side in a tight embrace.

"Ladies and gentlemen, you've just heard Ashley's newest hit, "Fight for Your Dreams," and the official song of this year's Chicago Marathon. Ashley is very generously donating the proceeds from sales to the 150 charities supporting runners in this year's event. The single will be available starting tomorrow morning on iTunes and on the marathon and Ashley's websites. You'll be hearing a lot more of "Fight for Your Dreams" over the next few weeks as we get ready to run Chicago. And to make sure you remember this incredible experience, the staff will be giving you an autographed commemorative disc with this song and another of Ashley's hits as you leave today. Thank you for coming, and I look forward to seeing all of you on October 7."

The next thirty minutes were crazy. Even the most jaded sports media were patiently waiting in line to meet Ashley and ask her to autograph their credentials, notebooks, anything they could put their hands on. The camera crews were all frantically uploading to their nearby satellite trucks, making sure they could get their footage on the early evening news. I could imagine the teasers the local stations were going to use for this and wondered how soon the national celebrity shows would start pleading for footage.

And knowing Kate, her staff was already on the phone: *Access Hollywood, Entertainment Tonight,* and all the rest. If Ashley thought it was hard for her to get around town unrecognized before, this appearance made that an impossibility. Selfishly, I was thinking only of myself and the limited places we could go and spend time together. At least, I thought with a smile to myself, we still had her hotel suite and my home.

Hired and museum security eventually chased the reporters out, and the only people left in the big, glassy room were Ashley, Kate, and me. (And, of course, Ashley's security, but they were focused on the doors, not on us.)

I gave Ashley a quick kiss and was feeling generous enough to bestow a quick peck on Kate's cheek as well.

"Ashley, Kate, that was a magnificent performance. You made a huge impression today."

Kate smiled.

"Thanks, Erick. I hope you don't mind that I asked Ashley to keep it all a secret from you. I knew you wouldn't tell anyone, but it was great fun watching your face as the curtain rose."

Interesting. Kate had focused on me instead of the crowd. What's that all about?

Ashley smiled. "Erick, I'm so glad you liked it. I hope it raises millions for all these great charities!"

"I'm sure it will. It's going to sell like crazy. You're doing wonderful things for your own foundation and for all these charities."

"I wish we could include the Alex Project on the list."

"You and GrandHotel are being generous enough. I wouldn't think of it. Besides, we're all working together for a best-selling book, right? Since part of my book sales go to the Alex Project, we'll be in great shape. And speaking of great shape, where was Jack today? Kate, you looked like you were expecting him to be here."

She paused for more than just a moment, looking down at her feet. She suddenly looked up, concern on her face.

"I was expecting him, yes. He's been going through some things lately. I'm sure he'll be fine."

She didn't look sure at all.

Ashley turned to Kate.

"Kate, I've had it with Jack. He's been impossible to work with lately—mean spirited and downright nasty. I don't know what happened today, but it's the last straw with me. When you see him, tell him he's fired."

"Ashley, you can't do that this close to the race. You need Jack," Kate protested.

"No, I don't. We don't. It's over."

"I don't suppose you'll reconsider—no, I can see you won't. He won't take this well. Not well at all. He should be used to disappointment, but who ever is?"

With that, Kate turned and walked out past the guards. Ashley and I watched her leave, looked at each other for a moment, and then followed Kate out the door. It was a strange, unsettling way to end an incredible event.

77

The next few days were insane. Ashley mania had taken over the city and then some. As I suspected, the national celebrity circuit jumped on the story and did several remote interviews with Ashley, all plugging her new song and her Chicago Marathon participation. Pledges were coming into the websites at phenomenal rates of speed, with the Frederick Foundation needing to add server capacity after only two days.

Paparazzi were camped outside every entrance to the GrandHotel Chicago, desperate to catch a glimpse of Ashley. I was able to get in relatively unnoticed, but running outside was just about impossible. We kept moving at the private health club at the top of the hotel.

Ashley stayed firm about firing Jack. I half expected to see him turn up at the health club the next day protesting her decision, but whatever demons were bothering him must have kept him away, and we had to make do with following the training schedule he had laid out for us at the start and without his direct guidance. Guidance which lately hadn't been much help anyway. We knew we had challenges ahead of us, but after the big announcement, we also knew we had no option but to run smart and finish the race. Too many people were watching, and too much was on the line to do anything but succeed.

. . .

Ashley and I had a few more days—and nights—together before she had to leave for her Midwestern college campus tour. Tickets had sold out quickly for every show, which made Ashley and her managers very happy. A few tweaks had been made to the show, but it was essentially the same incredible evening that I had enjoyed back in Miami. That seemed like years ago.

We made the most of our time together and escaped, for the most part, the eyes and cameras of the omnipresent paparazzi. Quiet dinners in her hotel room were our mainstay, but we did escape for a few outings, mostly with the help of Charlie and Mr. Kaczmarek's beat-up car. Who would have expected one of the world's now hottest pop stars to be driven around in an old gray Chevy?

After one final, sweet night together, I left her in the middle of packing for an afternoon charter flight to Lansing for the inaugural campus concert at Michigan State's Breslin Center. From there, she had ten concerts in twelve days at the Midwest's biggest campuses: Michigan, Notre Dame, Ohio State, even my alma mater, Mizzou. She wouldn't be back until just before the marathon. I was hoping to join her for a day or two, but I was tied to tracking the last few weeks of marathon preparations and, of course, at the beck and call of the authorities for the insider trading case.

Not that you'd know anything was going on. I hadn't heard a word from anyone. I wondered if Ted's material had turned out to be a bust. And, like I did every day, I wondered where Ted was. And if he was alive.

78

Over the next few days, I tried to return to my normal routine, but that didn't seem likely. Paparazzi continued to show up at the front door and I was fielding calls from reporters wanting an inside scoop on Ashley's tour. According to Ashley, the tour was going well. The changes they made to the two previous incarnations made it a little more college friendly and the changes were being well received by the campuses.

I was still doing some shadowing at the marathon office, including joining one of the City Hall meetings. More Chicagoans should see how the City That Works does work when faced with something as logistically challenging as a marathon.

Having 26.2 miles of streets in the heart of the city closing on a shifting basis and one of the city's largest parks taken over by 45,000 runners and a 10,000-person support crew would have been too much for your typical city. Add to that hundreds of thousands of spectators. The marathon always said "one million" or "more than a million," which always sounded like poppycock to me. I mean, seriously. How do they count people lined up on curbs and in parks all across the city? Yeah, let's say a million. That sounds like a good number!

But watching all the city departments work together was truly impressive. Led by the police, of course, the teams worked together like clockwork. It was the biggest deployment of police at one time each year (well, except during the NATO summit and city-wide celebrations like the Blackhawk's Stanley Cup championship), but it also required huge resources from the fire department and its crack team of paramedics, Streets and Sanitation (hey, somebody's got to clean up that mess and make sure no last-minute road crews got sent out by mistake), and even the bridge tenders. Yes, those iconic Chicago River bridges are raised for boat traffic by a guy standing in the bridge house pulling on a lever or something. Can you imagine if signals got crossed and he raised the bridge for some dinky sailboat fighting the current as it came down the Chicago River toward Lake Michigan? Chaos. And yes, the Chicago River flows out from Lake Michigan, which is completely unnatural. It had been the other way around, but back in 1900, so much sewage was flowing into the Lake that they decided to build locks and reverse the flow. Pretty impressive for 1900, if you ask me. Next time you are in Chicago, ask people where the shoreline of Lake Chicago is. Even better, find a local in one of our taverns and bet him (don't bet with women; you always lose) that he can't tell you the location of Lake Chicago. You'll win.

But I digress. The teamwork the city showed—in conjunction with the marathon staff—was truly impressive. Yes, there was some infighting and a few turf wars. But everyone got marathon t-shirts and caps and were all happy. Ah, the power of freebies.

So I attended a few more meetings and did more work on the book, including early stages of dust jacket and book design. I was easily finding ways to keep myself busy without Ashley. And training, of course, following my own schedule in the absence of Jack. Initially, I was worried about keeping to this regimen, but I was so terrified of embarrassing myself in front of all those people—and Ashley—that I needn't have worried. Max was especially glad to have me back full time.

I know now that this was just the calm before the many storms of the coming weeks. Do I wish I had known what was coming? Handling death is easier when you can see it coming, right?

79

The day began with such promise. Sunny and pleasant, not too warm, not too cool. The beginnings of some fall color in the trees—fall is definitely one of my favorite Chicago seasons.

I took Max out for a run and came back to find Minu standing on my front steps with her boss, Art Erie, and a Cook County sheriff's police deputy leaning against a squad car parked in front of my house. I guess I should consider myself lucky that the lights weren't flashing, but it was still making quite an impression on my neighbors.

Minu walked toward me as I was turning through my front gate with Max. Believe me, Max was much happier to see Minu than I was.

"Erick, we need you to come with us. Right now."

"Minu, I'm sweaty and I stink. I don't know what's going on, but at least give me five minutes to shower and change."

"I'll ask. But you have to hurry."

"Why, what's wrong?"

"I'll tell you when we get downtown. Now let me go ask Art if we can let you shower."

A hurried conference between the two ensued. Meanwhile, several neighbors were either standing in front of my house or trying to be somewhat less obvious from their yards.

Minu came back. "Okay, you can have five minutes. But the officer is going to come in with you and make sure you don't communicate with anyone."

"Minu, goddamn it. I don't know what's going on, so how can I communicate anything to anyone? Is he going to watch me shower?"

"Erick, calm down. This will all make sense in a few minutes. Now go before Art changes his mind and takes you downtown as is."

I nodded and headed for the house. Faster than I thought possible, the deputy was at my side, almost walking through the narrow front door in unison with me.

"How can I make this easier, Officer?"

"Pretty simple, sir. Give me your cell phone and stay away from any communications device—house phone, laptop. And you heard the lady: hurry."

I let Max off his lead, filled his food and water bowls, and then headed up to the bedroom with Officer Friendly at my back. He pushed ahead of me to go into the bedroom, picking up my iPad from the bedside and holding it close. He then checked my closet and the master bath.

"Go ahead and get your clothes and shower. I'll stay here in the bedroom and give you some privacy. But don't push your luck."

Some privacy was right. At least he let me shut the bathroom door.

. . .

Somewhat less than five minutes later, I was back out front, and the deputy handed Minu my iPhone. With a practiced hand, she checked my recent phone calls and showed the screen to Erie. Nodding to me, she shut the phone off and slipped it into the pocket of her tailored black suit.

"Let's go. We don't have much time."

Erie got in front of the squad with the deputy, leaving Minu and me in the back. The car's sirens going off all the way downtown prevented intelligent conversation.

We turned off Dearborn Street into the underground garage below the Dirksen Building, home to the US Court of Appeals in Chicago as well as the US District Court. Someone knew we were coming because the barricades were up and a phalanx of officers was standing nearby.

"Minu, should I call my attorney? Do I need to? And why are we at a federal building? You guys hate the Feds."

"We don't hate the Feds. We have a friendly rivalry but work together when the occasion dictates. And this one does. And don't worry about Cynthia Ingwalson, Erick, we took care of that. She's waiting inside."

"What? You had my attorney come, and neither of you told me? Seriously, what the fuck is up?"

"In less than five minutes, Erick, you'll know everything. Just stay calm."

Stay calm. Isn't it funny? Every time I've been told to stay calm was just when things were getting their worst.

A small, wood-paneled elevator that said "Judges Only" was open and waiting, held there by a bailiff. Erie, Minu, and I were swept in, joined by an imposing, Marine-like guy in a Federal Protective Services uniform. He was so serious it made me almost miss my now close personal friend, Officer Friendly. The officer used his ID on the car reader that was built into the controls. When the small light turned green, he pushed one of the unmarked buttons (how did anyone know what floors they were for?) and the doors closed. Even I knew better than to speak. Hard to speak when you are scared shitless.

The doors opened on a hallway that looked like every other floor in every other modernist government building in the world. With the exception, of course, of the additional FPS officers and a very worried young woman in a killer black suit.

"Is that him?" she asked.

"Yes," answered Erie.

"Oh, thank God. We're getting ready to start, and you know how he is when he's kept waiting."

"Yes, Margie, I know. Lead on."

Without introductions, we followed her nervous flight down the hallway and into a suite simply labeled, "The United States Attorney for the Northern District of Illinois."

Shit. The US attorney's office. This had to be bad. Really bad.

80

We walked through a large reception area and then back through a series of hallways to a simple, unmarked door. As we walked in, I saw that we were in a large, high-tech conference room. I tried to gather myself, but looking around the room did nothing to calm me down.

I felt like I was in a bad version of the old "This Is Your Life" from the golden days of television. Seated close to the door were Detective Hanson of the CPD and my favorite FBI agent, Drury. Someone who appeared to be older and more senior accompanied each. In the corner of the room speaking with someone who looked vaguely familiar was a very welcome sight, Cynthia Ingwalson. She came over to my side as Minu and Erie were pulled into conversations at the side of the room.

"Erick, I know you're upset. I'm sorry this is how things turned out, but don't worry. You aren't in trouble. Well, at least not in legal trouble."

"What the hell does that mean?"

"You'll understand everything in a minute. Remember, I'm here to watch out for your interests in this mess."

I started to ask her why everyone kept telling me that I'd understand soon, but just as I started to question her, the familiar-looking man took his place at the head of the table and began to speak.

"Please be seated so we can finally begin." With that, he looked at me as if I had been holding up the show. And why did one look from him make me feel guilty of something?

"Thank you all for coming," he began. "I know all of you have been putting in incredible hours on this case, and I want you all to know how much that work is appreciated. This has been a great example of interagency cooperation, and Chief Patrick and Director Henderson are as grateful as I am."

The mention of the Chicago police chief and the director of the FBI suddenly gave me a clue as to where I'd seen the man before. On TV. He was the US attorney. No run-of-the-mill assistant US attorney. *The* US attorney. Peder Arnold. As in appointed by the president, confirmed by the Senate US attorney Peder Arnold. Double shit.

As I was trying to get my head around this, I realized that he was speaking to me.

"Mr. Anderssen, we are extremely grateful for your help in our investigations. Without the information you turned over to us, we certainly wouldn't be ready to take action today as we are. Cynthia, why don't you and Mr. Anderssen use my office while we get the operation started from here."

"Peder, thank you. We'll do just that."

Minu mouthed a small "thank you" at me from her seat across the table. I expect this—whatever it was—was quite a coup for her. Standing up, I followed Cynthia through a side door, leaving the group behind.

We found ourselves in a corner office befitting the US attorney. Big desk, big sitting area, big windows that had that funny underwater look of bulletproof glass. Great. Just where I wanted to be.

81

I'm afraid I wasn't very nice to Cynthia for the next couple of minutes. I started out demanding to know why I was practically kidnapped by the state's attorney and then dragged to the US attorney with no explanation, no warning, no nothing. And why was she already here? Whose side was she on? And then I got really angry.

Cynthia sat patiently in one of Arnold's overstuffed chairs and let me work through my anger. When I started to lose steam, she looked at me as if to say, "Okay, that's enough. Are you ready to listen?" But she never said a word, never moved a muscle. Finally, I flopped down in the chair across from her.

"I'm sorry. I know this isn't your fault. But can you tell me what's going on? Please?"

"Of course. You deserve a full explanation."

And with that, she began to fill me in on what had been happening since I had given Minu the envelope of material from Ted. The wheels of justice had been grinding swiftly after I turned over the papers.

"Erick, you're here because there are going to be a number of arrests today, and the US attorney was concerned that you might get word of them and inadvertently alert one or more of the individuals that this was going down. They don't want any of the fish to escape the net, as it were."

"Well, I guess that make sense. But couldn't they have done it in a way that didn't feel like a kidnapping?"

"By sending Minu, they thought they were. After all, she is your next-door neighbor, and she should have been somewhat reassuring. I'd have come, but I was just summoned here a few minutes ago myself."

"So, what's the story behind this big plot?"

"From what they've told me, it's a classic insider trading scheme that started in New York with a couple of people, but it quickly spread across the country. There seem to be a couple of key players: Ken Hamlar, who handled all the record keeping and distributing the funds after the accountant in New York was killed; your friend Barbara, who seems to have been the recruiter; and, of course, the person who's the mastermind behind this whole thing."

"You mean Thunder? Who is it? Don't tell me it's someone I know."

"I'm afraid it is someone you know. Lord Peter Greene."

"What the hell? Lord Greene? What in God's name is some multi-kazillionaire British lord doing with an insider trading scam?"

"It's more than that, Erick. Turns out that Greene isn't just involved in an insider trading scam. He's using that scheme to prop up Regency Holdings, one of his major investments that's in real trouble. He's using the insider traders to keep activity—and the price of his stock—artificially high while he scrambles to keep the company solvent. The SEC apparently has some pretty convincing evidence that he's been taking money from several of his other companies to keep the hotel afloat."

"But Regency Press has done so well. It's one of the biggest publishers in the world."

"Very successful. And he's got highly successful publishing companies in the UK, Germany, France, and Australia, and he's negotiating to buy one of the largest publishers in China. But he's been branching out lately—diversifying, if you will—and it hasn't gone well. His Regency group tried office equipment in Korea, package delivery in the Netherlands, and a steel plant in Germany. All are teetering on the edge of bankruptcy. But his big gamble—the one he leveraged the most in order to get—was GrandHotel. He was convinced that he could turn GrandHotel into the Ritz Carlton or Four Seasons for the millennial generation by investing big in upscale décor and celebrity names. Rumors have been swirling around the stock for weeks but something was keeping the price up. The US attorney and SEC are convinced that Greene's highly complicated corporate structure, combined with this insider trading group, have been artificially propping up the stock price. Supposedly, Greene has borrowed everything he can with the stock as collateral. When this gets out, the stock will collapse, and so will Greene's empire."

I was stunned. To hear that my friends were being used to prop up some rich guy's ego added another layer of tragedy.

"What's happening with Ken and the rest?"

"They're all being arrested today, including Greene who is in New York for a board meeting. The SEC is conducting a raid on Greene's US headquarters as we speak. The Financial Services Authority and Crown Prosecutor are doing the same for Greene's London offices. The New York Stock Exchange halted trading in the stock a few minutes after the open. By the end of the day, Greene will be ruined. And in jail."

"I still don't understand why Greene pushed so hard for me to write the book."

"Because Ashley insisted that you write it, and no one else. If you refused to write it, the entire Ashley endorsement deal would fail, and Greene needed that deal to succeed in order to save his entire scheme. He must have felt that it was his last chance, which explains the amount of pressure he put on you to write it."

"But why didn't he simply cancel the book once he realized that I was digging into Regency and GrandHotel?"

"He probably knew that canceling the book would only make you even more suspicious. And if he canceled it outright, he'd lose Ashley and jeopardize the scheme. But after threatening you to quit—the bomb threats, the shooting attempt at the hotel, everything—his only choice was to have you killed before you could publish anything linking Regency and GrandHotel to the scheme. We suspect he was running scared."

"How do the Feds know they have everyone involved? What if there are more people in on this?"

"They know they don't have everyone—at least not yet. There are a few coded names that they haven't broken, but they're hoping that one of the people they're arresting today will cooperate and fill in those names."

"And what about Ted?"

"No news. He's completely disappeared. I'm sorry. I know how close you two were."

"Are. How close we are. I'm not giving up on him."

"Of course. But it's very difficult to drop off the grid these days. There's no credit card activity, no ATMs, no nothing. I wouldn't hold out too much hope, Erick."

"Well, there you're wrong. I do hold out hope. He'll be back. I know he will."

"Right now, you have to worry about yourself first. The US attorney is concerned about your safety. Unfortunately, too many people know about your involvement in the unmasking of this scheme. Someone may try to retaliate. We're working on a protection program for you. Once everyone is in custody, you can leave here, but you'll have 24/7 protection for the foreseeable future."

"That's ridiculous. I just gave Minu some papers and told her about the rumors I had heard. No one is after me. I can't hurt anyone; I'm not a witness."

"There are a lot of people who are going to have their lives ruined by this. One of them may blame you. It won't hurt to have someone keeping an eye on you for the next few weeks. As much as I regret the intrusion in your life, I have to strongly recommend you accept the protection."

"What about Ashley? And the marathon?"

"I don't know anything about that, Erick, but we'll figure it all out. In the meantime, let's go back into the conference room and see how the arrest program is going."

I followed Cynthia back into the conference room. Everyone was on the phone, urgently talking to somebody. As they finished their conversations, they'd hurry to the US attorney, lean over him, and quickly make a note on a long list he had in front of him. Cynthia and I watched this little ballet for a time, and then things began to slow. As people leaned back in their chairs, we walked over to where Minu was sitting.

"Minu, how is it going?"

"Pretty well. The New York leg was flawless; Greene and all his key players were nabbed just as we planned. Of course, Greene is trying everything from thinly veiled bribes to serious bluster, but the team is moving him into interrogation now. The Chicago end isn't going as well. We have almost everyone, but there are still two outstanding who slipped their watchers, and now we have to track them down."

"Who's missing?"

"Hamlar's number two on the bookkeeping side, one of his old controllers from the utility company. Retired guy, likes to take the dog for long walks. Dog turned up on the front step, no guy. We don't know if he made our watchers or what happened. He's a minor player in the scheme, so I'm not too worried. The other one does have me worried—and worried for you, Erick."

At this point I dreaded even asking the question, but I knew I had to.

"Who is it? Who else did I know so little about?"

"Jack Clark."

"My Jack Clark? Kate's husband?"

"Yes, I'm afraid so."

I was beyond shocked. And then I began to think about Kate and Jack's lavish lifestyle. Even given her marathon paycheck and his Nike deal, they were living the high life. Did they need money so badly? At least this explained his recent deterioration. In a strange way, I was glad his involvement in this scheme was finally coming to light. Whatever was eating at him might finally be put to rest. For his sake and for Kate's.

I wondered aloud why no one had ever tried to enlist me, especially given how close I was to so many of them.

"The only thing I can think of is that they thought of you as someone whose sense of right and wrong would not only keep you from participating but maybe even turning them in. I guess that should please you."

"I find all of this so hard to believe."

Cynthia interrupted me.

"Erick, let's get you out of here."

"But how did Jack get involved? Did Kate know?"

"We don't know for sure, but we have some ideas. However, having you here doesn't help anyone. We're going to get you home where you can take all of this in. Let's go."

I allowed Cynthia and Minu to lead me out of the big corner office, through the crowd of closely packed cubicles, past the big reception area. As we walked to the elevators, there were suddenly two large men on either side of me.

"What the hell?"

Minu held up her hand, as if to stop me.

"I told you were in danger. These are deputy US Marshals. They'll be with you 24/7 until we're satisfied that everyone involved in this scheme is in custody and that you are out of danger. This is a given and not up for debate."

"But I—"

"What did I just say? If necessary, we'll take you into protective custody, and you won't like that. This is your best alternative, so just deal with it. You are in danger, and you need to be protected."

She seemed serious, so the best I could do was nod and leave. Cynthia, the deputies, and I got on the elevator. Minu gave me a small smile.

"You've done the right thing all along. Go on, now. Run that marathon, finish your book, and enjoy your life. You're in good hands with the deputies, and we'll take care of the rest. Your role in this won't be made public. And Cynthia will make sure that you'll be protected from a legal perspective."

One more small smile as the elevator doors closed.

"And I'll see you and Max running in the neighborhood!"

I thought about Max. His unconditional love and trust. Suddenly, I wasn't worried about Jack, Lord Greene, or anyone else. I wanted to be with my dog.

82

I should have known that I wouldn't have to worry about how I was getting from the Dirksen Building to my house. My ride home was courtesy of the US Marshal service. Cynthia put me into the car with a small hug.

"Everything will be fine, Erick. This will be a big deal for a few days in the media, and then they'll be onto something else."

"No, everything won't be fine," I said. "My charity will be permanently scarred by Hamlar's involvement in this scheme. No one will trust us with their money. I'll spend months straightening everything out. And Jack's involvement will devastate Kate. And what's going to happen to Ashley and her big deal to be the face of GrandHotel? This is going to change lives, lives of people close to me. And on top of all of that, my best friend has disappeared."

"Erick, I know this is going to be hard. But you can't change what these people have done. You need to take care of yourself and the people closest to you. You're free to tell Ashley what's happened as long as you don't divulge any details about who or what. Take care of yourself, take care of Ashley, and we'll take care of the rest."

I knew it wasn't that simple, but I needed to get home. I nodded and slipped into the backseat of the black Navigator with the blacked out windows.

A few minutes later, we pulled up in front of my house. Through the dark haze of what I assumed was bulletproof glass, I saw someone walking in the front yard with Max. Recalling that time so long ago—and yet just a few short months ago—I was sure it was Ted waiting for me.

I hurried to get out of the car, only to find that the doors were locked and I couldn't open them. I pounded at the glass as one of the deputies got out of the front and carefully looked around him. As his colleague headed toward my house and the person waiting there, the first deputy opened the car door slightly.

"Mr. Anderssen, do you know that person?" He pointed at my front steps.

"Yes, I do, deputy. I used to be married to her."

"All right, we're clear," he shouted to his colleague, who was close to pulling a gun on Kate. Max growled at the deputy. He'd always been fond of Kate, regardless of the nasty things I would tell him about her.

"Mr. Anderssen, we'll be here if you need us," the deputy said.

"And even if I don't, right?"

No response, just a stare.

"I understand," I sighed.

Both Kate and Max watched me as I walked toward the steps. Kate let go of Max's collar so the big dog could run to me. As he raced toward me, I looked over his head to see the devastation in Kate's eyes.

"Erick, I—"

"Kate, let's get inside. I want to feed Max, get us both a glass of wine, and then we can talk."

As we walked inside the house, I realized that my phone was still turned off. As I turned it on, I saw that there were several missed calls from Ashley and a couple of matching voice mails. With apologies to

Kate, I called Ashley back and explained a little of what had been happening. She was appropriately concerned, but I promised her I would be over as soon as I finished talking to Kate.

She had already moved to the living room when I got off the phone. I poured two glasses of Barbara's Kistler chardonnay from the wine fridge and joined her.

"Erick, I don't know what to say. Jack, involved in insider trading? I knew we had money problems, but not this bad!"

"What kind of money problems?" Hey, she was my ex-wife. I could ask intrusive questions.

"It's never been made public, but he lost his Nike endorsement earlier this year, and he hasn't found anything to replace it. He was trying for another book but was turned down everywhere. He's lost a few training clients and he's been drinking a lot, calling himself a has-been. But insider trading? And for months? I don't even know where the money is, and now he's missing. A bag, a few clothes, and he's gone."

"Now that the Feds are looking for him, he'll only make matters worse by running. You don't have any idea where he could be?"

"None. He doesn't really have any friends. And he hasn't touched our credit cards or bank account . . . not that he'd need to, given the amount of money they say he got illegally and stashed somewhere."

"Kate, are you safe? Do you need to stay with someone?"

"I don't know where that would be. I don't think Jack's a violent man—"

"You bought a gun."

"I know, but I think I overreacted. You know I tend to do that. In fact, I don't know why I came here and bothered you. I'll be fine. Thanks for the wine. I know you need to get to Ashley."

"But, Kate—"

"No, I really have to go. We've only got a couple of days left before the race. I have too much work to do to be sitting here drinking with you."

I didn't know if she was posturing or hiding, but I let her go. Frankly, her problems paled in comparison to mine, so I headed over to the hotel to tell Ashley what I could.

83

Kate was right on one point. We were only days away from the marathon. Ashley and I were into our tapering mode now, which meant that we were running less and building energy for the race itself. Stocking up on carbs (what a great excuse to eat pasta) and fluids (okay, perhaps a rich cabernet wasn't what the training manual meant), but enjoying every moment together. We weren't able to get out much, but again thanks to Mr. Kaczmarek and his livery service, Ashley and I enjoyed some quiet strolls around the neighborhood and a beer or two at River Shannon. I'm sure we weren't supposed be eating large quantities of peanuts, but they were so delicious, and being able to drop the empty shells on the floor was just too much fun to resist.

84

Kate had ensured that our race bibs and commemorative t-shirts were delivered to the hotel, saving us a trip to the Health and Fitness Expo. For the purposes of the book, however, I needed to make that pilgrimage, so I set out on the Saturday morning before the race to see what this whole Expo thing was all about.

McCormick Place is the largest convention center in the United States, and once you get inside, it feels even bigger. Many of the nation's largest conventions and trade shows are held there, some hosting up to 60,000 or more attendees. The three-million square feet of exhibition space was conveniently located just south of the Loop.

After making my way down the long concourses, I entered the Expo and found myself in the modern-day equivalent of a county fair. Balloons, music, sound, and light gave the hall an almost holiday feel. Row upon row of exhibitors, vendors, and sponsors beckoned to the runners, their friends, and their families. I knew that almost 250,000 people would come through the Expo in its brief two-day lifespan, and it felt like most of them had chosen this hour to attend.

Getting into the spirit of things, I tried on a new pair of running shoes (I bought), looked at a number of new t-shirts (I didn't buy; none of them featured the greatest rock bands of all time), and saw a number of famous runners (at least famous to other runners) signing autographs in sponsor booths. I was tempted to buy the marathon logo nipple guards, guaranteed to protect from bloody nipples (hours of rubbing against fabric, don't you know) but was ultimately grossed out by the subject.

Wanting to get the ordinary runner's experience, I was disappointed to run into Paul O'Bannon, who was there keeping an eye on things. Within seconds, I was in the midst of a guided behind-the-scenes tour, which in retrospect wasn't all that impressive. There wasn't much behind the scenes, and it was nearly as interesting as what was in front of the crowd.

One of the big draws was the big GrandHotel booth with its massive eighty-five-inch screen showing the sped-up course video that I had seen filmed not that long ago. There was also a main stage with speakers talking about blister treatment, shin splints, and other topics of interest to the die-hard runner. Fascinating stuff.

Although O'Bannon was trying to steer me toward the sponsor booths with their bright lights and generous giveaways, I pushed back and wanted to see the actual bib pickup. Relenting, he guided me through the maze of booths toward the very back of the hall, where I found a queue of runners with confirmation tickets in hand, waiting for their bibs. I asked why this so-important function was tucked way back here. After a bit of hemming and hawing, I got my answer.

"Vendors pay good money for their booths, and the booth is important to the sponsors. If this was in front, the runners would just scoop up their bibs and goodie bags and take off."

After doing months of research and interviews, this was the first I'd heard of the concept of a "goodie bag." It reminded me of an eight-year-old's birthday party. As it turns out, I wasn't far off.

Each runner receives a personalized bib from a volunteer. It's a roughly five-by-seven piece of weatherproof paper with the runner's unique bib number (and sponsor logos) on it. They then proceed to pick up their event t-shirt—highly prized by the runners—and a large plastic bag with a drawstring filled with samples, magazines, coupons, and other random items. The runners then have to work their way back through the maze of booths to exit the hall. Simple, devious, and effective. I had to admire that.

Escaping my guide, I headed back to the GrandHotel for a final carbo load of chef-inspired pasta and an early bedtime so as to be well rested for the next day's race. I'm not sure how much rest Ashley and I would get, but we'd certainly make the early bedtime.

85

The day—Marathon Day—dawned cloudy and cool with just the hint of a breeze. Perfect running weather, but far from optimal for the hordes of media that came out to watch Ashley run. Yes, of course, some of them were there to cover the actual race and the Kenyans who would actually win, but you can't tell me that *People*, *TMZ*, and *Access Hollywood* had suddenly developed an interest in endurance racing.

We left early from the hotel via an unmarked Chicago Police Department vehicle from the hotel's underground garage. As always, Kate's pull got us that special treatment and, of course, a drop off right at the entrance to the VIP runner compound. As befits those of us with special status, we'd have a private place to stash our gear, have a bite to eat—no, no champagne for me before I run 26.2 miles, thank you—and most importantly, access to a heated and air-conditioned trailer with attended washrooms. Experienced runners tell me that even the best events in the world don't have enough port a-potties for that last half hour before race time. Too far back in line as the clock ticks down? Use a tree. Didn't go in time and have to get to your assigned place in the start section? Pee down your leg. You have no idea how disgusting a marathon start can be.

Sarah Peters welcomed us and a pair of highly attractive young hosts who would cater to our every need, including getting us to the

VIP start section well before the starting gun would go off. I saw a few familiar faces in our special little area: an alderman, a couple of local TV anchors, and one of our disgraced governors trying for an image makeover. I introduced Ashley to the few people I knew for no other reason than to distract her. I saw she was nervous, as was I. Would we—could we—finish this marathon? A month ago I was certain, but the distractions of the last few weeks had taken their toll.

Fortunately for everyone's nerves, the start was almost upon us. One of the young guides came to get Ashley and me and took us down a fenced-in path in the park to the start. The crowd and the noise were overwhelming. We knew that there were more than 40,000 people lined up behind us along Columbus Drive, with the start corrals so big they had to snake down Balbo Drive on the side. The announcers were giving last-minute instructions, music was playing over the loudspeakers, and the media were everywhere.

We were in the second section of the start, right behind the elites who would be competing for $750,000 in prize money. When combined with the appearance fees paid by the Chicago Marathon for their participation, winners could find themselves with a half a million-dollar payday. Like I said, too bad it was too late for me to change careers.

The national anthem was sung by one of the Lyric Opera's hot new tenors, and then it was just a matter of waiting for TV to run their intros before we'd be off. I was eyeing the crowd, looking for both the obvious police presence and the undercover officers that were there to supplement Ashley's protection. One of her runner-security guards was immediately in front of us, and I could see the other just behind Ashley and slightly to the right. As we were waiting for the starting gun, I could see a man pushing his way through the crowd. Was he trying to get to Ashley? Our protection thought so: Just as her guard turned to intercept the man, a Chicago Police Department uniformed officer pulled him down to the ground. Two more cops came flying just as the starting pistol fired. We took off, both guards keeping an extra vigilant eye on Ashley and the crowd around us.

Despite being in the VIP start section, it was crowded and chaotic as we headed north on Columbus Drive under the amazing Frank Gehry-designed bridge. The bridge was closed to the public but packed with photographers and camera crews, all of them capturing the start and, of course, Ashley. I could feel her two bodyguards tensing as we went under the bridge, trying to judge which was the greater threat: the people on the bridge or the huge crowds lining the course. I looked over at Ashley, who was extremely tense, staring tightly at the ground as she ran.

"Ashley, look at me."

She glanced up, then down again.

"Ashley, now. Look at me."

She slowly lifted her head, meeting my eyes.

"You've got half the Chicago Police Department and some of Charlie's best people keeping an eye out for you today. Don't worry about what you can't control. Let's focus on running this marathon, okay?"

A small smile crossed her face.

"All right. I can do that. Give me your hand."

"Always."

"Then I can do it."

And so the race began.

86

The first part of the course was crowded, but the field of runners was enthusiastic, buoyed by a combination of adrenaline and the massive crowd of spectators lining the streets. Up Columbus, across Grand, down State Street, and into the canyons of the Loop. Up the financial district of LaSalle Street, into Lincoln Park and my neighborhood. Ashley and I kept up a good pace, smiling over at each other as we saw a familiar landmark, a sign encouraging her, a friendly face.

The course left the park, turned just south of Wrigley Field, and began the run south along Broadway. I heard a commotion ahead of us, louder than the spectators had been before. As we approached the noise, I heard Ashley begin to laugh, a challenge when you've run 8 miles or so. Then, suddenly, I saw why she was laughing.

The Frontrunners, a group of gay, lesbian, bisexual, and transgender runners, are one of the many groups that volunteer to work water stations along the course. What sets the Frontrunners apart—and what contributes to their many wins as best water station of the event—is their incredibly popular team of male cheerleaders with their matching cheerleader skirts and pom-poms. Often, they'll choose a theme to accentuate their station. It could be Elvis, Disney, or, in this case, Ashley.

Yes, the guys were saluting Ashley with matching Ashley wigs, tight sweaters (suitably filled out), and pleated skirts. The crowd went wild when they realized that Ashley was right there. True to her spirit, she ran over and hugged and kissed many of the cheerleaders, which just made the crowd go even wilder. And made Ashley's security team—and me—incredibly nervous.

But there was nothing to fear from this crowd; they showered love on my diva. With one or two last hugs and more cups of water than we could handle, we were off again.

Down through Old Town and River North, the crowds remained strong, and we kept up a good pace. Bands hired by the marathon were stationed every mile or so along the course, playing everything from polkas to punk rock.

As we turned to the west, the crowds thinned, as did our energy. Our pace had dropped and I worried that I was slowing Ashley down. I suggested she go on without me, but she claimed that she was running at the pace she needed to run.

Fortunately for our motivation, the crowds picked up in Little Italy, and that gave a boost to our energy. We had been running for nearly two hours and we still had nearly 10 miles to go. Not for the first time, I wondered if we'd make it.

. . .

We moved into Pilsen, with mariachi bands and huge crowds. Chinatown was next, with dragon dancers and the big arched Gateway over Wentworth Avenue. Those crowds quickly thinned, as we hit one of the hardest parts of the course.

We were now at mile 23 or so, only 3 miles to go. We'd been running for more than three hours, and the toll it was taking on our bodies was tremendous. My legs were leaden, and lifting one foot after another seemed to be an enormous task. Despite taking plenty of fluids, I was dizzy and dehydrated, almost nauseous at times. I was working through cramps in one calf, and we'd had to stop for a moment to work out a similar problem with Ashley's legs. Blisters, chafing, and an almost deadened feel to my arms had been a constant for the last several miles.

The security team had swapped runners out three times already, ensuring that they would be sharp and focused on protecting Ashley rather than entering the near hallucinogenic state I was in. Frankly, it was now just about moving forward, picking up one leg and putting the other one down. There were very few people along the course and the field of runners had thinned. I was sure I was hallucinating when I saw the gay Ashley cheerleaders again, only to find out later that the marathon bussed them down to this semi-desolate stretch of street to encourage us on.

We fought our way up Michigan Avenue as if in a battle. And, I guess we were. Battling against our bodies, which were telling us to stop putting ourselves through this agony. Our natural defense mechanisms were saying that we had gone too far, depleted too much, crossed a line that shouldn't be crossed. Despite all the training and planning, the cost to our fragile physical vessels was too high. Stop now and save yourself, our bodies were saying. You've pushed yourself too far.

Then, suddenly, the crowds began to grow, dramatically so. Bleachers were packed with family and friends, more bands, and noisemakers.

Finally, we made the turn off of Michigan Avenue onto Roosevelt Road. Just yards to go and the crowd was immense. One last turn and the finish line, with its huge superstructure of green and gold, was in sight. I could hear the public address announcers calling out runners' names, culled from the runners' bib numbers by spotters. Then it was Ashley's name being called out; then it was mine. With a burst of energy, Ashley raised her arms and waved triumphantly to the crowd. The succeeding roar propelled both of us across the finish line.

We had done it. We completed the marathon distance. We were marathoners.

87

We only had a moment to relish our success, needing to move down the finish line chutes to make room for other runners. Before we could do so, Kate rushed over to embrace us both, Charlie at her side.

"That was phenomenal, just phenomenal. Your time was awesome for first-time marathoners, you finished together, and you both look great!"

I took the "look great" part with a grain of salt, seeing as how runners on either side of us were throwing up, bleeding, and generally looking like something from *The Walking Dead*.

Ashley, ever gracious, responded.

"Kate, this has been the most amazing experience of my life. Thank you for giving me—and all of us—this incredible opportunity."

For my part, I wasn't quite as gracious. Not because I felt any animosity toward Kate; that was gone, given all that we'd been through this summer. No, instead I was leaning over, hands on my knees, trying to catch my breath. Leaning toward me, a hand reached over to me with a bottle of water. I saw the gold and green of a marathon official jacket on the arm, and so I gladly accepted it.

As I was about to drink it, I noticed Ashley's complete exhaustion. So, ever the gallant, I passed the bottle over to her. She accepted it with a grateful look. She took a deep drink, draining nearly half the bottle with one pull. Suddenly, her face contorted as if she was in excruciating pain. With a desperate cry, Ashley collapsed to the ground.

. . .

As Kate, calling for the medics, rushed toward Ashley, I looked back to see where that bottle of water had come from. I was shocked to see Jack standing there, resplendent in the gold and green marathon jacket, a look of horror on his face.

"That was for you, you son of a bitch," he cried out. With a roar, he spun away from me and ran, pushing people aside.

"Grab him," I said to Charlie, who was stunned, watching Ashley writhe on the ground. But he regained his senses, and with two of his sweat-soaked guards, he pushed through the crowd to grab Jack. In the confusion, Jack almost got over the security barricade and into the spectators, but with a final push, Charlie brought him to the ground in a tackle. The other guards had to restrain Charlie as he brought his fist down on Jack's face.

Meanwhile, the medical crew in their bright red jackets was swarming over Ashley. A stretcher was on its way down the runners' chute, and security was clearing the way through the crowd of runners. Kate pulled me with her as the medics continued to work on Ashley on the stretcher. I could hear the roar of the crowd, oblivious to what was happening. Looking back at Ashley and her drawn, pained face, her mouth pulled back in agony, I couldn't do anything but pray that this wonderful woman wouldn't be taken from my life.

88

But she was.

89

The doctors told me later that there wasn't anything they could have done for her. The poison—cyanide, they believe—acted too quickly for them to take any countermeasures. She was dead before we got to the hospital.

They gave me a few minutes with her, alone. A chance to say good-bye. But this lifeless, pain-filled face wasn't that of my love. It was a shell, an empty vessel. Everything that made Ashley who she was: that was gone. I stood there for a minute or two and then walked back into the waiting room.

Detective Hanson and a uniformed officer were there waiting for me.

"Mr. Anderssen, I'm sorry for your loss. But we need to get your statement."

"Now? Really? I can't, I just can't."

"We need to do this now while your memory is fresh. I promise we'll do this as quickly as possible."

As quickly as possible turned out to be nearly an hour of me in an exam room repeating my story three or four times as the officer took notes. Finally, emotionally drained and physically exhausted, I had to stop.

"Detective, I can't go on. You must have everything you need ... please."

"Fine. We know how to get in touch with you if we need you."

"Yes, you certainly do." And with that I walked out of the exam room and saw Kate in the waiting room, standing quietly by the exit.

"Erick, I—"

"Kate, there's nothing to say. Nothing. Don't even try."

"But I'm horrified that we've lost Ashley, that Jack may have had something to do with it—"

"May have? HE gave me the *fucking* bottle of water that *killed* her. I handed Ashley's death to her. Don't ever mention his name to me again. And I don't want to see you again. Ever."

"Erick, please—"

I shoved past her and was out the door onto the street. Unable to focus on the streets around me, I blindly began walking, trying to get away from what had just happened to Ashley, to us. To the rest of my life.

. . .

Some time later—an hour, maybe two—I realized that I was back in Lincoln Park, near the South Pond. I dropped to the ground, and for the first time, I cried. I sobbed. I moaned. I had never felt so alone.

. . .

I must have fallen asleep, for when I looked around next, it was approaching dusk. I pulled myself up and began to walk toward my house. I wasn't thinking; I wasn't mourning; I was just moving. Like a robot, I stumbled down Hudson Street toward the house. And, as was often the case, someone was sitting on my front steps waiting for me.

It was Minu. She stood as I approached.

"Oh, Erick—"

"I know," was all I could say. She wrapped her arms around me, and I began to sob again. Like a mother comforting her child, she made soft, gentle, soothing sounds until my sobs quieted.

She helped me into the house, where Max came bouncing to meet me. He had been staying at Minu and Amar's for the race, and clearly Minu thought that I could use another friend. Seeing Max made me cry again. He knew nothing of my sorrow or my loss. Only that he loved me. And I loved him back.

Minu hung gracefully in the background for a few minutes while I tended to the dog. Finally, as Max was noisily gulping down his kibble, I turned to her.

"So, what do we know? I assume that you aren't here just because you live next door."

"No, I'm not. But you know that Amar and I are terribly sorry about your loss and will do anything we can to help."

"I want you to tell me that you have Jack and that he'll pay for what he did to Ashley."

Minu paused before she answered.

"Yes, Jack is in custody. Turns out his money troubles were the cause of much of what's happened. He's the one who first suggested the marathon book to Barbara, hoping the proceeds would help get him out of the debt he and Kate have built up trying to maintain their lifestyle. Barbara brought the idea to Greene, but the endorsement deal with Ashley was already in the works, and when Ashley heard that a marathon book was under way, she insisted that you'd have to be the one to write it. And Barbara, not wanting to endanger her status with Greene's organization, went along with the idea—throwing Jack under the bridge. That pissed Jack off, so he killed Barbara. When

Greene realized what a loose cannon Jack was, Greene had Jack beaten as a warning. But Jack didn't take the hint. Instead, he did what he could to point you in Lord Greene's direction like making you think the beating was intended for you.

"But, in the end, Jack saw that his life was ruined and blamed you. Watching you die in front of Kate and Ashley was to be his revenge. He probably thought he was going to get away with it, but he didn't plan on you handing the water bottle to Ashley."

"You don't have to remind me that I killed her, Minu. I'll never get over that."

"Erick, it wasn't your fault. You had no idea that there was anything wrong with the bottle. Jack should never have been in the finish line compound, but the hired security force didn't know that he was a threat. Everyone knew Jack and let him pass without credentials. Kate is devastated, by the way, simply horrified that it was Jack who did this to you."

"I really don't give a shit what Kate feels. She knew Jack was a problem and should have dealt with it a long time ago."

"I don't know whether Kate knew what was going on with Jack. She's blaming herself for everything."

"Unless she put the cyanide in the bottle, it's clearly not all her fault. What's going to happen to that son of a bitch?"

"He'll be tried for two counts of murder, as well as your attempted murder. He claims that Lord Greene hired someone for the New York killings, so we're pursuing that.

"Does he know where Ted is?"

"No, but he did help us figure out how Ted got his hands on the file he sent you."

"How?"

"When Jack confessed to killing Barbara at O'Hare, he says he was almost spotted by a TSA inspector going by the parking garage where he had killed her. He ran before he could get the file from Barbara's bag. We think Ted was at O'Hare and came across Barbara's body when he was looking for her there. Ted took the file, knowing that it would incriminate him if the police found it. Obviously, he had a change of heart later and sent it on to you."

The thought that Ted had trusted me that much, in the end, almost made me smile. But I didn't want to think about Ted right now.

"That son of a bitch confessed," I said. "What happens now?"

We'll do everything we can to make sure he goes away for the rest of his life."

"Small comfort, frankly."

"I know, but it's all I can offer."

"I really loved her, Minu."

"I know you did."

"What am I going to do now?"

"Is there someone I can call to stay with you?"

Someone to stay with me. My love was dead, my best friend missing, my agent murdered, and my ex-wife out of my life forever. No, there was no one. Just Max and me.

"No, thanks, Minu. I'll be fine. I need to get cleaned up."

"We're just next door. If you need anything, even if it's just a shoulder to cry on . . ."

She didn't need to say anything more. She slipped out the front door, leaving the dog and me. Max—as always—sensed something was wrong and came over to sit next to me. He put his big head on my knee, trying to comfort me. And it did, a little. But nothing would ever fill the void that Ashley's death left in my life. Nothing.

90

The next weeks were a muddle of memories and memorials. A CPD patrol car stayed in front of my house for a few days to keep the media away. The neighbors were solicitous, bringing food and staying with me as long as I needed them to.

Two days after Ashley's death, Charlie stopped by. He was on his way to the airport to pick up Ashley's parents, who wanted to accompany their only daughter's body back to San Diego.

We greeted each other at the front door silently, and then the big, stoic man began to silently cry, reaching out to me. As we hugged in the doorway, I could feel his massive shoulders moving with his tears. After only a minute or two, he broke away, cleared his throat, and was back to business.

"Mr. and Mrs. Frederick would like to meet you if you are available. Dinner in Ashley's suite at the GrandHotel?"

As much as I wanted to avoid the pain, I knew I owed it to Ashley to meet them. I nodded yes and got the details from Charlie.

Getting dressed for dinner, I pulled on some of Ashley's favorites. The Brooks Brothers navy blazer, Thomas Pink crisply starched robin's egg blue shirt. How she had loved buying that shirt for me.

Charlie showed up as promised and drove me to the hotel. Minutes later he was introducing me to John and Monica.

"Erick, I'm so happy to meet you. Ashley told us so much about you, and I know how much she loved you," said Monica. Ashley's father seemed to be unable to speak.

"And I loved her. I'm going to miss her so much," I said.

As usual, the mothers are the stoic ones. Monica nodded and smiled.

"But we'll always have our memories of Ashley, and she'll always have a place in our hearts. We're blessed to have had her in our lives."

With that, we moved to the dining room and enjoyed a simple supper from the GrandHotel's kitchen. Within a few minutes, we were telling Ashley stories and even laughing a bit.

By the end of the evening, they had invited me to stay with them when I went out to San Diego for the memorial service. With hugs to both, I accepted a ride home from Charlie.

As I walked up the sidewalk, Charlie spoke.

"Erick, you know you made her very happy."

"I do, Charlie, I do."

"Thank you for that."

And with that, Charlie got back into the car and drove off.

91

The months slowly passed. The insider trading trials had begun, and it looked like the prosecutors were going to be very successful. Lord Greene fought the hardest, but the evidence was overwhelming, thanks to Ted. God, I missed my friend.

Jack's confession brought about a swift guilty plea and a sentence of life in prison without parole. It didn't make me feel any better.

I finished the marathon book, and it was now in editing. I helped Martha get a job with my new publisher. Turned out Lord Greene did know Martha—and better than any of us had suspected. They'd been having an affair, more of Greene's manipulations. After using Martha to keep track of Barbara, he dumped her unceremoniously the day after the funeral. She was devastated to find out how she had been used, but she was settling into her new job quite well. Of course I was assigned to her. She was very complimentary about my work and confident it would be another best seller for me. I had dedicated the book to Ashley, and the publisher and I were donating part of the proceeds to Ashley's foundation.

I had a few months before I needed to start the next one, but I was already getting nagging emails from Martha wondering whether I had found a topic yet. It would just be a matter of time before she would start suggesting topics, just like Barbara used to do.

With my spare time, I returned to California to see John and Monica and spent a few enjoyable days sailing with John.

I reacquainted myself with friends who I'd ignored during my Ashley days, and I started running again when the Chicago weather permitted.

I was coming back from one of those runs when I again saw someone waiting for me on my front steps. Hoping against hope, I wanted it to be Ted, waiting for me with a bucket of cold beer.

But it wasn't.

It was Kate.

"What do you want?" I asked.

"Just to talk. Just for a few minutes."

I didn't have the energy to fight her, so I opened the front door. Max, of course, greeted her happily. I walked into the living room, started a few logs burning in the fireplace, and sat down. Kate came in a minute later.

"That's a very sweet dog."

"He likes everyone. Don't take it personally."

"Erick, I'm not here to fight. I want to say something, and then I'll leave."

"So, say it."

"Erick, I knew Jack was in trouble, and I knew it was bad. I *was* afraid of him—you saw the gun at the hospital. I should have told you then. And if I had, a lot of things would have turned out differently. But I didn't, and I'm going to have to live with that for the rest of my life. I'm here to tell you how deeply sorry I am. I know that won't help, but I had to tell you."

"Thank you for that. Is there anything else?"

"No." She paused. "Yes, there is. I really enjoyed the time we spent together last summer. It reminded me how much I loved you, and why we were so happy together. And reminded me how badly I treated you. It just kills me that we'll never have that back again. Even friendship is out of the question, I know that. But I'll go now."

"I'm still angry that you hid Jack's problems. We might have done something about it if we'd only known."

Now it was my turn to pause. "But maybe we should give it a little time. Maybe . . . we could have lunch together at Nellie's when the weather gets better."

"That would be nice. Thank you."

She turned and left. I heard the big front door close. Max walked over to me and sighed, as if sad to see Kate leave. He was always the forgiving one. Maybe it was a quality I should learn.

When I began this tale, I said that I was born under a lucky star. But losing Ashley made me wonder what had become of that luck.

As I sat by the now roaring fire with Max's big head lying on my leg, I thought about it a little more and it came to me. For one brief summer, I had known and loved Ashley. And that made me a very, very lucky man.

92

A few months later, as spring was starting to grace the city and I was starting to feel alive again, a postcard showed up in the mail. The picture was of the US Capitol building, and on the other side, one word: *Freedom*. In Ted's handwriting. It had been postmarked just a few days earlier.

About the Author

Mark A. Nystuen, in the second smartest thing he ever did, moved to Chicago in the late 1970s and promptly fell in love with the city. In a nearly thirty-year career with LaSalle Bank, one of the Midwest's largest financial institutions, Mark headed up the creation of the bank's sports marketing business. For more than a dozen years, those responsibilities included leading the organization, marketing, and operation of the LaSalle Bank Chicago Marathon. During that time, Mark and his team turned a mid-level race into one of the world's largest participatory events. Mark is now a principal at The Kineo Group, a Chicago-based strategic marketing, branding, and communications firm.

In *the* smartest thing he ever did, he married Susan, and they have three amazing sons: Kevin, Connor, and Scott—Chicagoans all.

» *Photograph by John Sundlof*